Mending Fences

CARRIE JACOBS

for Dottie, my wonderful mother-in-law
and for Claire, the beautiful girl who made me a mother-in-law

Chapter One

Saturday, April 10

Chandler sat in the third row of the crowded theater, slowly breathing in and out. The twinge in her extended belly grew more intense. She tried to pay attention to her husband Oren, up on the stage, fully immersed in his role as Claudio from Shakespeare's *Much Ado About Nothing,* but the baby launched a foot up into her diaphragm.

"*And I'll be sworn upon 't that he loves her,*" Oren/Claudio was saying from the stage.

Beside her, Maddie yawned and swung her feet, her four-year-old's attention span near its end. Chandler put a hand on Maddie's knees to remind her not to kick the seat in front of her.

"*Peace! I will stop your mouth.*" Alan, the actor playing Benedick, declared.

Chandler mentally calculated the remaining lines. The play would be over in just a minute.

"*...if my cousin do not look exceedingly narrow to thee.*" Oren delivered his last line as he always does – perfectly.

A band wound around Chandler's entire middle and squeezed. Hard.

"*Strike up, pipers!*" Benedick's booming words were the last of the production. Music played and the characters danced as they exited the stage.

The audience erupted into raucous cheering and applause with a standing ovation as the actors ran back onstage and took their bows.

Chandler held the seat back in front of her and tried to stand. Instead, she cried out, the pain stealing her strength. She sank back onto the seat.

"Are you okay?" David, her dad, asked from the other side of Maddie. "Chandler?"

She still gripped the back of the seat in front of her. Sweat trickled down the back of her neck and beaded across her forehead.

"Chandler?" David's voice was full of concern, but she couldn't answer.

She felt her dad swoop Maddie up and hand her off to her mother. He put a hand on her back and leaned down. One look at her face and he stood bolt upright and yelled, "Oren!"

Directly behind her, someone else called for Oren's attention.

People crowded the aisle, asking if she was okay. She flapped her hand, waving them away, until Oren pushed through and took her arm. "What's wrong?"

Alan was right behind him, telling people to back up and give her space.

The contraction relented and she tried to wave away the concerned faces around her. "It's fine, thank you."

Her father said, "I think the baby's coming."

She gripped her belly and argued, "No. He's not due for another week."

Another contraction doubled her over, an effective counter-argument.

"Mommy?" Maddie sounded scared.

"It's okay, honey," David and Lisa, Chandler's mom, both spoke softly to Maddie. "I think your brother's coming."

Oren smoothed her hair back. "Breathe, honey."

Chandler managed a pained smile. "At least he waited until the play was over."

Alan more firmly directed the gathered people to clear the area. "Head out, folks, this isn't part of the show."

"We need to get you to the hospital," Oren said.

Chandler took advantage of a lull in contractions and pulled herself to her feet. Oren put his arm around her and Alan stationed himself at her other side, gripping her arm. They'd gone a few steps when she stopped. "My purse."

Ashley, her best friend, was nearby. "I got it."

Chandler took another step and the vice gripped her middle. "Shit," she growled through gritted teeth.

Warmth trickled down her legs.

"Nooooo." Mortification heaped on top of the pain. Her water breaking in public was the stuff of nightmares.

Alan said, "Uh oh, I think you sprung a leak."

She managed to laugh at that. Whether it was the pressure from laughing or the start of another contraction, the trickle down her leg became a gush. At least it didn't last long.

A woman's voice demanded, "Get her over here."

Alan and Oren turned her and steered toward the stage.

"Oh, great," she grumbled. "Am I the encore?"

On the stage, Gretchen had some blankets and pillows at the ready.

The panic rose in her chest. "I am not having this baby here!"

Gretchen, a volunteer for the fire department and in full Shakespearean costume, firmly guided her to the floor. "It's here or in the car."

"What? No! We have time!" The word ended in a wail as the strongest contraction yet hit her and the urge to push was too strong to resist.

Oren squeezed her hand.

Gretchen barked, "Get these people out of here!"

Alan jumped off the stage to the floor and yelled for all the looky-loos to move their asses out.

There was no time to be embarrassed as Gretchen hiked Chandler's skirt up.

The next massive contraction hit and Chandler pushed for all she was worth.

"You're doing great," Gretchen coached her. "His head's right there. One more big push, Chandler."

Chandler pushed.

Alan yanked the theater door open to let the EMTs through. "Almost there."

Chandler pushed again, gripping Oren's hand like a vice.

"Got him!"

Chandler dropped back against the pillows as the baby wailed, his cry taking full advantage of the theater's acoustics. She heard cheering from the lobby.

The EMTs loaded Chandler and the baby onto the stretcher, securing them. Gretchen covered her with a blanket and tucked it securely around her legs. They wheeled the gurney up the aisle. Alan grabbed the door handle. "You took 'Friends and Family' night a little too far, Chandler."

"Stick to Shakespeare, Alan. You suck at comedy."

He laughed and held the door open for them to pass

through. "Let me know if you need anything," he said, clapping Oren's back. "And congratulations!"

"Mommy!"

Off to the side, Chandler's parents, Lisa and David, held Maddie. They rushed over, relieved. The EMTs paused for just a second.

Chandler reached out and touched Maddie's arm. "Mommy's fine, princess. Your little brother just ccouldn't wait, but now we have to go to the hospital so the doctors can check us both over."

Maddie clutched her stuffed animal and constant companion, Princess Giraffe, and shoved her thumb into her mouth.

"We'll meet you at the hospital," her dad said.

Alan yelled to the remaining crowd, "It's a boy!"

<h1 style="text-align:center">Chapter Two</h1>

Two hours later, Oren hovered near Chandler, now wearing a clean hospital gown, the baby nestled in her arms. He was still in full Shakespearean costume, to the great amusement of the hospital staff. At least he'd been able to wash off most of his makeup in the hospital bathroom.

Ashley and Elliott, their best friends, had popped in to coo over the baby and drop off Chandler's purse and some clothes they'd picked up at the house. Too bad for Oren they had only grabbed Chandler's hospital bag, so he was stuck in his velvet robes and tights until he had a chance to go home.

Chandler's parents brought Maddie in, accompanied by Oren's parents, Janice and Theo.

Beaming, Oren stood by Chandler's bedside and said to the gathered crowd, "I'm glad you're all here."

Chandler smiled up at him.

"We'd like everyone to meet Finnegan Samuel Turner." Oren addressed both of their dads, whose eyes welled with tears. "It worked out great since both of your middle names are Samuel."

Lisa sighed, "Oh, that's so sweet."

Janice made a noncommittal grunt.

Everyone took a brief turn holding the new baby. While he was being passed around, Oren helped Maddie up onto the bed beside Chandler. She snuggled close, holding Princess Giraffe tight and sucking her thumb.

Lisa was the last to hold the baby. "Maddie, do you want to hold your baby brother?"

Maddie's face scrunched up. "Eww, no."

"Madelyn, that's not nice," Janice scolded.

"Mom, it's fine." Oren waved away her concern and took Finn from his mother-in-law.

Ashley said to Chandler, "We'll let you get some rest. Love you."

"Love you, too." Chandler gave her a tired smile.

Oren hoped the rest of the group would take the hint and follow suit.

David touched Lisa's shoulder. "We'll give you a few minutes with Maddie. We'll grab some coffee downstairs and be back to get her shortly." They followed Ashley and Elliott out of the room.

"I suppose you want us to leave so you can spend some time with *her* parents," Janice said.

"What? Everyone's leaving so Chandler can get some rest."

Theo put his hand on Janice's back. "Let's go, we'll see them again tomorrow."

"If we're even invited," Janice mumbled.

Oren ignored the snarking and hugged his parents. "Thanks for coming. I think the regular visiting hours start at ten tomorrow." He not-so-subtly edged them toward the door.

Theo waved at Chandler, then walked into the hallway. Janice followed him without so much as a glance back at her daughter-in-law.

Oren gently rocked Finn in his arms, just outside the room.

"I just don't understand why she chose to honor the fathers. Madelyn's middle name doesn't have anything to do with me."

He really didn't want to deal with this nonsense. "It doesn't have anything to do with Lisa, either," Oren explained. "And Finn's middle name wasn't Chandler's idea, it was mine."

"I doubt that."

His dad said, "C'mon, Janice. He needs to get cleaned up and changed."

Oren sighed. "I'll see you guys tomorrow. Love you." He turned and went back into the room and rolled his eyes. "Finally. Some peace and quiet." He sat on the bed near Chandler's hip, close to Maddie's feet. "Ready to hold your brother?"

Maddie stared at the bundle and slowly nodded.

Oren gently arranged the baby in Maddie's arms. Chandler reached around her, helping to hold him.

"What do you think, pumpkin?"

Maddie made a face. "He smells weird."

He and Chandler caught each other's eye and laughed.

Finn squirmed and started to fuss.

Maddie tried to pull back. "Eew."

A small dribble of spit left Finn's mouth and landed on Princess Giraffe.

Maddie shrieked.

Oren hurried to take Finn.

Maddie started to cry, staring helplessly at the stuffed animal her new brother had just defiled.

Chandler brushed at Princess Giraffe with the corner of the blanket. "It's okay, sweetheart. Princess Giraffe just needs a bath. She's fine."

Maddie scowled and crossed her arms. "Put it back."

"What?"

She glared at the baby. "Put it back in your belly." She

poked Chandler's belly and made another face. "It's squishy now."

"You know what?" Chandler said softly. "I bet he feels bad about spitting up on Princess Giraffe. I bet he'd like to give her one of his new blankies to say sorry."

Maddie eyed him suspiciously.

Oren nodded as he gently swayed. "Mommy's right." With his free hand, he wrestled with a pink blanket his parents had given them just in case the four hundred sonograms had been wrong.

Chandler took the blanket from him and swaddled Princess Giraffe. "There. Does she feel better?"

Maddie took her stuffed toy and cradled it. "Yeah."

"How about we switch and let Mommy feed the baby while you sit on my lap?"

Maddie scrambled down off the bed with her giraffe.

Oren helped Chandler get the baby situated, then sat on the chair beside her, scooping Maddie and Princess Giraffe onto his lap. He was exhausted, but had to admit the timing was pretty darn good. Tonight had been their final performance and practices for the next one wouldn't start for a little more than a month.

He looked over to Chandler and she took his breath away. Nursing their brand new son while their daughter rested against his chest.

Nothing could be more perfect than this life they'd built.

Chapter Three

Chandler sank down the wall until she sat on the cold tile bathroom floor. The shower blasted scalding hot water, filling the room with steam. Finally, *finally*, the baby stopped screaming. She ran a protective hand over his soft, fine hair and choked back a sob.

He whimpered in her arms, so she settled him in to nurse, now that his nose was clearing and the poor boy could breathe. With her free arm, she stuffed towels under her nursing arm and tried to relax. She shifted to see her watch, but her eyes were so heavy and scratchy from the lack of sleep that the face was a blur.

Finnegan suckled himself to sleep. Chandler's eyes were too heavy to hold open. Her head lolled back and smacked against the tile wall.

She jerked upright at a soft tapping on the bathroom door. The interruption made her want to scream, "LEAVE ME ALONE!" but she said nothing. The door opened a crack, letting a rush of cold air in. Goosebumps popped up on her arms.

Oren slipped inside and quickly closed the door behind him. He turned off the shower and sat on the floor beside her. He whispered, "Let me take him?"

Chandler looked blearily down at Finnegan, who'd fallen off her breast and was fast asleep. She was too tired to move or object or assist when Oren reached over and gently took the baby. He cradled Finn in his arm and reached over to stroke Chandler's cheek. "Go to bed."

Instead, she slumped down onto the towels, dead to the world.

For all of thirty minutes.

"MOMMYYYYYYYYYYY!!!!"

"No, Maddie," Oren's voice was stern but quiet through the bathroom door.

Chandler's eyes scratched like she was blinking with sandpaper.

Maddie screeched, "I WANT MOMMY!" and a second later, Finn wailed.

Chandler pressed her face into the towels and hoped her family couldn't hear her sobbing. Finn had had a rough start to his short two-month life, with back to back to back infections – one ear, then both ears, now sinus. Maddie was feeling jealous and neglected, not that anyone could blame her. Chandler hadn't slept more than an hour at a time for at least two weeks. And Oren had to go to work.

Too exhausted to cry anymore, Chandler got up. Her arm and hip hurt from laying against the tile, and her bladder threatened to burst, even though she'd barely eaten or drank anything for days. She peed, trying not to nod off as she sat on the toilet, then got up and washed her hands and wet a washcloth to wash her face. Her reflection horrified her. Deep, dark circles lay under her bloodshot eyes, making her always pale face even more gaunt. Her lips were pressed in a tight line, turned down at the corners.

It looked like the face of someone who would never know happiness again.

The thought piled misery on top of misery as her exhausted brain insisted her children would grow up tormented and neglected because their mother couldn't get it together. Women had been doing this for thousands and thousands of years, right? All without modern conveniences or medicine.

This shouldn't be so hard.

She brushed her dyed blonde hair and pulled it back into a pony tail. That was all the effort her appearance would be getting today.

Pushing away from the sink, she took a deep breath and went into the fray.

Oren sat on the bed, bouncing a wailing Finn, while Maddie lay facedown on the mattress, kicking her feet as hard as she could, screaming into the bed. At least it muffled her. Chandler wished she could have a fit like that. It might help.

"Honey," Oren began.

Chandler was pretty sure she wasn't going to like whatever he was about to say. She fleetingly wondered if this is where he announced he was leaving her because he couldn't stand this life anymore.

"I called my mom. She's coming to stay for a couple of days."

She wasn't sure which was worse.

"Just so we can get Finn's sinus infection under control and get your routine back on track."

Routine. He knew it was one of her magic words. If Chandler liked anything, it was routine. Organization. A plan.

"You need some sleep, and I can't get any more time off until Seth and Corey get back at the end of the month." He'd taken two weeks off when Finn was born, and several days since then. He was completely out of PTO, and it was only June.

It was Wednesday. Okay, maybe having Janice come until the weekend wasn't the most horrible idea ever.

Her last few functioning brain cells balked at that. It *was* the most horrible idea ever, but she was too tired to fight it.

"I'm sorry, I know you probably hate the idea, but I tried your mom first and she can't come until next week."

His words came to her through mud. Her eyes fixed on a frayed spot on their bedspread until dots danced in her vision.

"Chan?"

Her eyeballs felt like sandpaper as they slid up to look at him. "I don't care."

"About what? Chan?"

"Anything."

Her world went dark.

Chapter Four

Oren saw it coming, but with Finn in his arms, he couldn't move fast enough to keep Chandler from hitting the floor.

Maddie was still sobbing into the pillow at the injustices of her world. Oren laid Finn down and by the time he got to his knees beside Chandler, she was coming to.

He brushed her hair off her face and suddenly realized how sunken her cheeks were, how dark the circles under her eyes were. "Hey."

Her bloodshot eyes darted around, frantic. "What happ—where's the baby?"

Oren grabbed her shoulders and helped her sit up. "He's fine. Chandler. Look at me."

Her wild eyes couldn't seem to focus on anything. A stab of guilt sliced through him. He'd been so busy with work and getting ready for the theater's upcoming production of *Hamlet* that he hadn't seen how bad things had gotten for his wife.

The doorbell chimed.

Maddie stopped crying and sat up. "Who's here?"

"It should be Nanny."

"Yay!" Maddie bounded off the bed and danced to the stairs.

"Careful!" Oren warned. He picked Finn up. They all went downstairs, where Maddie was jumping up, trying to unfasten the childproof latch on the door. He moved her out of the way and unlocked the door, opening it to his mother's beaming face. She grabbed him in a hug, and over her shoulder, he noticed two huge suitcases. And a tote bag. And her massive purse.

Oh, no.

"Mom, that's a lot of stuff for a couple of days," he said, wheeling the bags into the kitchen.

She ignored him, bending to lift Maddie into her arms and plant kisses all over her face. "How's Nanny's girl?"

Maddie giggled and squealed with delight for a few minutes, then squirmed to be put down. "Nanny, I'm hungry."

Oren cringed a little inside as Janice shot a side-eye at Chandler. "Hasn't she had breakfast yet? Goodness."

He jumped in. "Yes, she did. I gave her a Pop-tart about an hour ago."

"A Pop-tart is hardly nutritious." Janice sighed and opened the fridge. "I guess I'll have to make some breakfast before I'll even be able to hold the baby."

Oren glanced over at Chandler, but she didn't seem to notice. Oh, well. His mom's snide comments would be a small price to pay for Chandler to get some sleep. He went to the living room and pulled the bassinet into the kitchen. He put Finn in the bassinet, then turned the dial for it to gently rock side to side. Ah, the magic of modern technology.

He gently squeezed her arm. "Go to bed. I'll see you tonight."

"Okay." Chandler sounded like a zombie, toneless and raspy.

He put his hands on her shoulders and physically turned her toward the doorway. "Go."

She shuffled away to the stairs.

Oren listened until he heard the bedroom door close. "Mom, I can't thank you enough. We really appreciate you coming over to help."

She cracked an egg into a pan. "Of course. Some people have a rough time being a new parent."

"Please don't."

"What?" She raised her shoulder – and a spatula – in innocence. "Just because I went back to work at six weeks doesn't mean I can't understand it's harder for some other people to adjust."

"You didn't have a sick baby."

"You had colic for months."

"I give up. Just… be nice." He gave Maddie a hug and a kiss. "Daddy's going to work. You be good for Nanny. Love you."

"Love you, Daddy." She scrambled up on her stool at the sink. "Can I help, Nanny?"

Oren kissed his fingertips and lightly brushed them against Finn's cheek. Part of him hated to leave and go in to the office. A bigger part of him was relieved and anxious to go. That part of him also felt like a giant coward.

"Finn's antibiotics are in the fridge. He already had his dose for this morning. There's also bottles on the bottom shelf when he gets hungry."

"Oh. Chandler isn't nursing?"

He bristled at the judgment in that comment. It seemed like everyone on the planet had an opinion on how his son got fed. "She is. And pumping for situations just like this. Please. Just let her sleep."

"Don't worry. *I* can handle an infant and a little girl."

Maddie said, "I'm a *big* girl."

"You sure are." He didn't have time to deal with his mom's thinly-veiled condescension. "I'll see you tonight. Thanks again."

"And be careful. This rain has the roads slick."

"Thanks." He let himself out, glad that his household was peaceful, for the moment at least.

As he flipped the windshield wipers on, he couldn't help but feel like the summer storm brewing across the sky was some sort of harbinger of what was brewing at home.

Chapter Five

Chandler woke and stretched. She startled, panicking for a second until she remembered that Janice had the kids. Relaxing into the pillow, she felt almost human again. She got out of bed and checked the clock. Six o'clock. A little twinge of guilt nagged at her. She'd slept for nine solid hours without moving from the position she'd started in.

Deciding she might not get another chance, she stripped and got into the shower. For the first time since Finn's birth, she shaved her legs and took her time shampooing and conditioning her hair, biting back frustrated tears at the clumps of strands that remained stuck to her hands. Her thick, lush hair had turned to crap sometime in the third trimester of her pregnancy, and the unrelenting stress after Finn's birth made it worse.

She let the hot water pour over her and tried to be grateful. Maybe this was the turning point. Maybe getting a little sleep was just the start of an upswing. She certainly felt a lot better after one good sleep. With Janice here for a few days, she'd even be able to sneak in a few naps. By the time Janice left on Saturday, or maybe Sunday, everything would be good as new.

She'd just have to ignore a few barbed comments and try not to bite her tongue in half. Easy peasy.

Her breasts ached painfully at not being emptied for so long, so she cut her shower short and dried off. She skipped the bra and pulled on a super-loose button-down shirt because she had to either nurse or pump like *right now*.

The power flickered as she got dressed. Her pre-pregnancy jeans slid on easily. She tried to feel smug about the fact, but she knew it was only because of stress and starvation that she'd fit back into them so soon.

She hurried downstairs. Janice was reading to Maddie, doing a range of voices for each character in the book.

"Hey."

"You showered during a storm?" Janice clucked, then admitted, "Well. You look much better."

Chandler didn't point out that Janice would probably be quite happy to see her electrocuted and out of the picture. Oh, the stories Janice would be able to tell. In reality, though, she hadn't even noticed the steady low rumbling of thunder until she started getting dressed. "I feel much better. I can't thank you enough for today."

Janice ignored the comment and went back to the book.

Finn stirred in the bassinet, so Chandler lifted him out and offered him a breast, which he greedily accepted. She settled onto her favorite chair, wedging a pillow under her arm while the baby nursed. The instant he paused his suckling, she switched him to the other side and nearly wilted with relief.

Maddie climbed down from her grandmother's lap and got another book. "Here, Nanny."

Janice situated Maddie in the crook of her arm and began to read. It was easy to see where Oren had gotten his love of theatrics. One could easily envision Princess Poppy and her friends with Janice's distinct voices.

Chandler shifted Finn to her shoulder and patted his back until he burped. A whiff of stink came from the direction of his diaper. She got up and, with one hand, flicked a blanket out and onto the floor. She put the baby on the blanket and slid the basket of changing supplies they'd put under the coffee table toward her.

As she changed his diaper, Maddie announced, "He has a penis. Cuz he's a boy. I don't have a penis, Nanny."

Chandler heard Janice suck in a breath. "No, you don't."

"Mommy, what's my penis called? I forgetted."

"You don't have a penis, Maddie. You have a vagina."

"Yeah. I have a bagina, Nanny. Do you have a bagina?"

Janice cleared her throat. "Let's finish our book, okay?"

"Mommy has a bagina. It's how Finn came out of her belly."

Chandler was glad her back was to Janice because she couldn't contain her grin at her mother-in-law's discomfort. Once she finished changing Finn, she was relieved to see him look around the room, bright-eyed, instead of wailing in pain. Hopefully the antibiotics were finally working and the poor little guy would kick these infections for good.

Janice finished reading to Maddie. "I made a meatloaf and potatoes for dinner. I put plates in the fridge for you and Oren. Maddie and I already ate."

Chandler's stomach rumbled at the mention of food. "Thank you. Oren always says your meatloaf is the best."

"When he was at home, I used to make him his own meatloaf or nobody else would get any." She chuckled.

Finn cooed and gurgled, reaching to grab his toes. Janice scooped him off Chandler's lap and bounced him. "Go eat. You need to get some meat back on your bones."

She stood and went to the kitchen. She microwaved the plate. When it was done, she sat down and attached her double breast pump. Sitting at the table, she ate with one hand

and scrolled through her phone with the other, feeling a bit like a dairy cow while the machine emptied her breasts.

Oren came through the kitchen door. When he saw her, his smile widened. "Hey, babe." He leaned down to kiss her. "Mmm. Meatloaf."

"Your mom made it. There's a plate in the fridge for you, but you can finish mine, too. I can't eat it all."

He grabbed her fork and speared a hunk of meatloaf. "How'd today go? Did you get some sleep?"

"It was great. I didn't get up until about six.'

He touched her cheek. "You look so much better."

"Gee, thanks," she snarked.

"No, I mean you look like you *feel* better."

The pump finished, so she released herself and buttoned her shirt while Oren slid easily into the routine of getting the milk to the fridge and washing the pump pieces.

"Thanks. I'll take Maddie up and get her ready for bed. I'm sure your mom could use a break."

"A break?" Janice said from the doorway. "From what? All I've done is watch the children and make dinner."

Chandler tried not to bristle and read into Janice's comment. *Think nice thoughts. Think nice thoughts.* That was one of Princess Poppy's nauseatingly repetitive mantras, and it wasn't working very well. *Think nice thoughts.*

"We appreciate it," Oren said, flicking water from his fingertips. He put the pump pieces in the dish drainer and dried his hands.

Maddie grabbed onto his leg. He reached down and whisked her up into the air.

"Again!"

He lifted her again. And again. And again.

"Mommy's going to take you upstairs and get your jammies on."

"No. I want Nanny to."

Janice scooped her from Oren's arms. "Okay, princess, let's go upstairs."

Chandler turned to get Finn from the bassinet, but Oren stopped her. "I haven't seen him all day."

"Oh."

She hung back, watching Oren gently lift the baby. He put a well-worn folder on the arm of the couch and settled in with Finn. Wrestling the pages open with one hand, he began to read.

"*'It faded on the crowing of the cock.*
Some say that ever 'gainst that season comes
Wherein our Saviour's birth is celebrated,
The bird of dawning singeth all night long:
And then, they say, no spirit dares stir abroad;
The nights are wholesome; then no planets strike,
No fairy takes, nor witch hath power to charm,
So hallow'd and so gracious is the time.'"

Chandler leaned on the door frame, watching him affectionately. "Horatio?"

"Close. Marcellus."

"Ah." *Hamlet* wasn't her favorite, but she'd been with Oren long enough to recognize most of Shakespeare's plays from short bits of dialogue.

Finn was the perfect audience. He stared up at Oren, captivated by the rhythm and flow of the words. How well Chandler knew the feeling. She loved listening to her husband practice his lines. His troupe performed two plays each year, one in the spring and one in the fall. Finn had been born on closing night of *Much Ado About Nothing*, and they would be performing *Hamlet* in September, three months away.

Oren was a tad obsessive. As the head of the troupe, he

took it upon himself to know every part inside and out as well as keep the back end organized and running smoothly.

"I feel a little useless right now," Chandler admitted. "I have some energy, but nothing to do with it."

He looked up from his pages. "You could always work on costumes, if you want something to do."

"Good idea. Let me know when Finn's hungry again." She went down to the finished basement they'd converted into a sewing room slash costume room slash office slash prop room slash whatever else she needed it to be room.

The main living area had a huge island where Chandler cut fabrics. Counters and cabinets lined the longest wall. The second-longest wall had a sturdy bar where she hung costume gowns and robes. Along the short wall that had windows near the ceiling was her sewing machine, and the other short wall was a massive white board where she sketched ideas, made notes, and a corkboard where she tacked her color-coded to do lists and purchase orders.

The basement was her sanctuary, one she hadn't stepped foot into since Finn was born. She'd originally planned to only take a few weeks off, but with his infections and her exhaustion, her online costume shop had been closed for a little more than two months. Lightning lit up the world outside the French doors that opened to the patio for a second.

Chandler breathed deeply. It felt like coming home to be in her space again, surrounded by things that belonged to her alone. Fabrics, tools, even the business paperwork, made her smile.

She spent some time just reacclimating herself to her space. She ran her hands over the completed costumes she'd made, touching the faux leather, the glass and plastic jewels, the velvet and muslin. They were reused for Oren's troupe's plays. A gown for a queen, a threadbare dress for a peasant. A plastic sword she'd covered with silver leaf to look real from the audience. Yorick's powdery skull that *Hamlet* would hold aloft. After each play, she lovingly fixed or recycled each piece, handed them off to the specialty cleaner she worked with, and then brought them here, to wait for their next performance. She made a mental note to schedule the pickup for the *Much Ado* costumes that were still waiting to be cleaned and repaired.

In her spare time – whatever that was – she designed Renaissance Faire costumes for her online shop. She'd become well-known for her gowns, but even more so for her hand-crafted corsets.

Chapter Six

Oren texted Chandler, letting her know Finn was fussing and probably wanted to be fed. She came upstairs and settled onto her recliner. Oren situated the baby. "I'll go up and get Maddie to bed."

"Okay." She smiled up at him.

It shook him how different she looked. Was it only this morning she'd been a zombie? She still looked tired, but it was the expected tired of just-had-a-baby. Again, the guilt prodded him that he hadn't even noticed how far down she'd spiraled. "I stopped and got distilled water for the humidifier, so hopefully he'll sleep tonight."

"Oh, good. I'd forgotten all about it."

He leaned down and kissed her, then watched her with Finn for a moment before taking the stairs two at a time.

His mom dried Maddie off while the tub drained. A ring of bubbles clung to the top of the tub, and soapy plastic animals floated toward the drain.

He scooped Maddie up, towel and all. "My goodness, did Nanny get in the tub with you?"

Maddie giggled and squirmed. "Nooo, Daddy!"

"I might as well have," Janice laughed, holding out her arms to show Oren her soaked shirt and pants.

Oren took Maddie to her room and plopped her onto the bed. "What jammies do we want tonight?"

"Poppy! Poppy! Poppy!"

He opened the dresser drawer and held up a set of pajamas with kittens on them. "Is this Poppy?"

"Nooooo," Maddie laughed.

"Is this Poppy?" He held up a set of Princess Felicia pajamas. He personally liked Felicia better. She didn't wear an obnoxious peacock feather tiara and have a billion expensive licensed accessories for sale.

"Noooo!"

"Is this Poppy?" Ducks.

Maddie giggled and clapped her hands. "Poppy, Daddy, Poppy!"

"This one, right?" Unicorns.

"Daddy!"

"No, these aren't pajamas of Daddy. Now you're just being silly." There was no question which pajamas were of Princess Poppy, the current most popular animated sensation. Poppy had five animated movies and a massive marketing team. No one with children could escape Poppy's grinning face and sparkling peacock feather tiara. It was on pajamas, sheets, board games, cereal boxes, dolls (and all their accessories), and even cell phone cases. Oren wasn't too sure about that one.

She clapped her hands, still laughing.

He picked a set of Poppy pajamas, and Maddie squealed in delight. She loudly sang Princess Poppy's theme song as Oren helped her put her pajamas on.

"Hush. It's time to quiet down for bedtime," Janice scolded as she came into the room.

Maddie clamped her mouth shut.

"Finish your song." Oren tickled her and picked up somewhere in the middle of the song. It took a minute, but Maddie sang along to the end, with much less volume and enthusiasm.

He held the comforter up so Maddie could crawl under it. He didn't want to ask his mom to leave the room, not when she'd been so gracious to drop everything and come over, but he wanted to make sure Maddie went to bed happy.

Maddie yawned and said, "Night, Nanny. Kisses." She held her arms up for hugs and kisses.

Oren was relieved that Janice delivered her hugs and kisses, then went to the guest room. He arranged Maddie's horde of stuffed animals, giving them each a kiss before snuggling them next to Maddie. Princess Giraffe had the best spot, tightly snuggled in Maddie's arms.

Next, he turned the light off and flicked on the soft night-light that glowed from Maddie's dresser.

He gave Maddie her hugs and kisses, then spoke softly, telling her a story about a princess who grew giant carrots in her vegetable garden. Spoiler alert: the princess wins a prize for her carrots.

Her eyes grew heavy. Her fingers twirled around Princess Giraffe's ear. With one last huge yawn, she closed her eyes.

Oren slipped out of the bedroom and closed the door with a soft click. He went to the master bedroom and sat on the edge of the bed to take his shoes off. Motion caught his attention, and he looked up just as his mom lifted her hand to knock on the open door.

"Can I come in?"

"Sure. What's up?"

"I have some concerns."

Chapter Seven

Chandler had been dozing while Finn nursed, until Janice's words "I have some concerns" filtered through the baby monitor.

She sat up, alert. The baby had fallen asleep, so she adjusted her shirt and waited.

Oren sighed in response.

Janice began, "When Chandler was changing Finn's diaper – on the *floor*, by the way – Maddie started talking about his… penis." The last word dropped to a whisper, like it was a dirty word. Chandler ran a hand down her face, trying to remind herself that Janice had done them a huge favor, and that she'd gotten some sleep thanks to her.

"Mom…"

"Then Maddie talked about… her parts, and then asked me about mine, and it was just all very inappropriate."

Chandler held her breath. Oren sometimes had a blind spot where his mother was concerned and agreed just to appease her.

He said, "I'm sure it was a little uncomfortable, but it was in no way inappropriate. It's developmentally spot on for

Maddie to recognize the differences between boys and girls and categorize them in her mind."

"Well. It may be developmentally spot on, but I don't understand why she needs to know those words. She's only four."

Chandler felt her chest tighten. Cutesy names for private parts were a complete deal breaker.

Oren's voice was patient. "The fact that she's four is *exactly* why she needs to know the correct terminology. It's something Chandler and I absolutely agree on."

This was one topic Chandler couldn't let go. She took Finn upstairs and went to the bedroom. She spoke gently. "Just FYI, the baby monitor was on." She settled Finn in his crib and stood straight. "I appreciate your concern, Janice. I do." She pulled in a deep breath, not wanting to offend her mother-in-law, but the subject was too important to gloss over.

"I'm not criticizing," Janice explained lamely.

"No, it's fine." It wasn't fine. She was definitely criticizing, but whatever. "You know I used to work in a daycare."

"Yes."

"Then you remember I was a mandated reporter. Any time we suspected any sort of abuse, we would report it as soon as we knew. We had one case where a little girl kept telling us her neighbor was touching her cookies. Janice, it took us months to understand she wasn't talking about cookies. It still turns my stomach to think how much sooner it could have been stopped if that precious girl hadn't been taught that ridiculous euphemism."

"That's awful."

"Anyway. I know it can be a little uncomfortable. For what it's worth, you redirected her attention brilliantly." Chandler gave Janice a smile.

Janice didn't return it, no doubt irritated at Chandler's appearance and speech.

Oh, well.

Oren broke the tension. "I think it's time to hit the hay since both the kids are asleep."

"Good night," Janice said. She reached over and gently stroked Finn's head. "Make sure that's not getting water on him." She gestured to the humidifier.

Chandler bit her tongue and made sure her voice was sweet. "Good night, Janice. Thanks again for coming." She grabbed her shirt and yoga pants and went into the bathroom.

Through the door, she heard Janice snark, "How many listening devices should I be aware of?"

Oren's reply was mild. "We only have monitors next to the kids' beds."

Chandler turned on the faucet to brush her teeth and drown out any further conversation.

A little while later, she snuggled next to Oren, resting her head on his shoulder while his fingers absently played with the seam of her sleeve.

"I, um," he began, "think maybe it might have been a little much to lecture Mom about the whole body parts thing."

She stiffened.

"Don't get mad. It was just the listening through the baby monitor when she didn't know you were listening that, I think, bothered her."

"I can appreciate that, but she doesn't get to accuse me of teaching my daughter something inappropriate."

"I was handling it."

"Okay."

"It's just that she's doing us a big favor. She didn't have to come."

"I know that."

"Show a little more appreciation, that's all."

She sighed. It was too late to get into a big discussion, and she didn't feel like defending herself. "Love you." She gave him a kiss on the cheek and rolled over.

By some miracle, Finn only got up once during the night, and it was because he was hungry, not because he was screaming in pain.

Oren got up with his alarm and got dressed for work. Chandler snuggled under the covers, unwilling to get up until the last possible second. Finn stirred in his crib, so she stretched and threw the covers back. "Guess that means I have to get up, huh?"

"Looks like it."

Chandler smiled down at the baby. "Hang on, sweet pea, Mommy has to go potty first." She grabbed her clothes and changed, then brushed her teeth and tied her hair back. When she came back out, Finn was just starting to fuss.

"Hurry up, Chan, he's hungry."

"He's fine." She scooped him out of the crib and tried to fight the rising annoyance. The baby wasn't crying, he wasn't upset, he was just letting the world know it was feeding time. She certainly didn't want to let a little tiff with Oren ruin what was an otherwise great start to the day. She felt rested and ready to get back to making her daily to do lists and getting things done.

She settled in her rocking chair to nurse, lifting her face for Oren's quick goodbye kiss. Finn was almost done when Maddie came in, dragging her worn "bankie" and Princess Giraffe with her.

"Do you have a book?" Chandler asked.

Maddie climbed up onto the bed and shoved her thumb into her mouth. "No."

"Your brother's almost done. Do you want waffles for breakfast?"

"Smiley waffles?"

"Of course." Smiley waffles were plain old frozen toaster waffles that had a face drawn with strawberry syrup. As far as Maddie was concerned, they were Michelin star quality cuisine.

When Finn was done, Chandler adjusted her shirt. "Okay, pumpkin, let's go down and make smiley waffles."

"Yay!" Maddie bounced off the bed and hopped the whole way to the stairs.

"Careful," Chandler warned.

"I know," Maddie sang. She shoved Princess Giraffe into her armpit, then gripped the handrail and slowly took each step until they reached the bottom.

Any hope that Janice might still be sleeping vanished. She stood at the stove, cracking eggs into a pan.

Maddie's face scrunched into a scowl. "I want smiley waffles."

Janice was firm. "No. Nanny's making eggs."

"I want SMILEY WAFFLES."

Chandler settled Finn on the table in his bouncy rocker. "Maddie, you can have some eggs with your smiley waffle. You like Nanny's eggs."

She glared, suspicious, but loosened her hold on Princess Giraffe's neck. "Okay."

Janice set the spatula down harder than necessary.

Chandler tried to ignore the gesture until Janice picked the spatula up and smacked it back down again. "Everything okay?"

Janice turned and planted her fist on her hip. "Obviously

not. I'm making eggs and pancakes. There's no need to have waffles, too."

Maddie's eyes widened.

"It's just a toaster waffle. She can have it with her eggs. Not a big deal."

"It *is* a big deal. I'm standing here making breakfast because you're—" she waved her hand to encompass Chandler from head to toe "—incapacitated or whatever, and I expect a little appreciation."

Chandler breathed against the tightness squeezing her chest. "Janice. I do appreciate you making breakfast. I appreciate you being here. I appreciate all your help. Maddie asked for a smiley waffle before we came downstairs and I had no idea you were already cooking. I'm happy to eat pancakes."

Janice grunted and jabbed at the eggs. A second later, she turned around and pointed the spatula at Maddie. Her voice was raised. "You're having a *pancake*, not a waffle."

Maddie's chin quivered.

"Don't yell at her," Chandler snapped.

"I want a smiley waffle." Maddie sniffled.

Chandler ran a hand over Maddie's mass of tangled brown curls. "You can have a waffle, but you have to eat some of Nanny's eggs, too."

"Forget it." Janice snatched the pan from the stove and scraped the eggs into the trash can.

Before Chandler could respond, Janice stormed past her, still gripping the spatula in her hand. For half a second, she considered going after her to apologize, until she looked at Maddie. Maddie's big blue eyes were full of tears.

"Okay, sweetie, let's make a waffle."

Maddie sniffled and the tears spilled down her cheeks. "No."

"Don't you want a waffle?"

She shook her head.

"Why not?"

Janice came back into the room and put the spatula into the dishwasher. Without a word, she dumped the plate of pancakes into the trash, along with the ruined eggs, and put those dirty dishes in the dishwasher as well.

Maddie sniffled loudly. "Nanny?"

Janice ignored her.

"Sorry, Nanny."

Janice turned. Her expression was cold. "Nanny's not mad at *you*, Madelyn." She flicked a pointed glance at Chandler.

Chandler saw red. There was no reason for her to be snippy with Maddie. She bit her tongue for a second, then it came out. "Nanny doesn't have any reason to be mad at all."

Janice glared.

Maddie started to bawl.

Finn wailed.

Chandler wanted to scream. She touched the side of Finn's bouncer to create the soothing motion for him in the middle of this chaos. It left a bad taste in her mouth, but she knew she'd have to be the one to back down, even though she'd done nothing wrong. "I'm sorry about the breakfast misunderstanding."

Janice crossed her arms and lifted her chin, needing an entire pound of flesh, apparently.

"We appreciate everything you're doing. Truly." She mentally choked on the words. Right now, Chandler would appreciate it if Janice went home, and little else.

Maddie sniffled. "Sorry, Nanny. I like eggs."

Finn stopped crying and tried to eat his foot.

Janice straightened her shoulders and made a satisfied "Hmph" sound. Then she started making a new breakfast.

Chandler gritted her teeth, but let it go.
Just like always.

Chapter Eight

Oren clapped his hands. "Good work, everybody."

"I thought we were starting with short rehearsals?" Gretchen joked.

He looked at his watch. Almost nine. "Shoot. Sorry, guys. I didn't realize it was so late." He shoved his script into his messenger bag.

"How's the baby?" Alan, who'd been with the troupe since its inception, came alongside the table where everyone piled their purses and bags and car keys and whatever else they'd carried in with them.

"Good. Poor little guy had an ear infection, but I think he's done with it." He crossed his fingers and held them up.

Gretchen interjected. "Aww, poor baby. How's Chandler doing?"

"Good."

She picked up a leopard print purse. "I hope it's not too much for your family, going to three times a week rehearsals."

"It's fine. My mom's staying with us for a while."

Gretchen and Alan shared a glance. "Oh," they said in unison.

Gretchen slung her bag over her shoulder. "Well, good luck with that." She waved and walked up the long aisle, past the rows of ancient wood-and-velvet audience seats.

Oren wasn't sure what that was supposed to mean.

Alan said, "Need any help moving chairs off the stage?"

"Nah, they'll be fine until we're back Tuesday."

"Okay. Night."

"See you next week."

Oren waited until Alan was gone, then took one last look around. He made the trek up the sloped aisle to the back of the theater and turned to look back. The red velvet curtains had seen better days, but hopefully they'd make it through the rest of this year's performances.

The wood floor of the stage was newly sanded and refinished, then waxed and polished to a high shine that amplified the stage lighting. The walls were dark, meant to fade away from view and keep the focus on the stage.

This building had originally been a church, built in the 1700s. It had fallen into disrepair and was slated for demolition until the Hickory Hollow Restoration Society took it on more than half a century ago. Rows of 1800s wood and velvet theater chairs, rescued from a demolition project three states away, curved toward the stage.

He pulled in a contented breath. He always felt most centered when he was here, on the stage, clothed in robes and tights, confidently speaking lines from Shakespeare's legendary pen. In those moments, he *became* Antony or Archidamus or Henry VIII or King Lear, or Hamlet… or in this season's case, King Claudius.

His phone vibrated in his back pocket. He didn't want to answer it. He knew the house was probably chaos, and his mom was probably on Chandler's last nerve, Maddie was probably running wild, and Finn was probably screaming his head off.

Steeling himself, he made the fifteen minute drive home.

He pulled into the driveway and shut the car off. The porch light burned brightly, but the only light on inside the house was in the living room. He let himself in.

The kitchen was quiet. It was almost eerie, a complete disconnect from the pandemonium he'd expected to find.

"Oren?" His mother's voice came from the living room.

He went down the short hallway and poked his head in. "Where is everyone?"

"Bed, I presume." Her tone was the dismissive, haughty one he'd despised for years.

Tossing his messenger bag onto the couch, he flopped down beside it. "Why'd you say it like that?"

"Like what?"

"Like you're irritated."

"No, I'm fine. Not irritated at all. I can't say the same for your *wife*, though."

Oren ran a hand over his face. She was definitely irritated. "What now?"

She closed her magazine and set it on the end table. "No matter what I do, it's not up to her hoity toity standards. It's fine, I'm just here to help, but she wants everything done her way and won't listen to anything I have to say."

Oren didn't doubt her, exactly, because Chandler's standards were pretty high, but he also knew his mom's approach often lacked even a modicum of tact. "I'll talk to her." He had no idea what he'd say, because he also knew that there was no way Chandler had complained about something his mother had done as far as cooking or chores or helping with the kids.

"Thank you, sweetheart. I'm only trying to help." She got up and smoothed her hands down the front of her shirt.

"I know." He watched Janice cross the room and listened to her footsteps heading up the stairs. He locked the doors, turned off the lights, and headed upstairs himself.

Maddie's door was closed. He peeked in, and she was fast asleep, her face mashed into Princess Giraffe's long neck. It was a wonder she could even breathe, but no matter how many times they moved the stuffed animal, she always found a way to pull it back to the same spot.

He clicked off the hall light. A thin line of light shone from under the door to the master bedroom. He slowly turned the knob, not wanting to disturb Chandler's much-needed rest.

He needn't have been so careful. She sat up in the rocking chair, nursing Finn.

"Hey."

She lifted her arm, not-so-subtly showing her watch. "You said you'd be home by seven."

"Sorry. Practice ran a little long."

"Sure."

"Chan, don't be mad." It had been a long day and he didn't want any conflict with her or his mother.

"You could have at least texted me back."

"Sorry." He had no defense to that.

Finn stirred. She lifted him to her shoulder and adjusted her shirt.

"I'll take him." Oren scooped the baby from her arms and bounced him on his shoulder, patting his back.

Chandler went into the bathroom and came back a few minutes later. She sat on the edge of the bed, rubbing moisturizer on her hands.

"How was today?"

"Long." She snapped the cap of her lotion shut and set the bottle on the nightstand.

Oren settled Finn in the crib and went to sit beside his wife. "Sounds like there was some tension."

"Really." Her voice was toneless.

"Mom's just trying to help. You can't be defensive and get mad at her just because she does things differently."

Her head snapped toward him. "Wow."

"What?"

"You have no idea what went on today, but you've already taken her side."

"There's no need for sides." He reached for her.

She yanked her arm away from him and stood.

"Okay, fine, tell me what happened."

"She said I'm a bad mother."

He stood and put his hands on her arms. "I'm sure whatever she said, she didn't mean it like that."

Chandler jerked back, her eyes filling with tears. "She literally said, 'Some people aren't cut out for mothering, Chandler. You're one of them.' Now please, Mama's Boy, tell me how I'm misinterpreting that. Go ahead. Tell me how she didn't mean what she said."

"'Mama's Boy'? Really?"

Her mouth dropped open as she gaped at him. "That's all you have to say?"

"I just don't see why you have to attack me. This is between you and Mom."

Her jaw worked a few times, like she had something to say, but in the end she just gave her head a shake and climbed into bed.

Oren took a shower, trying to work out a better way to explain it to Chandler, but by the time he got back to bed, she was asleep.

When he woke up in the morning, Chandler's half of the bed was empty. He felt a little wave of relief, immediately followed by a pang of guilt. He didn't want to argue, and it still stung that she'd called him a 'Mama's Boy.

He understood she was having a hard time, and his mother could be difficult. But if she'd learn to let things roll off her back, things would be easier for all of them.

Chapter Nine

Chandler sat in the living room, rocking Finn and dozing. Footsteps coming down the stairs roused her. Immediately, her chest, neck, and jaw tensed. Janice.

She shifted the baby and waited for the first verbal grenade of the day.

"Would you like me to take Finnegan so you can get dressed?"

Chandler pulled in a deep breath and handed the baby to her mother-in-law.

Janice clucked her tongue and spoke to Finn, who hadn't woken up during the exchange. "Goodness, how long have you been soaking in this full diaper? We have to get you nice and dry before you get a rash."

Chandler simply walked upstairs to the bedroom. Oren was in the bathroom, so she changed her clothes and picked up the full hamper, carrying it out and setting it beside the steps so she wouldn't forget to do laundry. Again. Like she was the only human living in the house that was capable of running the big scary washing machine, but whatever.

Maddie's door clicked open. Big blue eyes peered out of the cracked door.

"Hey, sweet pea. Do you want smiley waffles for breakfast?"

Maddie yanked the door open and shook her head. "I don't like smiley waffles."

Great. Janice's miserable attitude yesterday morning made Maddie think there was something wrong with waffles. Awesome. Just fricking awesome.

"What are you hungry for?"

Maddie shrugged dramatically. Princess Giraffe flailed along with the movement.

"Let's head down, okay?"

Maddie tromped down the stairs while Chandler lugged the overfull hamper.

Janice was already making breakfast, so Chandler went to the laundry room off the kitchen and separated the clothes. She opened the front-load washing machine, only to discover a forgotten load of laundry that had developed a bit of a funky smell.

With a sigh, she filled the detergent and color-safe bleach reservoirs and turned the machine on. The dryer was occupied by a load of towels. At least they were dry. She pulled them out and set them on the counter.

She'd just finished folding the towels and washcloths when Oren poked his head in the laundry room. "Are you going to eat breakfast with us?"

She'd rather not, but supposed it was necessary to keep the peace. Whose peace, she had no idea, since it definitely wasn't hers. "Sure."

She dropped the folded towels into the basket. The table was already set. Oren was flanked by Maddie on one side and Janice on the other, so Chandler sat across the table like an afterthought. She scooped some eggs onto her plate from the serving bowl. Seriously? A serving bowl for breakfast? No wonder Janice thought she was lazy, because there's no way in the world she'd serve scrambled eggs from a serving bowl on a regular old Friday. Or let's be real, *any* day.

Janice pushed the plate of bacon toward her. "Here. You need to put some meat back on your skinny bones. You look sickly."

"Please don't comment on my weight."

Janice harrumphed. "I'm not criticizing, Chandler. I'm concerned about your health. And if you don't take care of yourself, you won't have enough milk to nourish Finn properly."

Chandler looked to Oren for help.

Instead, he said, "Honey. Mom's just trying to help. And she's right. You have to take care of yourself to take care of the kids."

His tone and inflection sounded exactly like his mother.

Chandler's eye twitched. She swallowed a lump in her throat.

Oren glanced at his watch and gulped the last of his orange juice. Hand squeezed by Janice the night before, so it'd be cold. Just the way he likes it. "I gotta get to work. I'll see you tonight." He leaned over and gave Janice a peck on the cheek, then gave one to Maddie, then Finn. He didn't come around the table to kiss Chandler, and it felt like a sucker punch to her already fragile gut.

"Love you guys," he said over his shoulder on the way out.

Janice picked up her empty plate and put it in the dishwasher. "When you're done, I'm going to mop the kitchen since it hasn't been done in a while."

Chandler rolled her eyes at the dig. "I'm done." She scraped her barely touched eggs into the trash and put the plate and fork in the dishwasher.

Maddie scrambled off her chair and dragged Princess Giraffe toward the stairs. "I hafta poop," she announced.

Chandler picked Finn out of his bouncer and headed upstairs with Maddie. "Let's see if you can poop rainbows."

Maddie giggled and shrieked, "Like Poppy!" as she made a beeline for the Jack-and-Jill bathroom that connected her bedroom to Finn's nursery.

For some bizarre reason, Poppy rode a rainbow in every book and movie. Chandler and Oren often joked that she was farting them out. She missed those times, sitting together on the couch, making snide comments about Princess Poppy, her farted rainbows, and her hideous peacock feather tiara. And then they ridiculed themselves for the amount of money they forked over to the Princess Poppy empire.

Chandler sat on the edge of the tub bouncing Finn on her lap while Maddie took care of business on the toilet that was outfitted with steps and an adjustable backrest for toddlers.

"Mommy?"

"Yes, ladybug?"

"Why are you sad?"

The question smacked her right in the face. She cleared her throat once, twice, three times, trying to dislodge the well of tears that threatened. "Mommy's not sad, honey. I'm just really tired, that's all." She managed a pathetic smile and hoped it fooled Maddie.

It didn't.

"Don't be sad, Mommy." Maddie's big blue eyes locked on hers.

"I have an idea. After we take Finn to the doctor, how about we play dress up down in Mommy's shop?"

Maddie squealed and clapped her hands, her mouth open

in a wide grin. Chandler's costume area was off limits except for special occasions.

"I wanna be Poppy! Wif the big hat!"

No surprise there. "You can be Poppy. And it's called a tiara."

"You be Felicia."

Why not? A mashup of fairy tale movies sounded perfect. Chandler simultaneously felt pangs of happiness and guilt. Happiness because she adored playing with Maddie. She was bright and funny and energetic and sweet. Guilt because Finn had been so sick and required so much energy and attention that Maddie had been getting Chandler's threadbare leftovers.

Maddie finished on the toilet, and Chandler helped her change out of her pajamas. She put Finn on Maddie's bed, then helped Maddie get dressed – in her favorite bright green leggings and rainbow t-shirt dress – and brush her teeth.

Chandler had just rinsed the toothbrush (Poppy, of course) and reminded Maddie to wash her hands when she heard Janice shriek from the bedroom. She ran out, expecting to see something horrific.

Janice's eyes bulged with fury from within her beet-red face. She pointed to Finn, who was sucking on his toes. "What is *wrong* with you, leaving him unattended like this? He could have rolled onto the floor and smashed his head!"

She bent toward the baby, but Chandler was faster. She scooped Finn off the bed and said, "He's two months old, Janice. He's not rolling anywhere."

"Yes," Janice spat. "He's two months old and you left him *alone* on a bed with *blankets*. He could have *smothered*."

The last of her patience snapped. "Pack your shit and go home, Janice."

"And leave my grandbabies alone with you? Not a chance." She whirled and stalked out of the room.

Chandler stared at the open doorway, half-wondering if she'd just imagined the entire scene. How much bullshit did gratitude require that she endure?

"Can I watch Poppy?" Thankfully Maddie had missed the bulk of the exchange.

"Yeah," she said absently.

A few minutes later, Maddie and Princess Giraffe were settled on the couch watching *Poppy's Big Adventure*. Finn was in his swing, taking his morning nap.

Janice breezed in and cuddled next to Maddie. "Oooh, this is my favorite movie." Ah. So we switched from Hyde back to Jekyll. Great.

Chandler's phone dinged with an incoming text message from her best friend, Ashley.

I miss your face.

Chandler clutched her phone. The simple text felt like a lifeline thrown to her in the middle of the ocean. The kids were fine, even if they were being watched over by a wicked witch, so she ran upstairs to the master bedroom and locked the door. Her hands shook as she tapped the screen to connect to Ashley.

"Hey! How are you?" was Ashley's bright response.

Chandler opened her mouth to speak, but all that came out was a strangled sort of squeak. Words couldn't seem to pass through her throat.

"Chan? Honey, what's wrong?"

"I…" she burst into tears and slid to the floor, her back against the bed.

Ashley made soothing murmurs until Chandler could talk.

"I can't take it. I can't do this. I'm trapped in this house and

I miss you so much and I don't know what to do and I'm losing my mind."

"Hey, hey. Slow down."

Chandler sniffled and wiped her face on the edge of the comforter. "I can't talk here."

"Do you want to get together?"

"*Ohmygoshyes*," came out as one word. "When can we meet?"

"Any time you want. You can come over here. I'll be home all day, and I have snacks. Do you need me to come get you?"

The sweet offer brought fresh tears. "No. I'm taking Finn to his checkup in an hour. I can text you when we're done?"

"Absolutely. Chan, I'm so sorry. I didn't know you were having such a hard time. Why didn't you say something?"

"I don't know."

Ashley's soothing voice was the balm Chandler's soul needed. "Honey, it's okay. Elliott's home today, so he can take the kids and I'm all yours for as long as you need."

"Okay." She sniffled and tried to pull herself together. "I miss you. It's been forever."

"I know. These darn kids sure put a damper on girl time, don't they?"

"Yeah." She managed a weak laugh. "Okay. I'm okay. I'll text you as soon as we're done."

"Yay!"

"I can't wait to see you." All of a sudden, there was a light at the end of this dark tunnel.

"Me, either. Breathe, and I'll see you soon. Love you."

"Love you, too."

Chandler hung up and let out a deep breath. Meeting Ashley and unloading all the weight on her chest was just what the doctor ordered.

She washed her face and changed the shirt that was soaked

with tearstains. Good enough for a trip to the pediatrician. She adjusted the curtain that looked out over the side yard, toward the park. "Oh, crap."

Wednesday's storm had knocked a massive branch out of their old oak tree, which had crushed a section of their picket fence. She made a mental note to deal with it later. Along with everything else.

Downstairs, she double checked that the diaper bag was stocked.

"Okay, Maddie, let's take Finn to the doctor."

Janice glared. "Maddie can stay home. She doesn't need to be bothered with your meeting."

"I wanna stay home and watch Poppy," Maddie whined.

"Fine. You can stay home." She picked Maddie up and gave her a big hug and a million kisses all over her face until she was laughing and squealing. "Love you, love you, love love love you."

"Love love you, too!" Maddie yelled.

Chandler set her down and picked Finn up. "We'll be back later." She didn't wait for a response.

In the garage, she buckled Finn into his car seat, double checked the straps, and started the car. As she eased out, she hit the brakes abruptly.

Did Janice say "meeting"?

Chapter Ten

Oren sat at his desk, staring at a spreadsheet while Corey, his officemate, rambled about his big weekend plans. Something about a girl he'd met on Tinder and a boat. Corey was a great guy, and a hard worker, but he never shut up. Like, ever.

Oren's phone dinged with an incoming text. He swiped his phone to find a picture of Chandler and Finn smiling at the camera in the doctor's office waiting room.

He texted back,

Where's Maddie?

With your mom.

Oren sighed and shook his head, then replied,

Why? She needs a break.

Three dots appeared and blinked on the screen, then disappeared, then blinked again, then disappeared, like Chandler was typing and erasing and retyping a message. Then the dots blinked for quite a while before Chandler's response popped up.

She can go home then. She's not a hostage.

On the heels of that message was:

Dr called our name, can't text for a while.

He huffed out an annoyed sigh. Why couldn't Chandler just make the effort to get along with his mom? There had always been tension between them, but it had gone from zero to a hundred since his mom was staying with them. Oren didn't understand it. His mom was a huge help with the kids and around the house. Yeah, she could be a little – okay, a lot – rude sometimes, but that's just how she is. It's worth enduring a few obnoxious comments to have her help. Especially since Oren was about to get even busier with the *Hamlet* production.

The minutes ticked away until lunchtime. He left the office and walked down the sidewalk to get lunch at the sub shop. After he ate, he sat outside on a bench and dialed his mother's cell number.

"Hi, sweetheart."

"Hey. I just wanted to say hi to Maddie."

"Sure, but don't hang up. There's… something I need to tell you."

He rolled his eyes. "Okay."

A moment later, Maddie was telling him all about Poppy and Pink – Poppy's best friend, who happened to be a purple unicorn – and how when Mommy got home, they were going to play princess dress-up.

"That sounds fun."

"Uh-huh, and I'm gonna be Poppy and Mommy's gonna be Felicia."

"Who's Finn going to be?"

Maddie immediately dismissed that notion. "He can play with Nanny."

Oren chuckled. "Okay, princess, let me talk to Nanny. I'll see you after I'm done working. I love you."

"Okay! Love you!" she cheerfully yelled, nearly splitting his eardrum.

The phone rustled, then his mom was back on the line. "Do you have a few minutes?"

He looked at his watch. "Yeah, I still have twenty minutes until I have to be back from lunch."

"Well. I don't want to worry you." Then she paused.

"Out with it." He already knew he wasn't going to like this. A knot formed in his stomach.

"I'm concerned about the children's safety."

"Why?" He sat up straight. Had something happened?

"This morning, Chandler left baby Finnegan completely alone on Maddie's bed. Oren, I was so upset. He could have pulled a blanket over his face, or one of Maddie's stuffed animals could have fallen on his face and he could have suffocated. Maddie shouldn't be sleeping with those animals, either. It's dangerous, but I hold my tongue. Well, this morning I just couldn't. Finnegan could have smothered on that bed, or rolled over and fallen off and cracked his head open." She pushed out a huff. "When I told Chandler not to leave him on the bed, because I couldn't keep quiet about something so dangerous, she told me to pack my things and leave."

"Oh." Oren wasn't sure how to feel about that. He doubted the situation was as dire as his mom was saying, but if Chandler was lashing out and defensive because of some postpartum related hormonal thing, she needed to go see a doctor and get treated. And she needed his mom there, whether she liked it or not.

"There's more. I'm so sorry for having to tell you these things. It's not my place to meddle, but I'm pretty sure I know why Chandler's distracted and not taking care of the kids."

He pinched the bridge of his nose. "She *is* taking care of the kids, Mom."

"She wasn't on Wednesday. She slept all day long."

"And since then, she's been taking care of the kids." Good gravy, why couldn't either one of them just grow up and stop with the snide comments?

"With *my* help."

"Yes, of course. With your help. And we appreciate it."

"Anyway. Maybe I shouldn't say anything, but you're my son and I love you."

"I'm going to have to go back in soon. What is it?"

"I was in the living room with both of the kids and she went off on her own – again – and it wasn't my fault at all. I was just sitting there, and I heard her over the baby monitor. She was upset that I'd told her not to leave Finnegan on the bed, and she was crying and telling some *person* on the line that she missed him and loved him and couldn't wait to see him again. She was making plans to meet him after Finnegan's visit to the doctor. I'm so sorry, Oren, but I know what I heard."

Oren's world dropped out from under him. Right now wasn't exactly the best time in their marriage, but an affair? Chandler? His fingers clenched on the seat of the bench. It was a good thing he was sitting down.

His brain couldn't formulate any words, so he hung up and sleep-walked back to his office. He stared blankly at the spreadsheet while Corey yammered.

An odd silence caught his attention. He turned and found Corey looking at him, concerned. "You okay, man?"

"Um…"

"Bad food at lunch? You're looking kind of green."

Oren nodded, latching onto the excuse.

"Dude. You should go home. Are you okay to drive?"

"Yeah." Oren clicked to save his spreadsheet. "I can drive."

"Drink lots of water. I got food poisoning one time at the shore with this chick I met. She was so hot and we started making out but I had to throw up—"

Oren grabbed his messenger bag and left while Corey was still rambling. He drove toward the doctor's office, hatching half a plan to wait until Chandler came out and then follow her, but when he got there, he drove past the parking lot instead. He didn't want to be *that guy* – the distrustful husband who stalks his wife. No, he'd bide his time and gather more evidence.

Chapter Eleven

Chandler pulled into Ashley's driveway, and didn't even have Finn out of the car before the front door burst open. Ashley jogged over and scooped Finn out of her arms and handed him off to Elliott, then looped the diaper bag over his shoulder. She grabbed Chandler in a huge hug and said, "When I said Ell was on kid duty, I meant *all* the kids."

"Aww, I wish I had Maddie with me."

"Me, too." Ashley walked with her into the house. "Hannah was looking forward to seeing her."

Chandler and Ashley had met at the Hickory Hollow Campground, when she and Oren were there for their honeymoon. Oren had won the trip on a radio call-in contest. There, they'd met fellow winner Margo, who happened to be Ashley's sister.

Chandler and Ashley had hit it off immediately and became quick BFFs. They'd even coincidentally gotten pregnant at the same time. Maddie was born just two weeks before Ashley had Hannah.

Ashley led her to the living room, where the coffee table was covered with snacks and fancy glasses with ice water.

"Oooh, you're spoiling me with all your charcuterie skills."

"I would have gotten the wine out, too, but we can't have Finn getting drunk."

Chandler laughed. It felt so good, like it had been a lifetime since she'd laughed without faking or forcing it.

They sat facing each other on the couch, mirroring each other's position, legs tucked under them, arm resting on the back of the sofa.

Ashley didn't waste any time. "Talk to me."

"I might need that wine anyway," Chandler began. "I've been so miserable. Poor Finn has had a string of infections – he just got the all clear, by the way, thank God – and I was just exhausted. I mean, I've never been so tired in all my life. It was bad, Ash. I started having these thoughts…" She squeezed her eyes shut against hot tears that stung the backs of her eyes. "Like it would be better if I could just… slip away."

Ashley said nothing, but reached over and held her hand.

"So Oren called his mom to come over just so I could sleep. She came on Wednesday, and I swear I'm trying to be appreciative. I slept all day Wednesday, and that's only because of Janice. I know that. And I'm glad she came, because I was losing my ever-loving mind. And before you say anything, I *know* I should have reached out and asked for help. I should have called you or my mom or Kim or…" Tears slipped down her cheeks. "But Ash, I couldn't even lift my phone. I could barely put Finn on my boob. Go ahead. Tell me you told me so."

Ashley squeezed her hand. "I'm not going to say that. What I *am* going to do is apologize for not checking in on you. I was just trying to give you time to settle into a new routine, and I should have been doing more."

Chandler shook her head. "No."

"Yes. I promise I'll do better. Are you getting rest now? I know it's only been two days, but is it better?"

"It is. Finn's infection is gone and he slept for six hours Wednesday night and last night. I caught a cat nap yesterday, too, which helped. What's not helping is being stressed out over Janice, and I feel like such a user. Like here, come watch my kids and now go away."

"It can't be easy having her under your roof, though. How long is she staying?"

"I have no idea. I assume she'll be here through the weekend. I've had to bite my tongue so many times I've literally tasted blood. She said I'm not cut out to be a mother. Then she threw in how Oren's ex has three kids now and she's apparently the perfect wife and mother and Oren could have had that, but he's stuck with this hot mess." She waved at herself from head to toe, then filled Ashley in on the waffle drama. "This morning before I talked to you, she screamed at me because Finn was on Maddie's bed. I was helping Maddie brush her teeth. Like six feet away, and he's nowhere near rolling over. She went off about how he was going to roll off the bed and crack his head open. I appreciate her concern—"

Ashley cut her off. "You don't need to keep saying that. Of course you appreciate her help, but that doesn't give her the right to be mean. You're still recovering from childbirth, and you need to protect your mental health as much, if not more, than your physical health right now."

"I just…" Chandler sighed. "I know I owe her so much for dropping everything and coming to get the kids. I feel bad for snapping at her. She didn't have to help us."

Ashley made a "hmm" noise under her breath. "On another topic, I should probably keep my mouth shut, but I haven't seen you for weeks, and…" she took a deep breath and reached over to squeeze Chandler's hand. "Honey, you've lost a lot of weight. Are you eating enough?"

Chandler shook her head. "No. I've been so stressed out and my stomach just doubles over when I even think about food." Why did it feel like loving concern coming from Ashley, and nasty judgment when the same thing came from Janice? The old adage is so true: It's not what you say, it's how you say it that matters.

"Have you been in touch with your obstetrician?"

"No. I have a follow-up appointment next Tuesday."

"Make a list of things to talk over with her, okay?"

"I will. I promise." Chandler held out her pinky.

Ashley linked her pinky with Chandler's to formalize the pinky swear promise. "Are you hungry now? I had to try my hand at a charcuterie board."

Chandler looked at the coffee table, laden with meat, cheese, fruit and crackers. Her stomach rumbled. "I might inhale the entire thing."

"Nothing would make me happier." Ashley passed her a paper plate, then loaded her own with food.

Chandler only took a few pieces, but her stomach surprised her by demanding more, until she'd eaten what she considered to be a full lunch's worth of food. It was probably her first full, uninterrupted meal in weeks.

As they ate, Chandler unloaded more about Janice, and then confessed she felt a distance growing between her and Oren. "It's so different than it was with Maddie. I'm glad he's being respectful of my healing, but he doesn't even kiss me. It's like he can't wait to leave the house in the morning, and he dreads coming home at night. I mean, I guess I can't blame him because it's chaotic, but it still hurts. And now it feels like him and his mom are ganging up on me. She complains to him about something I've done and he won't even ask my side. All he does is tell me to let her comments slide, to let things roll off my back, to be appreciative. But he won't tell her to tone it down. I don't feel like he's got my back, and that hurts most of all."

Rapid footsteps thumped up the stairs from the basement, accompanied by shrieks of laughter. A second later, Olivia, eight, burst through the door and ran over to them. "Finn pooped ALL over the place and Daddy got poop on his shirt and then he dropped the diaper on the rug and there's poop on the rug and Daddy made a face like this." Olivia scrunched her face and stuck her tongue out. She put her hands on her throat like she was gagging.

"Oh, no," Chandler said. She started to get up, but Ashley grabbed her arm.

"He can handle it."

"Of course I can. I'm Superman," Elliott said as he appeared in the doorway, following Hannah. "Good thing we have a bathroom downstairs."

Ashley took Finn from him before Chandler could get up.

"I put the towels and Finn's clothes in the washer."

"I'm so sorry," Chandler said.

He waved away her concern with a laugh. "Babies gotta baby, right?"

Chandler was glad she'd tossed an extra onesie in Finn's diaper bag. "On that note, I should get home. I promised Maddie we'd play princess dress up after I took Finn to the doctor. She's probably got Janice run ragged."

Ashley held up crossed fingers. "Let's hope." She handed the baby back to Elliott and hugged Chandler tight. "I'll text you later."

"Thanks." She squeezed hard, feeling better than she had in weeks. Until she realized her boobs were leaking through her bra pads from the force of the hug. She got Finn buckled into his car seat and started the car. She was buckling her own seatbelt when the dash flashed with an incoming call and text message.

A grin split her face as she answered. "Ingrid? What a wonderful surprise! How are you?" This day was getting even better.

"Chandler!" Ingrid's thick Jersey accent filled the car. "How's that new baby of yours?"

"He's wonderful."

"Sweetheart, listen. Why I'm calling is, I'm getting out of the business. I said to Richie I was thinking about retiring early and he was all for it. He bought me a cruise to celebrate. I was looking at all this stuff, and I thought of you right away. That's the picture I just sent you."

"Oh." Ingrid designed elaborate costumes for Broadway shows, and had unofficially been Chandler's mentor in costuming. Chandler admired her talent and hoped she could be half as good. She tapped into the text thread and opened a picture of Ingrid's workspace with floor-to-ceiling *stuff*. Bolts of fabric, bins of accessories, ribbons, and stuff she couldn't identify from the little picture.

"It's not like I need the money, I need the space, right? So Richie said I should offer it all to you as one big package deal. If you want it, you have to take it all. It's already boxed up and in the back of Richie's truck, but if you want it, you can have it all for two thousand dollars."

Chandler was glad she hadn't pulled out of the driveway yet or she might have driven off the side of the road in shock. "Ingrid, that's crazy. You have to have at least twenty, thirty thousand dollars in it."

"Twenty-six."

"Why on earth would you sell it to me for less than ten percent of its value?"

"Because someone gave me a similar opportunity when I was young and starting out, and you know I love you and would do anything to help you. You remind me a lot of me when I was your age. You're so talented, and if anyone can make good use of this stuff, I want it to be you. I don't want to be pushy, but I need to know soon, and we'd want to deliver it this weekend because we leave on Monday for our cruise."

She didn't need to think about it. "Yes, of course. I'll take it."

"We can do payments if you need to. I know you're good for it."

Chandler did a quick mental scan of her business accounts. "No, it's fine." It'd wipe her business account to the bare minimum, but this was not an opportunity to be passed up. "I'll cash app you right now as soon as we hang up."

"Perfect, doll. Shoot me your address and we'll be there around eight tomorrow morning."

"Ingrid, this is incredible. I feel like I'm dreaming. Thank you so much."

"Hey, what are friends for, right?"

They disconnected the call. Chandler almost dropped the phone because hands trembled with excitement. She sent two thousand dollars via cash app to Ingrid. She couldn't wait to tell Oren. He'd always admired Ingrid's work, and her high-end fabrics. Fabrics Chandler only dreamed of as she worked with inferior – and much cheaper – materials. And they were being hand-delivered. Free. What an unbelievable stroke of good fortune.

She looked at the photo again and a grin spread across her face as she calculated how much must be left on the bolts of special flame-retardant red velvet. There looked to be enough to redo the theater's curtains.

Oren would be thrilled.

Chapter Twelve

Oren got home and went in through the kitchen. Janice was at the table with Maddie, playing a board game.

"Why are you home?"

"I couldn't concentrate. So I came home." He opened the fridge but forgot what he was looking for, so he closed it without getting anything out. He felt jittery and off-balance.

"Oh, honey, I didn't mean to upset you. I shouldn't have said anything."

He kissed the top of Maddie's head and remembered he'd wanted a bottle of water. "Stop." He didn't have the energy to deal with her doubts about telling him what she'd heard. He downed a couple aspirin to ease the pounding headache.

Nearly an hour passed before he heard the garage door sliding open. His phone dinged as he peered out the curtain to make sure it was Chandler coming home. He glanced down at the notification from the bank.

What the heck was this?

He fumbled and swiped onto his banking app, but in his haste, entered the wrong password. He tried again, and the app opened as Chandler came into the kitchen with Finn.

"You'll never guess what just happened." She sounded excited, but all he could see was a two thousand dollar debit from their checking account.

He shoved his phone toward her face so she could see it. "Two thousand dollars? Why would you spend two thousand dollars without even consulting me?"

"Oh." She waved a hand like it was nothing. "It was supposed to come out of the business acc—"

"It shouldn't have come out of anywhere! Two thousand dollars, Chandler?" He couldn't remember ever being so angry.

Chandler's voice was low. "This isn't the time or place for this." She cast a pointed look at the table, where Maddie and his mom still sat.

"Why? Is it supposed to be some kind of secret? You've got plenty of those, don't you?"

He expected to see some contrition or embarrassment at being caught, but her face blazed red with pure fury. *She* had the nerve to be angry?

"By the time I get home, that two grand had better be back in the account. Get it from your *boyfriend* if you have to." He shouldered past her into the garage, slamming the door behind him. His hands shook as he gripped the steering wheel and backed out of the garage. The tires squealed as he peeled out of the driveway.

He drove around aimlessly for a while, then pulled into the grocery store parking lot and hit a button on his dash to call Connor.

The phone rang, then connected.

"Gino's Sub Shop, how can I help you?"

Oren's mouth worked, flustered and trying to make sense of the greeting. "Wh—what? Wait. I'm sorry, I hit the wrong number. Sorry."

"No problem." They hung up.

More carefully, he scrolled to Connor's number and double checked before he dialed.

"Oren, what's up?"

"Are you—Can you—I..." He ran a hand down over his face. "I need to talk, are you busy?"

"Elliott and I are on our way to Sonny's. Do you want to meet us there?"

"Yeah." He slowly pulled out of the parking lot and drove to the diner, pulling in at the same time as Connor and Elliott.

Words threatened to burst off his tongue, but he waited until they were inside, seated at a corner booth. The place was packed, typical for a Friday night.

Oren's leg bounced with pent up nervous energy.

"Hey, guys, know what you're having?" the waitress asked.

"Busy night, eh Corinne?" Elliott said.

"Ugh, it's been crazy all day. Must be a full moon or something." She took their orders and came back a minute later with their drinks.

Connor asked her about her husband, Derek, and their new rescue puppy.

"He's tearing everything up. It's a good thing he's cute."

"Derek or the puppy?" Connor joked.

Corinne laughed. "Take your pick."

The small talk was driving Oren nuts. He needed to get this off his chest before he burst.

Corinne finally left to wait on another customer.

"What's up?" Connor asked. He and Elliott looked at him expectantly from across the table.

Oren clasped his hands and leaned forward. "I... we're having problems and I don't know what to do."

"We?" Elliott asked. "You mean you and Chandler?"

"Yeah. There's just so much going on. Finn's been sick, but

now that he's doing better, my mom and Chandler are butting heads and not getting along."

"Your mom?" Connor asked.

"She came to stay with us. She got here Wednesday after Chandler… well, she was exhausted and Finn wasn't sleeping at all, and I couldn't take any more time off work. I called my mom to come stay for a few days."

"Finn's doing okay now, right? But your mom's still there?"

"She's helping," Oren snapped. He didn't need his best friends questioning his mother, too.

Connor put a hand up. "Easy, I'm just trying to get every-thing straight."

"Sorry. Yeah. Mom's still there because things have come up, and Chandler takes everything the wrong way when Mom's just trying to help. This morning, Chandler left Finn laying on the bed and went off to help Maddie with some-thing. My mom walked in and saw this and Chandler flipped out when Mom told her it was unsafe."

"But he's not even close to rolling over yet, is he?" Elliott asked.

"No."

"How long did she leave him?"

"I don't know. Long enough to help Maddie brush her teeth." He felt the need to add, "So long enough for something bad to happen."

Connor raised an eyebrow and said, "What else?"

Oren continued. "Chandler took Finn to the doctor this morning, and was gone for the entire afternoon. Right when she got home, I got a notification that she spent two *thousand* dollars from our account. She never said boo to me about a big expense, but the bigger problem is that I'm pretty sure she was with…" He forced the words out. "Her boyfriend."

Elliott choked on his drink, coughing a spray of soda onto the table. He pounded on his chest and croaked, "What?"

"My mom overheard her on the phone this morning, telling this guy how much she missed him and how much she loves him and can't wait to see him. Mom kept Maddie so she wouldn't be around this guy. I mean, what else was she doing for five hours after Finn's appointment?" He slammed his fist on the table. "She took *my son* around some other guy. How do we come back from that?"

Elliott shook his head. "You need to slow your roll, bro." He wiped the table with a napkin.

Connor jumped in. "You're hearing all this stuff second hand about *your wife* and you're not even asking her about any of it?"

"Tell me how she could possibly explain—"

Corinne came to the table and set plates down in front of each of them. "Enjoy. I'll check on you in a bit."

"How can she possibly explain that phone call? Who else would she be meeting up with that she says she misses and then says 'I love you' to them?"

"You can't think of one single person she might say that to? Not one?" Elliott sounded annoyed. "Gee, I don't know, how about maybe her best friend?"

Oren froze. "What?" *Oh, no.*

"Chandler came over and spent the afternoon with Ashley. I was home, so the girls and I played with Finn. He had a massive diaper blowout, by the way."

Oren dropped his French fry back onto the plate, nauseated. *What am I doing??*

Elliott smacked his cup down. "There's also a great explanation for the money, since Connor and I were both already recruited to help unload a truck tomorrow."

"Unload what truck?" None of this was making any sense.

Elliott's angry tone also didn't make much sense.

"Dude. Talk to your wife. And maybe have your mom go home."

Oren shoved his plate away. Fries slid off the edge onto the table. "My mother is not the problem here."

"No," Connor said. "She's not. You letting her get in between you and Chandler is the problem."

He glared at both of them. "Some friends you are. You're supposed to have my back."

Elliott pinned him with a stare. "What kind of friends would let you blow up your marriage over nothing? You didn't want to know Chandler was with Ashley? Should I have let you keep thinking something so vile about your wife instead of telling you you're wrong and hurting your feelings? Would that make me a better friend? Cuz, bro, if that's the kind of friend you want, I'm out."

"We're here to help you," Connor added. He put a hand on Elliott's forearm, trying to balance his brother-in-law's anger.

"Help me? It sure doesn't look like it when you immediately jump on Chandler's side."

"Side?" Connor asked.

Elliott leaned forward, scowling. "Someone ought to be on her side, because you sure aren't."

Oren's hands clenched. He threw a crumpled twenty on the table and slid out of the booth. "Screw you," he said, then walked out.

He drove aimlessly for a while, his head pinging with all the conflicting information. True, his mom didn't exactly love Chandler, but she wouldn't do anything to sabotage their marriage. And even though she wasn't always the most tactful person, she wouldn't say things to be deliberately hurtful. Would she? No, of course not. It's possible, he decided, that his mom had misheard or misunderstood the phone call. And no, now that he thought about it, there's no way Chandler would have left Finn on the bed if he'd been able to hurt himself.

None of that explained the money, but it was true that he hadn't even given her half a chance to explain.

He looped back around to Prescott's Grocery and parked the car. He went inside and bought a bouquet of cut flowers and a bag of miniature Reese's peanut butter cups. Chandler's favorite.

When he pulled into the garage at a little past eight, he took a few deep breaths before he walked into what was sure to be a very uncomfortable conversation.

He let himself into the kitchen and overheard voices coming from the living room. He closed the door softly and slunk toward the hallway to hear better.

"I told you so," his mother was saying. "You're not good at being a mother, and you're not good at being a wife. You're such a mess Oren can't even stand to be around you."

He swallowed hard. What?! No, this was going to stop. Now. He strode down the hallway into the living room.

"Oren!" His mother brightened and smiled at him.

"Apologize."

"What?" Her face fell.

"I heard you. What you just said. I heard it. You can't talk to her like that." His heart pounded. It wasn't easy, standing up to his mother, but this was too far.

"Oren, I—"

"No. Apologize."

Her nostrils flared in annoyance. "Chandler. I'm sorry I pointed out that you're a bad wife and mother."

This was not at all what Oren expected to walk into. "Mom, stop."

Chandler stood with her arms crossed.

He expected her to be about to cry, but her eyes were dry

and hard. Instead of saying a word to his mom, she fixed her gaze directly on him.

"Chan, I'm sorry." He held out the flowers, but she ignored them. "You're an amazing mother and a wonderful wife, and I love you."

No reaction. Nothing.

He was tempted to get on his knees. "I'm sorry for—"

Chandler's cold voice cut him off. "This is not a conversation we're having with an audience."

"An audience. I'm his *mother* and I have every right—"

Chandler's glare swung to Janice. "You have no right to anything. Go. Home. Now."

"I will not," his mom insisted.

"Mom, she's right. It's time for you to go home."

"See? You see how she's turning you against me? This is exactly what I told you would happen. You should have married Belinda. *She's* a wonderful wife and mother and knows her place." She pointed at Chandler. 'She's trying to come between us."

The truth of everything his wife had tried to tell him landed like a cartoon piano from a ten-story window. Chandler never once said a bad word about his mother. Not even when she was enduring this kind of abuse. No wonder she'd called him a Mama's Boy. He'd been acting like one.

He swallowed hard. "Why don't we sleep on this and in the morning we can all have a rational discussion?"

"You don't get it," Chandler said. "She's leaving tonight. Now. And I think it's best if you go with her."

His heart seemed to stop, then pounded relentlessly against his ribcage. He couldn't possibly have heard her right. "You… you want me to leave?" His fingers crushed the stems of the cheap flowers.

"I *need* you to leave."

His mother's arms waved, gesturing wildly. "See? She's not only trying to come between us, she's trying to keep your children away from you! She can't make you leave your own house." She turned to Chandler. "We're not leaving."

"You don't get a vote." Chandler's voice was cold.

"*He* certainly does."

Chandler's gaze swung to him. She waited a beat and said, "Really, Oren? You're going to stand here and let her speak for you?"

"No," he said weakly.

His mother said, "Oren's right, we'll discuss this in the morning."

The calm vanished. Chandler screamed, "GET OUT!"

Oren jumped back a step, shocked. He barely ever heard Chandler yell, let alone scream. Finn startled awake in his bassinet and began to cry.

"Mom, get what you need and go home. I'll get the rest of your things."

When she looked like she wanted to speak, he barked, "Now!"

She shot him a filthy look, but went upstairs.

"Chan, baby, I'm sorry." He reached toward his wife.

She took a step back. "You, too. Oren, I swear if you ever loved me at all, you'll leave this house for tonight. Otherwise, I'll take the kids and go to my parents'."

Her parents lived a little more than two hours away.

"I'll… I'll go. But just for tonight."

She jerked her head in a half-nod.

He set the flowers and candy on the end table beside the couch and took the stairs two at a time. In the master bedroom, he tossed a change of clothes into his gym bag.

"Daddy?"

Maddie stood in the doorway in her Poppy pajamas,

clutching Princess Giraffe.

"Hey, cupcake. You should be in bed."

"It's too loud."

He scooped her up and kissed her cheek. "It's quiet now. Let's get to sleep." He carried her to her bedroom and tucked her back in bed.

She curled up, pulling Princess Giraffe close. "Daddy?"

"Hmm?" He smoothed her hair back from her face.

"How come Nanny hates Mommy?"

The question was a punch to the gut. What had he been missing? Or, probably more accurately, what had he been willfully blind to? "Nanny doesn't hate Mommy." He wasn't so sure that was true anymore. "Sometimes grownups are bad at communicating and they say things they don't mean."

She yawned and snuggled deeper into Princess Giraffe, seeming to accept his answer.

He kissed her cheek and tiptoed to the door. When he looked back, she was already sleeping. He pulled the door closed with a click.

In the master bedroom, his bag felt too heavy to lift. Every part of his being cried out, "This is wrong! This is wrong! This is wrong!"

He slung his bag over his shoulder and walked over to the guest room, where his mother was zipping her suitcase. "I'm not leaving anything here for her to steal."

Sudden exhaustion weighed down his soul. He grabbed a suitcase in each hand, leaving her to carry her tote bag and purse.

Oren dropped his bag on the kitchen table, then carried his mother's stuff out and loaded it into her car.

She got in the driver's side. "I'll see you in a bit."

It'd be easy to go home with her. Heck, she hadn't even dismantled his old bedroom. She'd boost his ego and make him breakfast and make him feel better. He shook his head. "No. I need some time to think. Alone."

"Can you afford a hotel room after she emptied your bank account? Of money *you* earned?"

How had he never noticed he'd let her stomp right past any boundaries around his marriage? Had he ever really put any up? Time to get the hammer and nails and build a fortress around his marriage if he had any hope of saving it.

"Drive safe." He closed the door before she said anything else.

Back inside, he wanted to ask Chandler to reconsider, to let him stay so they could talk, but he knew it was unfair. She needed some breathing room. He'd let her down a lot lately. Giving her a little space was the least he could do.

He found her in the living room on her recliner, nursing Finn.

"I, um, I guess I'll see if I can crash on Connor's couch."

Her eyebrows flew up. "You're not staying with your mother?"

"No."

"Huh."

"I'll call you tomorrow, then?"

"Whatever."

"I love you, Chan, and I'm so sorry."

Her eyes drifted shut. "I can't do this right now, Oren."

"Okay. We'll talk tomorrow." He wasn't sure if he should go over and kiss her or not. He stood, rooted to the floor, looking at his wife and his son.

If anyone had ever told him the day would come when Chandler told him to leave, he would have laughed and laughed at the absurdity until his stomach hurt.

That day was here. His stomach definitely hurt, but there was nothing funny about it.

Chapter Thirteen

Chandler expected to break down after Oren's car left the driveway. Instead of being overwhelmed by sadness, though, she was overwhelmed with relief. Janice's absence made the very air feel lighter, and the haze of negativity that seemed to weigh down the entire house had vanished, and it felt like home again.

Even though Oren wasn't home. Then again, lately it seemed like he avoided being home as much as possible, so maybe that's why it didn't feel as weird, as wrong, to have him not be here.

She still stood at the window, watching down the street Oren's car had driven down, but his taillights had faded into the distance a while ago. Suddenly, she was starving. She went into the kitchen and made a sandwich and followed it with a handful of grapes – already cut in half for Maddie, and then a snack cake Oren packed in his lunches and a few pretzels.

She cleaned up her place, then went around to lock doors and turn off lights. She carefully scooped a sleeping Finn out of his bassinet and went upstairs. Pausing to peek in on

Maddie, she was relieved to see her contentedly curled up with Princess Giraffe.

Finn stirred. Instead of putting him in the crib, she let him nurse again, hoping it would carry him through the night. While he nursed, she set the alarm on her phone. Ingrid and Richie would be arriving around eight, along with Ashley and Elliott and Connor and Margo.

After Finn was in his crib, soundly sleeping, Chandler changed and crawled into bed. The tears still didn't come. What did come was a replay of Oren's words. *"By the time I get home, that two grand had better be back in the account. Get it from your boyfriend if you have to." Get it from your boyfriend if you have to. Get it from your boyfriend if you have to. … your boyfriend…*

She swiped on her phone and, mostly for spite, went online to calculate one day's interest on two thousand dollars. She randomly picked eight percent, and if the money was a loan, she'd owe forty-four cents of interest for the day. Armed with that information, she logged into her banking app and transferred two thousand dollars and forty-four cents from her business account into the joint account she'd inadvertently paid the money from.

No boyfriend needed.

Her mind churned with a million thoughts. About the kids, the future, her marriage, where she was going to put everything Ingrid was bringing, and how she was going to get through another sleepless night.

At some point, sleep did come. Finn slept through until just after six, so Chandler turned off her alarm and started her day.

She'd gotten Maddie dressed and fed when she heard a

knock at the door. She glanced at the clock. It was seven twenty. She hoped Ingrid hadn't gotten there early.

Oren stood on the porch. "This feels weird, but I wasn't sure if I should come in."

"Of course you can come in." She stood back to let him pass.

"Daddy!" Maddie bounced into the living room and flung herself at him.

Oren swooped her up in the air and then pulled her close, planting loud growly kisses all over her face while she shrieked in delight.

Maddie squirmed to be put down, then ran off, probably to find Princess Giraffe.

"I was hoping we could talk."

"Now's not really a good time. The truck's coming in about twenty minutes."

"Truck?"

She didn't feel like explaining. "I put the money back in the account."

"I saw that, but it was an odd amount."

"Yeah. I added forty-four cents of interest, which is what a bank would charge on an eight percent loan."

"Interest?"

"Interest. I cash apped from the main account instead of my business account. It wasn't a big deal, despite your hissy fit." She crossed her arms and hoped he'd argue.

"Chan, I—"

A car door slammed.

Chandler itched to fight with him. The frustration of the past week – past few months really – welled up and threatened to explode.

He glanced toward the window.

"Don't worry, it's not my *boyfriend*," she said before she yanked the door open.

Connor and Margo were the first to arrive.

"I'm here for heavy lifting," Connor said, lifting his arm to make a muscle.

"And I'm here for a baby fix." Margo hugged Chandler. "If it's all the same to you, I'll entertain the kids while everyone else unloads the truck."

Chandler grinned. "You're an angel. I wasn't sure how I'd keep track of the kids in all the commotion."

"Hannah is over the moon about seeing Maddie."

"Right on cue." Chandler laughed as Ashley and Elliott pulled in.

They were getting out of the car as a huge U-Haul sized box van with "Ingrid's Costumery" splashed in bright colors along the sides slowly made its way up the street.

Theirs was the last house on a dead-end street. Chandler trotted down the sidewalk and waved.

The passenger window rolled down and Ingrid's loud Jersey voice carried through the entire neighborhood. "Chandler! We found you! Tell Richie where we're going."

Richie waved from the driver's seat.

She glanced over at the yard, glad the ground was dry, and noticed the still-broken fence along the far edge of the property. She pushed the chore out of her mind and motioned to a spot near the patio. "If you back along this side of the house, the basement doors are right there. You can park in the grass."

Richie gave her a thumbs up and maneuvered the van around so he could back up to where Chandler directed.

"What is all this?" Oren asked.

Chandler ignored his question and said, "Would you please go through and unlock the basement doors? And flip the lights on? Thanks." She went around the van to greet Ingrid.

"Hey, neighbor, you need some extra hands?" Nate called from his mailbox at the sidewalk.

"That would be amazing," Chandler said. The old adage was so true: many hands make light work. And she had a feeling there was a lot of work waiting in the back of this van.

"I'll grab Kim and Jared and we'll be right over."

"Awesome, thank you."

Elliott and Connor introduced themselves to Richie. Ashley came around to meet Ingrid.

Oren opened both of the French basement doors to the patio and propped them open.

"Let's see the space," Ingrid announced, then walked to the basement. She looked around for a moment, then clasped her bright-red tipped hands under her chin. "Oh, Chandler, this is just lovely. You have a wonderful setup here."

"Thank you." Chandler warmed under the praise of her mentor.

"Where are we putting everything?"

"Right through here." Chandler crossed the room and opened a doorway to a big storage room that currently only housed a few tables.

"Perfect!" Ingrid turned and clapped her hands, calling everyone to attention.

Nate, Kim, and Jared came in just as Ingrid began to speak. "Okay, everyone. We're unloading the truck straight through here. A lot of these things are delicate, so *please* be careful."

Connor elbowed Elliott's side. "You hear that? Delicate. Just like you."

Elliott snorted and elbowed him back. "I'm not the one crying over rescue kitten videos."

"Hey, you try being married to a veterinarian and not getting a little misty."

Everyone trooped back outside. Richie stood at the back of

the truck and grinned at Chandler. "You ready to see what you bought?"

Her heart flip-flopped with excitement. "Ready."

Richie shoved the bottom of the rolling door and it flew upward.

Chandler gasped. The truck was packed. *Packed.* There wasn't an inch of space. Plastic storage tubs in every color formed the foundation, topped with smaller clear plastic bins that revealed buttons and zippers and elastic in every color and size. On top of those were bolts of fabric. Tulle, velvet, cotton, chiffon, it was all represented in Ingrid's van.

One of the guys said, "Whoa."

Chandler swallowed hard and fought tears. All of this – enough to run her business for the next five years without buying a single straight pin – for a measly two thousand dollars? Unfathomable. She pressed her hands to her chest. "Ingrid."

Ingrid squeezed her shoulders. "You're welcome, sweet-heart." She winked, then turned and clapped her hands. "Okay! We'll start at the top. You. Start pulling these out. You. Load the fabric onto the tables, okay?"

Everyone murmured their acknowledgment, and Richie climbed up and started handing things down.

As soon as he cleared a spot, Connor hopped on the truck and helped hand items down as well.

Chandler's calves were tight and aching by the time they'd unloaded the van an hour and a half later. Her storage room was completely filled. She couldn't wait to start going through everything and organizing it and *using* it. Her fingers itched to lay out a piece of the lush corduroy and turn it into a pair of pants or a vest.

Outside, the air thickened with humidity. Oren handed out

bottles of water and herded everyone upstairs while Chandler walked Ingrid back out to the van.

"Ingrid, I don't even have words."

Ingrid patted her cheeks. "No words necessary. Just make beautiful things and do me proud. Send pictures."

Chandler couldn't speak. She nodded her head and reached out to hug Ingrid tight.

"I'll still be around if you need help with anything. Call me."

"I will. Thank you so much." She turned to thank Richie, but he was already in the van.

They pulled away and Chandler waved until they turned the corner at the end of the street and drove out of sight.

Back inside, she found the group congregated across the kitchen and living room.

"Love what you've done with the place," Nate said, nodding to the kitchen cabinets. They'd bought the house from Nate, after he'd moved next door with his wife, Kim. Kim's nineteen-year-old nephew, Jared, now their adopted son, said, "Chandler, you should do the costumes for Nate's new show."

Nate's eyes widened. "That's an amazing idea.' He ducked his head down, a little sheepish. "I knew you did costumes for the Shakespeare thing, but I didn't realize they were so… detailed."

Chandler laughed, knowing he was actually surprised at the quality, not the detail. Nate and Kim ran their own production company, producing small-scale shows using local talent, something Chandler would love to be a part of.

"What's the show?" she asked.

"It's a sort of medieval family saga."

Oren came alongside her.

"Wow. That's right up your alley, Chan." Ashley bounced on her heels. "You totally should."

"Hang on," Chandler said. "If you're serious, we'll have to get together and iron out some details."

"Absolutely." Nate beamed at Kim.

Kim nodded enthusiastically. "I'll email you some notes and see what you think."

"Perfect."

"And hey," Jared said, "if you need a babysitter, Isobel's been looking for some side work to save money for college."

Chandler grinned at him. "Definitely. I'll text her and see when she's available. You should be a broker or agent or something."

Kim laughed. "He has a way of coordinating, doesn't he?"

Jared blushed and waved his hand at them.

From the living room, Finn wailed.

"Uh oh," Margo said, carrying him into the kitchen. "Somebody's hungry."

"That's our cue," Elliott said.

"Can Maddie come?" Hannah yanked on Elliott's hand.

He looked at Ashley, who nodded over the girls' heads.

"Sure," Chandler said. Both girls squealed. "Nobody has to leave," Chandler told the group, but everyone filed toward the door, hugging and waving until the only person left was Oren.

She wasn't sure how to feel about that, and judging from his hands shoved deep in his pockets, he didn't either.

Chapter Fourteen

Oren stood awkwardly, hanging back while Chandler settled onto her recliner and nursed Finn. "So—"

"No."

"No?"

"I'm not having a big conversation right now."

"Why not? Seems like a good time to me."

"Of course it does." Her eyes blazed with anger. "You're not the one in a vulnerable position."

The words made no sense to him. "Vulnerable? You make it sound like you need to defend yourself or something. From *me*. That's ridiculous."

"Is it? Because I asked you to wait until I'm done nursing, but you're ignoring me and towering over me and making me very uncomfortable."

"Towering over you?" True, he'd walked over and now stood a few feet from her chair, but it wasn't like he was bending over her or getting in her face. "I guess I don't get how I'm making you so uncomfortable."

"Well, I'm sorry you don't get it. Maybe when I'm finished," she cast a pointed look at Finn, "I'll explain it."

Oren went over and sat on the couch. "Chan, just tell me what I'm doing wrong."

He watched her eyes squeeze shut. Her mouth pursed, and the baby shifted as she pulled in a huge breath and slowly blew it out.

"Are you giving me the silent treatment now? Really?"

"Can you seriously not give me five minutes?"

"Fine." He got up and went to the kitchen. Annoyed, he drummed his fingers on the counter, looking around for something to do while he waited. The red light on the coffee maker meant the pot was warm, so he poured a cup.

For the life of him, he didn't understand why Chandler was pushing him away so hard. Yes, the past few days had been rough, but his mom had gone home, so things should be back to normal.

He finished one cup of coffee, then half of another one before Chandler came into the kitchen.

"I put Finn in the stroller. I thought we could go for a walk."

"Sure." He didn't want to go for a walk. He wanted to get back to normal. But he waited while Chandler put on her sneakers. He jumped to open the door for her, then grabbed the front of the stroller to lift it over the little lip in the doorway.

"Thanks."

"Sure." He waited until she passed and pulled the door shut.

They walked down their small sidewalk until it joined the larger sidewalk running alongside the road. The silence between them pulsed in his head. He decided to start with a safe topic. "Did you see the fence?" He pointed. "Must have happened in all those storms Wednesday, huh?"

"Yeah. I saw it yesterday and forgot to mention it."

"I'll see if there's gas for the chainsaw. At least get the branch cut up and then see how bad the fence is damaged."

She nodded, but didn't answer.

The quiet tension was more than he could handle, so he scrambled to think of something else to say. "That's something about Nate's new show, huh?"

"Yeah. It sounds really interesting."

"Medieval costumes are really involved." He pushed forward and stated the obvious. "You aren't going to take it on, right? I mean, that's pretty time consuming."

"I'm waiting until I get the information from Kim, but I see no reason to turn it down."

"Chandler, come on. We have a dozen reasons to turn it down." He couldn't believe what he was hearing. "Finn. Maddie. Time. It's not like we need the money.'

Chandler made a "mmm" noise under her breath.

"What?"

She stopped abruptly and turned to face him. "I've learned a lot over the past few weeks. I need to be able to support the family on my own income."

His heart thumped in his throat. He swallowed hard around it. "Why?"

"Because my husband puts me behind his mother, who hates me, and then accuses me of having an affair."

"I don't put you behind my mother." He didn't comment on the affair part. He'd made a stupid, thoughtless comment, but never really thought she had a boyfriend.

Chandler turned back to grip the stroller handle and started pushing again. "Yeah, okay."

"Chan, seriously. I know it probably seemed like I was taking her side while she was here, but it's just because we owed her a lot for dropping everything and coming to help us. She didn't have to do that."

"No, she didn't." Chandler's voice was quiet.

He was glad she was finally coming around.

She stopped again and faced him. "Have you ever had a flat tire?"

"Huh?" He had no idea where this was going. "No."

"Let's say I'm driving along the highway and *boom*, I get a flat tire. I pull off the side of the road and some guy with a tow truck stops and fixes my tire."

"Okay?" Why was she talking about a hypothetical flat tire?

"Now the tire is fixed, and the guy hauls off and punches me in the face. Would that be okay with you?"

"What? Of course not." He found himself angry at a person who didn't even exist.

"Really? Why not? Because your mom came and helped me, and what she did was worse than punching me in the face, but you cosigned it because she helped us out. Helping us with the kids because I needed help doesn't give her a blank check to abuse me."

"I know she was being difficult, but I think it's a little much to call it abuse." He felt like he was walking a tightrope. Fall to one side and end up in a tank of piranhas, fall to the other and end up in a pit of vipers. The only way to survive was to inch across to the safety without making any enemies.

"Okay." She started pushing the stroller again.

"I'm not saying it was acceptable how she talked to you. It wasn't."

"Okay."

He saw her shoulders tighten. "Hey. I'm serious. It wasn't right."

"I know it wasn't. I'm not sure you actually believe it wasn't, because your words haven't had a lot of action behind them. Damn it, Oren, the first time she called me a bad mother, you completely ignored it and fixated on me calling you a

Mama's Boy. Do you hear that? The *first* time. Because it wasn't just once."

Her tone concerned him almost as much as her words. It was flat, measured, and emotionless. Like she'd already rehearsed the conversation a hundred times in her head.

They stopped at a corner and crossed the street to get to the community park. It was basically a huge field that housed two baseball diamonds on opposite corners and a soccer field in the middle, with a walking path around the entire perimeter, a tiny playground in the corner, and several pavilions covering picnic tables.

A handful of people were walking on the trail, and a youth soccer team ran drills on their field.

"I'm sorry if I haven't been supportive. I'm between a rock and a hard place, Chandler. I'm not trying to take sides."

"This isn't a situation where you can ride the fence. You've chosen your side, and it's not mine."

The stroller's wheels crunched against the gravel path.

"I have not chosen my mother's side. That's not fair."

"Fair?" She whirled to face him. "You want to talk about fair? What was fair about you accusing me of having a boyfriend? What was fair about your tantrum over the money? What was fair about telling me to just shut my mouth about your mother's abuse? What's fair about you trying to tell me not to take the costume job?"

"Chandler…"

Her eyes narrowed to slits. Her nostrils flared and her jaw clenched. "No. Don't you *dare* speak down to me like I'm an idiot who just needs something patiently explained before I get it. Lose that tone or don't bother talking."

Oren took a step back. He never expected this sort of venom from her. Sure, she had the right to be upset that he'd made some wrong assumptions. But nothing he did justified her oversized anger.

"Let's start with the first one. How dare you accuse me of cheating on you?"

"I didn't exactly say that."

She shook her head and resumed pushing the stroller.

"What? Are you done talking now?"

"If you're not going to be honest, then yes, I'm done."

"I don't even remember exactly what I said."

Her snort of derision suggested maybe that was a little too much honesty.

"I'm sorry for ever suggesting you had a boyfriend. That was rude and wrong and I'm sorry."

The stroller's front wheel caught on a stone and stopped rolling. Chandler cursed and went to the front of the stroller. She tugged the stone free and tossed it to the edge of the path.

"I'm trying to apologize."

"Try harder."

"What do you mean?"

"You're completely minimizing what you said to me."

He thought about that as they walked side by side for a few minutes. "You're right." He blew out a hard breath. "You're right, Chandler. I said some awful things to you. I know it's no excuse, but we're both under a lot of pressure and exhausted, and I just didn't stop to think about what might really be happening behind the things my mom told me."

"Hmm."

Oren touched her arm. They stopped walking and faced each other again. "Sweetheart, I'm so sorry for all the things I said. I hope you believe me when I tell you that I trust you completely. Despite what I said, I have no doubt Finn is safe with you. I trust you with the money. And I honestly do not, for one second, believe that you would be unfaithful. I wish I could take it all back. I hope we can move past this and start fresh because I trust you. I do."

Chandler's eyes welled and for a split second he thought that was a good thing because she didn't look angry.

She whispered, "You still don't get it."

Oren's blood ran cold. He put a hand on the stroller to steady himself because he was suddenly dizzy with an awful anticipation. Her words, when they came, landed in his gut like a wrecking ball.

"*I* can't trust *you*."

Chapter Fifteen

Chandler saw the wind leave Oren's sails. She felt bad for making him feel bad, but he needed to understand. He hadn't just said words. He'd attacked the very foundation of their marriage. And unfortunately, she wasn't quite done.

"I can't be with you right now."

Oren's face went white. He whirled and stumbled a few steps to the park bench, then sat with his elbows on his knees, his hands cradling his face, sucking in deep breaths.

She gave him a minute, then pushed the stroller over and sat down beside him.

"What… what are you… what… What are you saying?" His words were tight. "Do you… do you want…" A strangled sort of retch cut him off.

"I'm saying I need a few days to think." One of the rules in their marriage, from the beginning, had been to never use the "D" word. And she wasn't even thinking about… that. She just wanted some space. She didn't even want Oren to *leave*-leave. She just wanted to breathe. And recover. From both her mother-in-law and from the lasting effects of sleep deprivation. She was better, and improving daily, but still not back to one hundred percent. Right now, he was adding to the stress far more than helping to relieve it.

"How… how long?"

The anguish in his voice gutted her, and she almost backed down. But that wouldn't do either of them any good in the long run. "A couple of days. Just a little time to recharge and not spend every second of every day tiptoeing on eggshells and censoring every word."

He blinked half a dozen times, fast. "That's how you've been feeling? Around me?"

Chandler felt like she was running a dagger through his heart. "I'm not trying to be mean. Or overly dramatic. But yes, I've been feeling like I can't do a single thing right or you and your mom will gang up on me." She held up a hand before he could speak. "I know your mom's gone now, but I don't think you realize how hurtful it was for me to feel so alone, Oren. It's always been about not making waves with your mom, but having her under the same roof magnified everything, and even though she was helping with the kids – which I *do appreciate* – it was toxic for me. And your need to keep the peace meant I was on my own. I felt…" She swallowed the lump clogging her throat. "I felt like you abandoned me when I needed you. When she was policing my food, attacking my worth as a mother and a wife, and you backed her up."

"Chan." His voice was a whisper.

"You said the most hateful things to me. All because of lies your mother told you. You believed everything she said without question, without pause, without proof, without once stopping to give me the benefit of the doubt. I believed our entire life was built on a solid foundation of you and me having each other's backs through anything life could throw at us. And now my eyes have been opened and I'm questioning everything. I'm shaken, Oren. I'm rocked to my core because for the first time in our marriage, I'm utterly and completely on my own."

He ran a hand down his face and squeezed his eyes shut. "I'm sorry."

"I know."

"What can I do?"

Once again, Chandler felt like the villain. Because she didn't want to tell him how to fix this. She didn't tell him how to break it, and she needed her mental energy to heal and deal with the kids. "I'm sorry, but you're going to need to figure that out on your own. I don't have the bandwidth to give you instructions."

Finn fussed in the stroller, so she got up and pushed the handle back and forth.

"I don't know how to start fixing this." Oren's voice was thick with tears building just beneath the surface.

"You'll have to figure it out."

He rose from the bench and walked beside her, his hands shoved deep in his pockets. They walked in silence until they reached the house.

As soon as the door closed behind them, Oren's tears fell. "I… Chan, I…" He bowed his head into his hand.

"It's just a few days."

He shuddered a heavy breath. "It feels like forever. We've never… It's never been this bad and it's killing me." His voice hitched and tears flowed. "Our marriage – our family – is what matters most to me and I don't know how to fix this."

"You'll figure it out," she repeated. Chandler let herself be pulled into his arms. She closed her eyes and breathed him in. Everything about him was so familiar, and right now, so strangely foreign.

Finn squawked, tired of being restrained in the stroller. She pushed away from Oren and unbuckled the baby.

"I guess… um, I'll get some… stuff."

"Okay." Chandler didn't look at him as he walked away. She knew if she did, if she looked in his eyes and saw his pain, she'd relent. But if she did, nothing would change. Things would go back to normal for a while, but then if – when – there was another showdown, she'd stand alone, taking all the hits, while Oren appeased his mother in the name of keeping the peace. She just couldn't stand waiting for that moment to come, knowing somewhere in the back of her mind that it wasn't Chandler and Oren against the world anymore.

Chapter Sixteen

Connor said, "Oof, I'm really sorry, man. We'd let you stay, but Heidi's family is crashing here until their kitchen gets fixed."

"No, I understand." Oren sat in his car, parked at a gas pump at Sheetz. "Thanks anyway."

"Hey. Do you need to talk about it? Now, I mean? I can meet you wherever."

Oren forced a laugh. "You're just trying to get away from Heidi." He knew Connor wasn't super fond of Margo's sister.

"Shhh, you'll get me in trouble." Connor gave a little chuckle. "I'm serious, though. I'm here for you."

"I appreciate it, but I have a few more calls to make."

"You and Chandler were made for each other. It'll all work out."

Oren gulped back his emotions. "I hope so."

"I know so. Give her a little space, but not too much. Be proactive."

"How? I don't even know what she wants me to do."

Connor's tone was patient. "Yes, you do. She wants you to show her you've got her back, no matter what."

"I don't know how to show her that."

"You've known her better than anyone for years and years, right? You know what she likes, what she wants, what she needs. You don't need her to spell it out for you, man. You just need to take a breath and give it some thought." He paused, then ended with, "You *do* have her back, right? Rhetorical question, no need to answer."

Oren wanted to shout that yes, of course he had Chandler's back, and it was offensive and stupid to even ask the question. But that wasn't exactly what he'd shown the past few weeks, was it?

They ended the call and Oren sat, staring at his phone. He really wished he could have stayed with Connor and Margo. The last place he wanted to go was to Elliott and Ashley's. He knew he was probably very low on the list of Ashley's favorite people right now, and his every word and facial expression was sure to be scrutinized and reported back to Chandler.

So he sucked it up and tapped his phone. The call connected.

"Hey, Mom."

Oren sat at his parents' kitchen table. His mom's indignant outrage felt good for about two seconds, then it grated. She shoved a plate of warmed up supper in front of him – pork chops, mashed potatoes, corn, and a big scoop of peach cobbler for dessert.

Janice patted his shoulders as he cleaned his dessert bowl. "You're too skinny. It's like she doesn't feed you at all." The "she," of course, was sneered with all the derision one person could smash into three letters.

"Mom, don't start."

"I just don't understand. She's supposed to be your *wife*, for better or for worse. I'd say throwing you out on the street is worse for you and if you're going to keep paying the bills, it works out quite well for her."

"Stop!" He pinched the bridge of his nose.

Theo hollered from the living room, "What's going on?"

"Nothing," Janice snapped.

Oren put his dirty dishes in the sink and grabbed the dish soap.

Janice forcefully nudged him out of the way. "I'll do those. You need to relax and put all this ugliness out of your head."

Oren went into the living room and sat on the couch. His dad was on the recliner, *Wheel of Fortune* blaring on the television, quashing any chance of getting some sage advice.

A commercial came on. Theo muted the television and looked at Oren. "It'll be fine, son. Listen to your mother." He nodded his head once, then turned the volume back up.

Okay, sage advice wasn't happening. Oren might not be the most brilliant man on the planet, but he was pretty sure that listening to his mother is what got him in this mess in the first place. "Thanks, Dad."

The contestant won the bonus round and ended up with a hefty payday and a European cruise. As the credits rolled, Oren slid out of the room and went upstairs. His old bedroom was just as he'd left it. Sports trophies and medals lined one wall. His twin bed was still covered by a navy blue plaid comforter that matched the curtains. The closet still held a handful of his old clothes and jerseys from the various sports he'd played. A hockey stick leaned against the wall in the corner. The top shelf of his closet was home to his high school yearbooks.

There was no thin layer of dust, which meant his mom still came in and cleaned his room. Like she'd been waiting for him to come home. So she could fuss over him and console him and then twist a dagger in his chest with, "I was right about Chandler all along."

Even though it was barely eight o'clock, he showered in the attached bathroom – which still had his old body washes and overwhelming sprays in the linen closet – and crawled into bed thinking that he needed to cut the cord as much as his mother did.

Chapter Seventeen

Sunday dawned slowly. Chandler stretched and startled, jerking to the side to check on Finn in the crib beside her bed.

He was awake, sucking his fist and gazing up at the slowly spinning mobile.

Chandler smiled and reached over. "Hey, sweet boy."

He gurgled happily.

She hurried to the bathroom to take care of business, knowing his good humor would vanish as soon as he realized he was hungry.

Which he did while she was drying her mouth after brushing. She ran a comb through her hair and twisted it up as she walked back into the bedroom to feed her wailing son.

"Let's do this downstairs, shall we?" She scooped him out of the crib and he immediately turned the volume down to a moderate fuss.

Downstairs, she put Finn in his baby wrap so he could nurse while she supported him with one arm and pulled out the ingredients for breakfast with her other. She got the strawberry syrup to make smiley waffles for Maddie and poured herself a bowl of Cheerios.

By some miracle, Maddie was still asleep.

She'd just finished her cereal when the door clicked and startled her. She backed up against the counter, taking mental note of how far away the knife block was. The door creaked open and her hand inched toward the knives.

A second later, Oren popped into the kitchen

Relief coursed through her.

Oren held his hand up. "Sorry. I didn't mean to scare you. I was afraid if I knocked it'd get the kids wound up."

Chandler shifted Finn to her shoulder.

"Here, let me." Oren took the baby and flung a burp cloth over his shoulder, then bounced and patted Finn's back.

"How are you?" she asked.

"I've been better." He gave her a smile over Finn's head. "You?"

"I've been better." Chandler wasn't sure how she was feeling, having him here in the kitchen, like it was any other Sunday morning.

"I thought I'd take the kids this afternoon, if you want. Thought it'd give you some time to organize your new costume stuff or take a nap or whatever."

"Oh." It occurred to her that she wasn't sure where he'd spent the night. A sharp pang made her wonder if she *wanted* to know.

As if he'd read her mind, he said, "I'm staying at my parents'. Margo's sister is staying with them, and I didn't feel right asking Elliott if I could stay there."

"Why? It's not like Ashley would spy on you and report back."

"How can you say that with a straight face? She'd be like a pitbull with a notepad, sending you hourly updates and waiting for me to do something stupid so she could bite my head off." He laughed, and it felt comfortable, like any other time they'd shared a private joke. Because they both knew Ashley would absolutely report his every move back to Chandler.

"Okay, that's probably true," Chandler agreed with a laugh. "As for this afternoon, I promised Maddie I'd take her to McDonald's for lunch."

"Oh." Oren poked at the leg of the kitchen chair with the tip of his shoe.

"Maybe we could just take her to the park this morning and after lunch if you want to take the kids…"

"Okay."

She watched him for a moment, bouncing Finn and looking like he was feeling out of place. "I looked through the velvet. There might be enough for new curtains for the theater. I'll need to measure everything to be sure."

"Great!" His head bobbed up and down. "That'd be great. What if… maybe, if you're not too busy, maybe we could go do measurements and stuff after we go to McDonald's? Or before? Or whatever."

He looked so hopeful that it gave Chandler a little hope, too. "Yeah. I'll grab my tape measures and notebook and stuff so I'll have it with me."

"Great. Yeah. That's great. Those curtains are in rough shape. I was looking at them again last week and they looked pretty bad."

"I'll see if any of it can be salvaged. Maybe for a valence or something."

"Yeah. Great."

Chandler tapped her hands on the counter. "I guess I'll go see if Maddie's up."

"We'll get her." Oren took Finn and went up the stairs, leaving Chandler standing in the middle of the kitchen. She listened to his footsteps going up the stairs and squeezed her eyes against an unexpected sting of tears. Where had they gone wrong? How had they gotten so far off course, going from best friends to strangers? And how were they going to get back to where they needed to be?

A herd of footsteps coming downstairs shook her from her thoughts. She pulled in a deep breath and popped waffles into the toaster.

Her family stormed into the kitchen. Maddie climbed onto her chair like a spider monkey. "I'm allowed to have smiley waffles now," she announced to the room.

"What?" Oren asked with a laugh.

"Nanny doesn't like smiley waffles. They make her mad."

"Nah, she was just upset about the eggs."

Chandler tensed. The toaster popped, the sound making her jump. She put the waffles on a plate, then clenched her hands and flexed them. This. This reminder of Janice's overreaction about breakfast and Oren's defense of her. This is the bad place they need to come back from.

She poured the strawberry syrup on the waffles. "Shit!"

"Mommy said a swear," Maddie sing-songed.

"What?" Oren asked.

Chandler popped two more waffles into the toaster. "I got distracted." She'd poured the syrup all over both waffles instead of making smiley faces. "I, um… bathroom. I'll be right back."

"I'll get the waffles. Why don't you get your tape measure and stuff?"

"Yeah. Good idea." She fled the kitchen and went down the basement stairs to her domain. She felt a little calmer here, a little safer. In the kitchen, with Oren and the kids, it was easy to doubt herself and convince herself they were fine. That she was overreacting. That she was wrong. That of course it was okay for Oren to defend his mother. That it hadn't been *that* bad. That it was stupid to need space from an otherwise wonderful husband.

She sat down at her drawing table and pulled open a drawer. Her supplies were neat and orderly, everything in its place. It helped center her. Calm her.

She put her tape measure, notebook, and pencils in her small drawstring backpack. She'd take pictures with her phone and then come back and start sketching out some new curtains for the theater.

Chapter Eighteen

Oren was wiping Maddie's syrupy chin when Chandler came back upstairs from the basement. "I'll get her dressed and then change him before we go."

He followed Maddie as she bounded up the stairs to her room. "I hafta pee! Pee, pee, pee."

"Okay." He sat on her bed and waited. He knew better than to pick out any clothes for her. The last time he tried to convince her a safety orange dress didn't go with hot pink leggings it had ended in tears. Lesson learned. Leave the fashion to her.

When she flounced out of the bathroom, he held up his hands and wiggled his fingers.

Maddie groaned dramatically and went back to the bathroom to wash her hands. A moment later, she was standing in front of her closet, considering her options. "That one!"

Oren reached over her and touched a bright pink and yellow floofy tulle dress. "This one?"

"Yup."

He pulled the officially licensed Princess Poppy dress from the hanger and helped Maddie into it. She then opened a dresser drawer and grabbed a pair of lime green leggings that she tugged on herself. A pair of purple mud boots and bright pink rhinestone tiara completed the outfit. Because, duh, sparkle fashion.

Maddie twirled in front of her mirror. "What do you think, Daddy?"

"I think you're beautiful," he said, meaning every word. His heart clenched a little that he might not always be here for simple moments like this. And for what?

Downstairs, Chandler grinned as Maddie skipped into the living room. "Look at you!"

Maddie twirled for her mother. "Princess Giraffe is staying home because she just had a bath and she don't wanna get dirty at the park."

"I think Princess Giraffe is making a very good choice," Chandler answered.

The baby was already in the stroller, kicking his bare feet in the air.

"No socks?"

Chandler pointed to two tiny socks on the floor. "I tried."

"What is it with these kids and socks?" he chuckled. He and Chandler wrangled the kids to his car. He secured Finn while Chandler buckled Maddie.

A few minutes later, they unloaded at the park, a small community playground with a large lawn, swings, slides, monkey bars, a controversial sandbox that had been the subject of many heated discussions at township meetings, and a circle of six concrete animals on thick springs.

Maddie took off full speed and met Kinsley, another little girl from the neighborhood, at the animals. She scrambled onto the dolphin while the other little girl got on a raccoon. They rocked their animals back and forth, squealing and laughing as only little girls can do. Kinsley's mom waved, and they waved back.

The air was cool, but the sun suggested it would be hot before long.

He pushed the stroller. Chandler walked alongside him, her hands in the pocket of her hoodie. He grasped for something to say. Anything. "So Ingrid's done with the costuming business?"

"Yeah. She's retiring so they can travel. I think they're taking a cruise this week. Which is why I had to send her the money so quick."

He hated the defensive edge to her voice. Even more, he hated that he'd caused her to be defensive. In all their years together, Chandler had managed their money brilliantly, and had made nothing but good financial decisions for their family. He felt horrible for questioning her for a single moment, and being stressed out wasn't a good excuse for accusing her of mismanaging their money. Especially the *way* he'd questioned her. Without asking one single question.

No wonder he was stuck crashing at his parents' house.

Maddie was tired and dirty, but still wanted to play in the ball pit at McDonald's. By the time she got to her chicken nuggets, she could barely keep her eyes open. Oren carried her to the car, and she was asleep before he was done buckling her in.

At the house, he carried her inside. Chandler pushed the stroller into the living room and spread a blanket on the floor, where she laid the baby. He laid Maddie down next to Finn and tiptoed into the kitchen.

Chandler washed some dishes in the sink.

Oren wanted more than anything to go up behind her and wrap his arms around her, but he knew it would make her uncomfortable, and that was the last thing he wanted to do.

Instead, he kept his distance and said, "The kids are both napping. Do you want to grab a nap, too?"

She turned off the faucet and looked at him. "Um…"

"I think I'll put my headset on and catch a ballgame." He had no idea if there were any games on television or not. Or if anything was even in season. His thing had always been theater, not sports.

Chandler cast a glance at the stairs.

"Go on. I'll get you up when the kids get up."

"I have a lot to do…"

He chuckled. "Weak argument, Chan. Go take a nap. Whatever needs done can wait." He knew she still wasn't back to a hundred percent, and all he wanted in the world was for his wife and kids to be happy and healthy. Preferably with him.

As it turned out, there was, in fact, a game on television. He lay down on the recliner with his headset turned low so he could hear the kids but they couldn't hear the television. He dozed until Finn started gurgling and trying to swallow his own feet.

Oren put his headset on the end table and picked Finn up. He carried him into the kitchen and prepared a bottle with one hand, then carried him back to the recliner.

Wide-eyed, Finn took his bottle. He'd only gotten a few good slurps when Maddie woke up, yawned loudly, and went off to the bathroom, her hair a wild and messy halo around her head.

Once Finn was fed and back in his swing, Oren fixed Maddie a snack of cheese cubes and milk. He went upstairs and gingerly pushed the bedroom door open.

Chandler was laying in the bed, eyes open. She smiled when he came in and his heart skipped a beat. "I'm too comfortable to move."

"You can stay in bed if you want." More than anything, he wanted to climb in beside her and hold her close.

"Nah." She flipped the comforter back and slid out of bed. "Then I won't sleep tonight. Assuming Finn lets me."

Oren cleared his throat. "About that. I was thinking."

She froze, staring at him, waiting.

"Maybe I could take the kids overnight. I'll bring them back on my way to work. I figure that'll give you time to do whatever you want to do and get some uninterrupted sleep."

"That's really sweet."

"No matter what's going on here," he motioned back and forth between them, "I'm still the best dad ever, right?"

"Of course."

"Let's go to the theater."

Chapter Nineteen

Chandler watched Oren out of the corner of her eye as he changed Finn while Maddie hung on his arm. When both kids were ready, they took them out and got them situated in their car seats. Oren drove while Chandler made a few rough sketches in her notebook.

Satisfied with what she'd drawn, she said, "I have some ideas for the curtains. I think those gold tiebacks are still in storage. I might dig them out."

"They're probably on that shelf in the clear back of the prop room."

Chandler's mind flitted through different theater curtain styles. She wanted them to work for the Shakespeare plays as well as the modern plays Gretchen produced occasionally.

Oren parked in front of the theater. From the outside, it could easily be mistaken for an old church, which was its original purpose in the 1700s, 1800s, and early 1900s before it was gutted, abandoned, and fell into disrepair. The Hickory Hollow Restoration Committee took it on as a project in the 1970s and restored it as a community theater with a sloping floor and a large stage at the front of the room. White board siding, large stained glass windows, a small entry room with two huge oak doors. It even had a steeple that rose above the doorway with a long-silent bell.

He unlocked the front door and flipped on the lights. They walked through the small lobby and into the huge open room that was originally the sanctuary, but now housed rows and rows of theater seating that the Restoration Committee had rescued from a demolition project three states away.

Maddie ran down the aisle to the stage, Princess Giraffe flopping along beside her. She clomped up the steps and began dancing in the middle of the hardwood floor.

Chandler pushed Finn's stroller and parked him in the front row. "Do you know where the ladder is?"

"Yeah, I'll grab it." Oren disappeared behind the curtain to the storage room behind the stage. He reappeared a moment later with the folding ladder.

"Thanks. Make sure Maddie doesn't knock me over," she joked, nodding her head to Maddie, who was twirling in the middle of the stage, arms outstretched, her skirt swirling around her, not a care in the world.

He held the ladder as she climbed up and measured the top rod pocket of the curtain, then the rod itself. When she was done taking measurements, she carefully climbed back down the ladder.

"Thanks, I think I'm done with it." She took more measurements of the fabric and made rough sketches while Oren danced with Maddie and kept an eye on Finn.

When she was done measuring and making notes, they took Maddie in the back and let her root through the costumes and props. She laughed and played and pretended to be a princess while Oren practiced some of his lines.

Most of the afternoon had passed by the time they locked the theater and piled back into the car. The ride was quiet, except for Maddie's incessant singing of the Princess Poppy theme song.

"You okay with me taking the K-I-D-S tonight?"

Chandler appreciated he spelled the word out so little ears didn't get interested. "I mean, I'm not thrilled, but if that's what you want to do, it's fine."

"It is."

Emotions warred inside her. She could scarcely imagine an entire night to herself, curled up in her bed, not having to get up in the middle of the night. As wonderful as that sounded, though, she didn't like the idea of being away from the kids. "It'll give me time to look over the notes Kim sent me. I might even go over and talk to her and Nate about it."

"Oh."

For some reason, his careful reaction rankled her. "What?"

He turned into their driveway. "Nothing."

She peered into the back seat. "Finn's asleep. Do you want me to get their stuff together?"

"For what?" Maddie asked.

Oren grinned at her. "We're going to have a sleepover at Nanny's."

"Sleepover!" Maddie clapped her hands and danced in her seat.

Chandler said, "Will you help Mommy pack your bag while Daddy stays here with Finn?"

"Yeah!" She unbuckled herself with a dexterity and speed Chandler didn't want to think too much about.

They went inside and Chandler packed Finn's bag first, then helped Maddie pack her Princess Poppy backpack with enough stuff to last a week, let alone one night. When they were done, Maddie raced around her room, panicked. "Where's Princess Giraffe? She hasta go with me!" She flung pillows off her bed and yanked the comforter down, exposing her usual sleeping companions. Prince Monkey and Princess Hippo went flying into the air as Maddie searched. "Princess Giraffe!"

Chandler flipped the light off and back on to catch Maddie's attention. "Whoa, slow down. Princess Giraffe is in the car with Daddy. She's buckled in between you and Finn, remember?"

Maddie paused, then clapped her hands and jumped once. "Yes! I member." She picked up the monkey and hippo and carefully put them back on the bed, pulling the comforter up to their chins.

"Let's grab some bottles out of the fridge and then we're ready to go."

"Aren't you sleeping over, Mommy?"

"Not tonight."

"Are you hafta work?"

"Yup. I'm going to work on the curtains for the theater."

"You make pretty stuff, Mommy."

Chandler's heart warmed. She bent down and gave Maddie a bear hug. "Thank you, sweetheart."

Maddie gave her a loud kiss and squirmed away.

They went outside and Oren got out of the car. He opened Maddie's door and buckled her in her car seat. When he closed the door, Chandler felt a little awkward.

"I'll bring them by on my way to work."

"Okay."

He reached toward her, then dropped his hand back to his side. "Um…"

"Yeah. I'll see you all in the morning then. I packed extra bottles. You shouldn't need that many, but just in case he's off his routine being away from home or something…"

He reached again, catching her hand in his. "Okay."

"Okay." She squeezed his fingers. "Have fun.'

He snorted. "Unlikely."

She couldn't keep from smiling at that. Once again wondered if she should just tell him to stay home, but it was just too soon to give in if anything was to change.

"Maybe… maybe don't get in too deep with the Nate and Kim thing. That's a lot of work we don't have a lot of time for right now, right?"

"Oren. It's fine. I can handle it."

"I'm just saying it's a lot with the kids and your online store and the theater, especially with the play starting up."

She bristled. "The theater isn't my priority."

"It's a *family* priority."

She didn't want to argue, but she couldn't ignore it. "It's *your* priority, and I support that. I'm happy to volunteer my time and donate my supplies to do the curtains, but it takes a back seat to a paying job."

Maddie knocked on the window.

"We can talk about it later," she said.

"Don't sign any contracts."

Why did that sound like an order? Chandler gave him a tight smile and pulled her hand away. She opened the car door and gave Maddie kisses. "Be good for Daddy." She waved and closed the door.

Oren leaned over to kiss her. "See you in the morning. Love you."

At the last second, she turned her face and he kissed her cheek. "Love you, too." She waited on the porch, waving, until the car was out of sight. Then she grabbed her phone.

Are you busy?

She texted to Ashley.

Half a minute later, her phone vibrated with an incoming call. "Everything okay?"

"Yes. No. I don't know. Maybe." She curled up on the corner of the couch and spilled her heart and soul. She ended with, "Am I being too harsh? Too unreasonable?"

Ashley pushed out a breath. "Chan, I love you. And I'm probably the wrong person to ask, because I'm really biased. After all the problems Ell and I have had with my dad and Jean... I can't see any way that you can allow Janice to keep treating you this way, and Oren has to back you up, one hundred percent. If I hadn't made a stand with Jean, Elliott and I wouldn't be together right now, and he wouldn't have been wrong for leaving."

"I know."

"I told you about Jean trying to hire a divorce lawyer for me when I announced my pregnancy, right?"

"Yes."

"Janice is doing the same sort of crap, trying to sabotage your marriage, and Oren has to take a stand. I'm not saying he has to choose, exactly. I mean, he doesn't have to cut his mom off, but he can't stand for letting her treat you this way. Boundaries."

"I know." Her eyes drifted shut. "It's been much better now that she's gone and when it's just me and Oren, I feel like the stuff with Janice is... I don't know, insignificant."

"I get that. But Oren needs to have your back when she *is* there, just as much as he does when she's not. Basic respect in your own home isn't an unreasonable boundary."

"I know."

"And he needs to chill out about the work with Kim and Nate. There's nothing wrong with you taking on that work if you want to. You know better than anyone what you can handle."

Chandler nodded even though Ashley couldn't see her. "You're right. I feel awful saying this, but it's like no matter what happens, this has been eye-opening, and I've realized that I need to be able to support myself. It'll be great if all this work is just extra money for fun stuff for the family, but what if everything falls apart? My online shop could barely cover the bills at this point, but if I focus on building it, I can build it up and replace my old day job income by the end of next year."

"Why do you feel awful saying that?"

She thought for a minute. "Because if I'm planning to be able to support myself, it feels like that means I've got one foot out the door."

"But you don't."

"No. I don't. I know it might look bad that I want some space right now, but it's not like I'm thinking about... you know. I don't even want to say the word."

"There's nothing wrong with needing a little space to breathe and clear your head. And there's nothing – *nothing* – wrong with intentionally growing your business. Even if you weren't having some issues right now, it's smart to look ahead, even to when the kids are ready for college or buying their first house. Heck, it could be to save up for a family trip to Disney. It doesn't have to have anything to do with the current tension."

"You're right." The relief at having someone *understand* was almost overwhelming.

"Of course I am. Go work on your color-coded business plan while you have the house to yourself."

"You know me so well."

After the call ended, Chandler went to her office in the basement and pulled out a calendar. It wasn't long before she lost herself in making plans for the future of her business.

Chapter Twenty

"Okay, stinky, let's get a bath."

Maddie giggled and made a show of loudly sniffing her arm. "I'm not stinky! Finn's stinky."

That was accurate. Oren changed the baby's full diaper and deposited the mess in a plastic bag. "Hang on, I'm going to take this outside."

"I'll get my towel!" Maddie hummed to herself as she dug through the small pink backpack.

Oren carried Finn downstairs in one arm, with the foul bag dangling from his opposite hand. "Mom? You want to take him a sec?"

"Of course." Janice came around the corner from the kitchen and took Finn. "Is Maddie by herself?"

"She's getting her stuff out for her bath. I need to throw this away outside."

"The cans are already at the curb."

The streetlights gave the neighborhood a nice glow in the deepening darkness. He jogged down the sidewalk and tossed the bag into the trash can at the edge of the road. How on earth can a kid so little make a stink so big?

Inside, he expected to take Finn back from his mother, but they weren't in the living room.

"They went upstairs," his dad offered from his recliner.

Oren took the stairs two at a time and found his mom filling the tub for Maddie. She sat on the edge of the tub bouncing Finn on her lap.

He felt the water. Satisfied with the temperature, he reached over and turned off the faucet.

"Daddy, can Princess Giraffe sit here?" She patted the counter across from the tub.

"Sure," he said, at the same time his mother said, "No."

Janice shook her head. "You don't want it to fall in the water."

"She won't fall in, Nanny."

Oren shrugged. "It's not a big deal. Maddie likes having her in sight."

"Whatever," his mom said.

He got the stuffed animal from the bedroom and settled her on the counter. "Ready?" He helped Maddie climb into the bathtub, then handed her a small basket of rubber bath toys that stayed at Nanny's house for occasions just like this.

Maddie hummed the Princess Poppy theme song for a while as she splashed and played with her bath toys.

Oren knelt beside the tub and helped her wash, while Janice held Finn.

"Nanny, he pooped in the water."

Janice looked at the water. "Don't tell lies. He did not."

Maddie rolled her eyes. "Not *now*. When he took a bath last week."

Janice's mouth pressed into a thin line. "He hasn't had a bath since last week?"

Oren could barely control his own eye roll. "He had a bath Friday."

"Why not yesterday?" She held Finn closer to her chest, as if protecting him from something.

"Because his skin is sensitive and he doesn't need a full bath every day." He shook his head. "Before you argue, that was advice straight from the pediatrician."

"Can we call Mommy before bed?"

Janice gave a rude snort.

Oren side-eyed her. "Of course we'll call to say good night to Mommy."

"I wouldn't," Janice muttered.

Maddie dumped sudsy water from one plastic cup into another. "You don't like Mommy," she said, very matter-of-fact.

"Of course I do."

"No, you don't," Maddie argued.

"I'd like your mommy more if she wasn't mean to your daddy."

Oren's head snapped up. "Mom."

Maddie frowned. "Mommy's not mean."

"Mommy threw you all out of the house. That's mean *and* selfish."

"Enough!" Oren roared.

Maddie dropped her plastic cups. Her eyes went wide, no doubt shocked to hear Oren raising his voice in anger.

"Well, she did. If she was a good wife and mother, she never would have thrown you all out on the street."

Oren's throat constricted. He choked around a flood of words that fought to come out. Sucking in a sharp breath, he swallowed them before he unleashed a torrent he'd end up regretting. He reached into the water and put Maddie's toys in their basket, then wrung out the washcloth. When he was calm enough, he said, "Okay, princess. Let's get you dried off."

She let Oren lift her out of the tub and wrap her in her towel. Her little face was pinched and unhappy.

When she was dry, Oren helped her into her Princess Poppy pajamas and led her to the bedroom. He just wanted to get the kids to bed so he could have a discussion with his mother about the inappropriate things she was saying.

Janice followed him, still carrying Finn. "I don't know why you're getting upset with *me* for stating the obvious."

In a flash, Oren realized a discussion wasn't going to cut it. This is what Chandler had been talking about. His mother had been disrespectful and hateful about her – in front of their *children* – and he was planning to… what? Reprimand her? Ask her to be nice? Put his foot down? And then what? Back down when she pushed back.

His stomach clenched as the full force of realization landed on him.

His attempts at keeping the peace rolled Chandler straight under the bus. All by herself.

Janice flipped the corner of the comforter back and patted the mattress for Maddie to climb in. "I'll tell you a bedtime story. Since your mother probably doesn't do that, either," she muttered.

Resolve straightened his back. It was time to show Chandler he was on her side. "No. We're going home."

Maddie looked back and forth between him and the bed, confused.

"What are you talking about?" Janice stood straight.

"I've had enough. I will not tolerate you saying things about Chandler, especially to our children." His throat and chest went tight with anxiety. Standing up to his mother was harder than he'd anticipated. He tossed all of Maddie's belongings in her princess backpack and pointed to her boots. "Maddie, put your shoes on."

Her eyes brimmed with confused tears, but she did as he told her, sitting on the floor to pull her boots on.

"Oren, you're being ridiculous."

"No. You're being disrespectful of my wife." He slung the diaper bag over his shoulder, picked Finn up, and grabbed Maddie's backpack with his free hand.

She talked at him as they walked downstairs into the kitchen. "Why should I be respectful of her when she threw you out of the house *you* pay for? She's being disrespectful to my son and my grandchildren, but you act like I should be kissing her feet."

Oren grabbed the bottles out of the fridge and awkwardly wedged them into the diaper bag. Maddie was glued to his leg.

"Oren. Be reasonable. There's no sense in dragging the kids out at bedtime."

He ignored her and nudged Maddie out the door. He set the backpack beside the car and fumbled in his pocket for the keys.

Janice stood on the porch and shouted, "Oren! You're making a huge mistake! Don't choose that woman over your family who loves you!"

He buckled Finn into his car seat, then lifted Maddie up into the car and secured her in her car seat. He double checked both buckles and set the backpack and diaper bag in the back of the vehicle.

"Oren!"

He froze, his fingers curled around the door handle. Slowly, he turned and looked at his mother. "You need to stop. Now."

"If you drive away, you're making a choice, Oren. You won't be able to take it back!"

"Mom, I love you, but I will always, *always* choose my wife." He slipped into the driver's seat and started the car.

He just hoped there was still a chance that his wife would choose him.

Chapter Twenty-One

Chandler sat at her drawing table, sipping a glass of red wine. Her first in nearly two years. She drafted out a very bare bones, high-level business plan to cover her goals for the next two years and felt really good about it. She'd let it settle for a few days, then revisit the plan and make tweaks as necessary.

That done, she sketched out some ideas for costumes for Nate and Kim's upcoming show. She made the base of the costumes fairly basic and multi-purpose so they could easily pivot across various time periods, then penciled in some intricate accessories.

She finished her wine and grabbed a bottle of water from the fridge. Her mind hummed with ideas for costumes and accessories and props. It was the best creative buzz she'd had in at least a year.

It was almost nine when something thumped upstairs. Heart pounding, she tiptoed up the stairs and heard Oren's voice. "Let's tell Mommy we're home."

She pushed through the basement door, which was ajar. "Hey. I wasn't expecting—"

Maddie launched herself at her. "Do you love us, Mommy?"

"What? Of course I do." She squeezed Maddie and planted kisses all over her face. "What a silly question. Mommy loves you more than anything in the whole wide world." She looked at Oren, questioning.

Maddie burst into tears.

Chandler petted her hair and made soothing noises. She looked over Maddie's head. "Did someone not want to do a sleepover?"

Oren shook his head. "I'll fill you in after we get settled." He gently bounced Finn, who was fast asleep.

That sounded ominous. Chandler carried Maddie upstairs. "Where's Princess Giraffe?"

Oren said, "She's in the car. I'll put Finn down and get her."

Chandler took Maddie into the bathroom and encouraged her to use the toilet and wash her hands. She put a dot of toothpaste on Maddie's Princess Poppy toothbrush and waited while Maddie brushed.

"Did you have fun at Nanny's?"

Maddie's chin trembled. "No." She rinsed her toothbrush and slowly put it in the Princess Poppy toothbrush holder. "Nanny's mean."

Chandler's entire body clenched. "She was mean to you?" Her inner mama bear was ready and willing to come out and maul someone.

"Nanny said you said you don't love me and Finn and Daddy and you don't let us live here no more."

Blood pounded behind her eardrums. She took a few breaths and made sure her voice was calm. "I love you so, so much. I love Finn, and I love Daddy. And we all live here together." Despite whatever the future held, it was true now.

"Nanny made me sad."

"Don't be sad." Chandler lifted her into her arms and carried her to her bed. She sat down with Maddie cradled on her lap. "Mommy loves you. Daddy loves you. We love you very, very much, and we love Finn very, very much."

"More than the whole world?" she quietly whimpered.

"More than the whole, whole world," Chandler confirmed.

Maddie yawned.

Chandler lifted the blankets for Maddie to crawl under, then kissed her forehead.

Oren slid around the doorway and tucked Princess Giraffe under the covers with Maddie. He gave her kisses, too.

She yawned again. "Love you."

"Love you, too," both of them answered.

Chandler checked on Finn while Oren closed Maddie's door. The baby slept soundly, his tiny fists raised beside his head like he was cheering for his favorite sports team. She didn't want to wake him, so she resisted the urge to reach down and touch him.

Oren stood awkwardly in the hallway, as if he couldn't cross the threshold to their master bedroom. Quietly, he said, "Can we go downstairs?"

"Yeah." She wasn't sure if she wanted to scream or cry or drive to Janice's and deck her. Or all of the above. She also wasn't sure if she wanted to hear Oren's version of how he'd handled the situation.

Baby monitor in hand, Chandler walked down the stairs to the kitchen.

Instead of stopping, Oren opened the basement door and gestured for her to go down.

She passed him and said, "Is there going to be yelling? Is that why you're taking me two floors away from the kids?"

He shook his head, but didn't smile at her joke.

That concerned her as she flipped on the light switch and

went down to her workspace. A small sofa and her drafting chair were the only pieces of furniture, so she settled onto the sofa and Oren sat beside her.

"Tell me everything," she said.

Oren leaned forward, his elbows on his knees. He clasped his hands together. His knuckles whitened as he squeezed. "I have a lot to say, and I'm not sure where to start.'

Her throat tightened.

"I'm sorry. I... I've been so wrong. I finally... ' he trailed off and ran a hand through his hair. "You're right. This whole time, you've been right and I've been blind. Worse. I didn't believe how... I never once thought you were *lying*, but I convinced myself you were exaggerating."

Chandler waited while Oren put his thoughts in order.

"The whole time we've been married, I knew there was tension between you and my mom. She's difficult. I know that. I grew up with her. I thought we could just ignore it. After Maddie was born it seemed like she backed off because she was so happy to have a grandbaby. When Finn came along and she dialed it up to a thousand, I thought it'd pass. I never thought she was doing anything more than being an obnoxious, meddlesome, but ultimately harmless in-law."

She gritted her teeth, feeling a lot of different things at his speech. A little glad he was seeing the reality of the situation, a little mad, a little sad, and a whole lot frustrated

"Tonight, when she told Maddie you threw us out and that you didn't love us, it hit me. Chan, it hit me like a punch to the gut. She's always been this way, she's just better or worse sometimes. I thought it was postpartum hormones or something you just needed to deal with. But when I was standing there, and I heard the words coming out of her mouth, it hit me that it's not up to you to deal with her. It's not even up to her to change. It's up to me to protect you, and I've failed so miserably."

She didn't say anything. Just waited.

"I've failed you, and I've failed our family. I should have listened and been a better partner. I'm sorry. As soon as I heard everything she was saying, I realized that everything you'd said had been exactly how it went down. I realized that I've been allowing you to be mistreated and I didn't do anything to protect you. I'm so sorry. I know where I went wrong, and I'm sorry it took me this long to realize it." He gave her a shaky smile. "I set a hard boundary with my mom. I told her I won't ever tolerate her disrespecting you. It wasn't easy, but I'm really glad I did it. Now we can get back to normal and move forward since I pulled my head out of my backside."

Yes, she was glad he'd had an epiphany, but it didn't change one very simple fact. Her anger burned brighter. Once again, she felt like the bad guy, like she should just smile and be grateful that he finally understood. "I'm glad."

His brows pressed inward. "You don't sound glad."

"I am. But I can't just snap my fingers and be over this. I'm glad you realized what your mother was doing. But you only had this great awakening after you heard it with your own ears. What if she'd never been so blatant in front of you? What if she'd have said those things to Maddie when you weren't right there? You'd still be thinking I'm overreacting and maybe even trying to poison Maddie against her grandmother. You only believe me now because you witnessed it firsthand, and that's just another slap in my face."

His mouth was open, stunned. "I thought you'd be happy. I'm on your side, Chan. We're a team, and I lost sight of that. I thought that was a good thing."

A niggle of impatience wound its way through her chest. "It *is* a good thing. I'm just saying it doesn't erase the past few weeks, and to be honest, I'm a little angry that you expect a trophy for realizing I'm not a liar. You should have known that all along."

"A trophy? I just wanted a little appreciation for admitting I was wrong."

That one word made her see red. "Appreciation? 'Hey, Chan, guess what, now that I have solid proof, I know you're not a liar.' You want appreciation for that? Really?" She stood up and walked around her drawing table just to put some distance between them. "It's late. I'm going to bed."

"I'm not leaving again. It's my house, too."

"Fine. I'll stay in the guest room." She padded up the two flights of stairs and got changed for bed. When she was done in the bathroom, she came to a stop in the bedroom.

Oren stood in the doorway with an armful of clothes. Quietly, so he didn't wake Finn, he said, "I'll take the guest room. Good night." He paused, his hand on the doorknob. "I love you."

He pulled the door shut before she could answer. Which was a good thing, because she wasn't sure she would have.

Chapter Twenty-Two

Well, *that* hadn't gone the way he'd expected. Oren flung his clothes onto the bed in the guest room with unnecessary force. His balled up socks bounced off the bed and rolled across the room.

Grumbling, he rounded the bed and picked them up. He replayed the argument in his head, trying to figure out where he'd gone wrong this time.

In the morning, he was no closer to an answer. It stung that he couldn't quite figure out when he'd stopped being able to read Chandler and understand her, almost telepathically. Two months ago, he could have accurately predicted her every move, and she his.

Now, as he straightened the comforter on the small, stiff guest bed, he couldn't guess what might happen next.

Stepping lightly down the stairs, he wasn't sure if anyone was up. As he reached the bottom, he heard voices in the kitchen. Chandler's back was to him. Maddie was in her booster seat, her feet swinging as she happily ate her smiley waffle. Finn cooed in his swing.

"Hey," he said tentatively.

Chandler half-turned and smiled at him. "Good morning."

"Daddy, look. This is my second smiley waffle!"

"My goodness, you must be hungry."

"Mommy said I'm the hungry hungry caterpillar."

Oren lightly tickled her belly. "You look like a caterpillar."

She giggled and went back to her waffle.

Oren opened the fridge and checked the shelf on the door. "Are we out of peanut butter?"

"There's a new jar in the pantry."

He got it and made himself a peanut butter and jelly sandwich.

"Is that what you're taking for lunch?"

"Breakfast. I'll probably eat out of the vending machine today."

"There's leftover meatloaf if you want it."

He reopened the fridge.

"It's in the blue container. Take the whole thing because I won't eat it."

He cracked a little smile. Okay, so his wife hadn't changed so drastically after all. Chandler had a very short list of things she considered acceptable to eat as leftovers. Meatloaf didn't make the cut.

"There's macaroni and cheese in that bowl, too." She pointed.

He pulled the bowl out.

Chandler opened a drawer and set two plastic containers on the counter for him. While he dished leftover macaroni and cheese, which she would totally eat, by the way, she got his insulated lunchbox out of the pantry.

"Thanks." He stopped himself before he said "sweetheart" even though he wanted to use the term of endearment.

"You're welcome."

The whole morning felt oddly formal, like they were tiptoeing around the elephant in the room. He finished packing his lunch and stood in the doorway for a second, watching Maddie swing her bare feet while she happily ate her smiley waffles and Finn tried to eat his toes. Chandler stood at the sink, eating a bowl of cereal while the sink filled with soapy water. In that moment, two things were abundantly clear.

One, this was the best possible life he could ever imagine.

And two, he'd do whatever he had to do to make things right again.

Work dragged, and he found himself spending more time than usual texting with Connor and Elliott, brainstorming ways he could win his wife back.

Try dating her again

was Connor's suggestion, followed by a thumbs up emoji from Elliott.

The idea implanted itself in his brain and for most of the afternoon, he did his job on autopilot while he thought back to the early days of their relationship. Most of the time, they watched movies at home or went for walks. Of course, they'd met when they were still teenagers, so they were pretty broke. His part-time job bussing tables after school covered his gas and the occasional meal out, but even if they'd have had a ton of money, he was sure they would have done mostly the same things.

Elliott followed his thumbs up with,

> Don't overthink it. Simple dinner and a movie
> is a good start. We'll watch the kids.

Oren texted back his thanks. Yeah. He'd start simple. He looked at the phone in his hand. Couldn't get much simpler than sending a text, could it? Up until a few weeks ago, he and Chandler texted back and forth throughout the day, every day.

He opened the text thread with Chandler Most of the messages were mundane, impersonal clips about things to pick up at the store or something about the kids. The last text was days old. No wonder he felt distant from her. Even this electronic connection had been missing.

He typed,

> Thinking about you. Hope you're having a
> good day.

A few seconds later, little dots appeared that showed she was typing a response.

> Day is good. Hope yours is, too.

> Frank broke the coffee machine so 'm dying
> for caffeine

She sent back a photo of herself holding up her favorite travel tumbler that held half of a homemade iced coffee.

> Sorry about your luck lol.

He chuckled and set his phone down. Baby steps. It felt

good to connect with her, even over something as small and simple as coffee and a little laugh. It gave him hope. And made him feel like a complete fool for letting things run this far off the rails.

<h1 style="text-align:center">Chapter Twenty-Three</h1>

The kids were being adorable, so Chandler snapped a few pictures she sent to Oren, then slipped her phone into her pocket.

"Mommy? Can we go to the park?"

"We can go to the little park." The tiny park near their house wasn't as equipped as the one across town, but it only required loading up a stroller and not the whole car.

"Okay."

She helped Maddie down from her booster seat and put the dirty plate in the sink, along with last night's supper dishes to be dealt with later.

Finn was happy and fed, so she scooped him up and into the stroller.

Maddie reappeared in the kitchen with her purple mud boots on the wrong feet.

"Switch your shoes, or your feet will grow on backwards."

"Will not," Maddie groaned and grumped as she flopped onto the floor to pull her boots off and put them on the correct feet.

"Doesn't that feel better?"

She shrugged, noncommittal, refusing to admit her feet felt better now.

Chandler double checked the contents of the diaper bag and headed out the door.

Maddie skipped happily along the sidewalk, then into the grass that led into the park.

Chandler paused and looked at the broken fence. She sighed and looked away. There was too much turmoil in her mind to even think about cleaning up the branches and broken pickets. She watched her daughter run to the sliding board and scramble up the ladder. She pulled her phone out again and took some pictures. Sending them to Oren felt nice. Normal. She pushed Finn's stroller in big circles around the playground equipment, keeping an eye on Maddie and feeling pretty darn good about finally getting some fresh air and exercise.

"Mommy! Push me!" Maddie scrambled onto one of the swings and pumped her little legs furiously, to no avail.

Chandler finished her lap around the perimeter and parked the stroller to the side of the swing set. Finn was wide awake, taking in the sights and sounds. She took hold of the chains and pulled back. "Hang on," she warned, then let go.

Maddie cried, "Higher! Higher!"

"Hey, guys," a voice called out.

Chandler grabbed Maddie and set her on the ground to keep her from jumping off the swing.

Maddie ran full speed at them. "Jared!" Then she yelled, "Isobel!" as an afterthought.

Jared swooped her up into the air. "You're an airplane, Maddie!"

Maddie squealed, and Chandler had to laugh.

"What are you guys up to?" she asked.

"We were out for a walk and thought we'd come hang out with Maddie-girl." Jared swung her into the air again.

Isobel said, "Jared said you might need some babysitting." She bit her lip and added, "I was also kind of hoping you might be able to show me some costume stuff. Like, sewing stuff."

"Sure." A little twinge of excitement pinged in Chandler's belly. She'd learned so much from Ingrid and she'd always wanted to be an inspiration and mentor like that for someone else. It would be great if that someone was Isobel. She was bright and enthusiastic, and as her relationship with Jared continued, she became more involved with Kim and Nate's production company and would put her new skills to good use.

Then again, she might be getting a little ahead of herself. "Have you ever sewn?"

"Yeah, I've made some basic stuff like pillows, and I can fix holes and stuff like that."

"That's a great start. I'm hoping to measure out fabric for the theater curtains this afternoon if naps go well."

"I'd love to help."

Jared piped up. "I can babysit if you need to get some work done."

Maddie jumped up and down and clapped her hands. "Yes! Play with me, Jared!"

"Quit climbing on him. He's not your personal set of monkey bars," Chandler admonished with a laugh.

Jared's dark curls bounced across his forehead as he bent to lift Maddie into the air again. "I don't mind."

"If you really want to, and you really don't mind watching the kids, sure." This was an unexpected but most welcome change of plans. Chandler had assumed Isobel would be the babysitter.

"Yay!" Maddie cheered. "Jared! Look what I can do!" She ran for the sliding board.

A while later, they headed back toward the house. Inside, Chandler said, "I'm going to feed Finn, and then we can get started. If you're sure. You don't have to do this."

"We're sure," Jared said.

Isobel nodded her agreement.

Chandler herded everyone down to her basement area and opened the French doors leading to the patio. Jared took Maddie out to the lawn beyond the patio while Finn napped in his stroller in the shade just outside the doors where both Jared and Chandler could see him.

She laid a bolt of fabric on the island and pulled her notebook out. "These are the measurements I took at the theater."

"Whoa, is this what you're making?" Isobel pointed to a sketch of the curtains Chandler had in mind.

"That's the plan."

"They're huge. How can you do that?"

"In pieces." Chandler flipped the page to a more detailed drawing of the curtains in sections, with measurements.

"What does this mean?" Isobel asked about numbers scribbled on the side of the page.

"Those are my hems. I'll show you."

"This seems so complicated."

Chandler smiled at her. "You'll see that it's not. With these curtains, everything is done in straight lines."

"Even the ruffles?"

"Yup, they start out straight, then we gather them." She flipped to a blank page and made an even simpler sketch, talking Isobel through every step as she scribbled on the paper. "It boils down to a series of rectangles."

"Oh. I see it now." Her voice was excited. "And then for the top ruffled part, you just kind of scrunch it up?"

"Exactly."

Chandler unrolled the velvet from the bolt and had Isobel help her measure the length they needed. That done, they unfolded the fabric and pinned the amount needed for the hem on one of the long sides.

"Aren't we doing the top and bottom?"

"Sides first." Chandler held the side at the top and folded it over. "See? Once this part is hemmed," she folded over the top, "we can hem the top. If we hem the top first." she demonstrated, and Isobel caught on immediately.

"Oh, the side hem would close the top part."

"Exactly. We need that open to add the loops.'

Isobel nodded enthusiastically. "Makes total sense."

For a while, Chandler was lost in her work, going slow, making sure to show Isobel every smallest step along the way.

An hour, maybe two, had passed before Jared appeared in the doorway with a dirty, sweaty, but quite happy Maddie in tow. He pushed the stroller toward the island.

Chandler glanced up and caught his concerned expression. "Everything okay?" She looked in on Finn, who was gurgling and playing with his feet.

"Yeah, it's probably nothing."

"What?"

"Some car stopped at the dead end and sat there watching us for a few minutes. They turned around real slow and I thought it was weird, so I brought the kids in."

Isobel said, "Probably lost or something."

Goosebumps rose on Chandler's arms. "Did you notice what kind of car?"

He shook his head. "Not really. I was paying more attention to Maddie. Sorry."

"No, no, don't apologize. I'll just keep it in mind. Isobel's probably right and their GPS just brought them down the wrong street." She had a sneaking suspicion it was Janice, trolling by to check on her and manufacture some 'evidence' to tell Oren.

She smiled at Isobel. "Well, we have all the panels cut and pinned for the side hems. I have to run to JoAnn's and get more thread before we start the actual hemming." There was probably plenty of matching thread somewhere in the things she'd bought from Ingrid, but she knew if she started looking for one thing, she'd get the urge to organize it all and not get the curtains done for another month.

"Can we do that tomorrow?" She sounded excited and hopeful.

"Absolutely."

"What time should we come over?" Jared asked.

"Are you sure you're up to watching the kids again?" She shook her head at a filthy Maddie clinging to his leg, grinning up at him.

"Of course. They're great."

"I'm a princess!" Maddie interjected loudly.

Jared winked at her. "I'm a dragon."

Maddie giggled and made a series of dragon roars and growls, capped off with a massive yawn.

"Well, Princess, let's get you in the magical bathtub," Chandler made a face at the head to toe sweat and grime covering her daughter.

Chapter Twenty-Four

Oren realized with a start that he was looking forward to getting home. His thumbs tapped the steering wheel. There was no dread, no unease, no wondering what he might be walking into. Sure, there was still the underlying question of how to get things back to the way they should be, but now that Finn was healthy and his mom was back home, it seemed doable.

As if summoned by his wisp of a thought, his dash lit up with an incoming call from his mother.

"Hi, Mom."

"Are you done being ridiculous?"

What a way to start the conversation. "You want me to hang up now?"

"You'll do whatever you want. I thought you'd like to know that your children were outside, but your perfect wife was nowhere to be found."

"What are you even talking about?" *Why did I even ask?*

"I went by your house today."

"Why?"

"To make sure everything was alright. And clearly it was

not. Because sweet little Finnegan's stroller was parked in the sun and Maddie was in the grass covered in filth and their *mother* was not present. I sat there for ten minutes waiting, but she never came out."

Oren turned down the street to his house. "That's ridiculous. She'd never leave the kids alone outside."

Her tone turned triumphant. "Oh, I never said they were *alone.*"

He didn't listen to the little voice in his head telling him to just hang up. "What are you getting at?"

"Your children were in the company of a *man.* Doesn't that bother you? Another man spending time with your children?"

"This conversation is over."

"Suit yourself. Just remember that you picked her. I'm not so sure she's picking you, but whatever. I guess you'll have to learn from your own mistakes." She disconnected the call.

Oren pulled into the driveway and into the garage. What was she up to now? There's no way Chandler would leave the kids with some random man. She wouldn't even have a man at the house. Right?

Of course not. Oren shook his head, getting angry at himself that his mother could so easily sow little seeds of doubt. Well. He wasn't going to stew and assume and let things fester. Not any more. Resolved, he went into the house.

Chandler and the kids were in the kitchen. She and Maddie were making funny faces at Finn while something cooked on the stove.

"Hey."

She looked up and smiled. "Hey. How was your day?"

"Great." He took a chance and leaned over to kiss her cheek.

"My turn!" Maddie threw her arms around his neck and demanded kisses all over her face while she giggled.

Chandler turned back to the stove and stirred the pot.

"Smells good."

"Spaghetti and garlic bread."

"Salad?"

"No, the lettuce was bad, and I didn't feel like running out to get more."

"Oh."

Apparently, he failed to keep his disappointment out of his voice, because Chandler gave him an annoyed side-eye.

While Maddie was entertained by making faces at her brother, Oren took the opportunity to stand beside Chandler. He kept his voice low. "Got a phone call from Mom on my way home."

She made a noncommittal grunt.

"Since I'm one hundred percent not making any assumptions or taking her word for anything, I just wanted to let you know she was trying to tell me you left the kids outside alone with some guy. But I one hundred percent know that's ridiculous and you wouldn't have anyone here without me knowing." He made a dismissive "pssht" noise to emphasize how absurd he thought the notion was.

Chandler's stirring slowed to a stop. She turned the burner off and slid the pot off the hot surface. "I wouldn't have anyone here? Without letting you know? What, like getting permission?"

Uh oh. "Permission? Of course not. I just meant that you'd tell me if there was anyone here."

"Why?"

He blinked a few times. Why on earth did she sound annoyed? "Well... I... I mean, I'm sure it would come up in conversation."

She shrugged. "Most likely."

"But, I mean, if anyone was around the kids, of course you'd tell me." He waited for her to agree.

She shook her head and fixed a bowl of spaghetti for Maddie, cut the noodles and meatballs, then sprinkled parmesan cheese over the top. Her movements were so careful he knew she was mad, but he had no idea why.

"You seem annoyed. I'm telling you I know she was lying. I didn't have to even wonder."

She got plates out of the cupboard. "See, here's the problem. She wasn't *actually* lying, but she left out enough detail that your imagination ran away with this whole scenario. And now you're being the white knight swooping in to rescue my reputation and instead of just dismissing her outright, we've got a whole new *thing* again, and quite frankly, it's exhausting and insulting."

"Wait. If she wasn't lying, then who was here?"

Chandler smiled. Actually smiled. But somehow Oren knew it wasn't a good smile.

"You just admitted to having a guy around *my* kids."

She slowly and carefully enunciated every word. "Jared and Isobel came over. He watched the kids – *our* kids, by the way – while Isobel and I were cutting fabric."

"Was that so hard? Why didn't you just tell me?" He was relieved it had been nothing.

"When exactly did I have the opportunity? Or would you like me to check in with you immediately every time I encounter another human being? What's my time limit? Do I have to notify you within thirty minutes, or is that too long? How about I wear a camera on a hat so you can livestream my every move?"

"What?" This was going downhill fast.

"You know what? I think I'm gonna run out and get that lettuce."

"I don't need a salad. It's fine."

"No, I'll be back. Go ahead and eat." She grabbed her purse and kissed Maddie on top of the head. "Mommy's running to the store. Daddy has your supper."

Oren watched her head out into the garage without a second look back. He helped Maddie into her booster seat. She chattered while they ate, but his mind kept wandering. What the heck did he do wrong this time?

Chapter Twenty-Five

Chandler drove around town for a little while, working through her thoughts. Something about the way Oren seemed so proud of being certain she hadn't had anyone around *his* kids just got on her last nerve. And then it flat out pissed her off when he jumped to being suspicious.

She pulled into the Target parking lot and scrolled through social media for a while, letting her mind wander as she skimmed a million posts from the million mommy groups she was in. She stopped and read through another mommy-wars post about breast vs bottle and rolled her eyes. People were so rude and judgmental.

Sufficiently calmed down, Chandler went into the store and pushed a cart up and down the aisles, not looking for anything in particular. She picked up some laundry detergent and splurged on a bottle of nail polish for herself. She went through the grocery section and got milk and actually remembered to grab lettuce and a tomato. When she was done, she still wasn't in the mood to go back home, so she went to Caretti's Coffee Shop and sat in the car sipping an iced latte.

Her phone buzzed with an incoming text from Ashley.

Just checking in. How's today?

Chandler started to type a reply, then backspaced over it and called instead.

Ashley picked up right away. "What's up?"

"I had too much to type." She told Ashley about Oren's speech and then his jumping to suspicion, demanding to know what guy was around *his* kids. "Am I overreacting? Tell me I'm being ridiculous."

"Well…" Ashley began carefully. "I suppose it's possible you're overreacting and misunderstanding what he's saying. It's also possible he's the one being ridiculous because he's telling you to tell him if anyone comes over, but he literally just walked in the door, so like, are you supposed to send him a running live feed of your entire day or everyone you see or text or talk to or run into at the grocery store? What's the time limit? Like, if I come over at ten, does he need to know that by ten fifteen? Or maybe you should just get a nanny cam so he can monitor your activities at his leisure?"

Hearing Ashley's second hand outrage made her feel better, especially since she so closely echoed her own thoughts. "I'm not crazy thinking he's being a bit much?"

"Not at all. What pisses me off the most is that you haven't done anything to give him one single reason to be suspicious. It's all because of his mother's interference and that's not okay."

"Thank you for validating me." Chandler leaned her head back against the headrest. "I feel like I'm so frustrated and on edge waiting for something to happen that I'm looking for offenses where there might not be any."

Ashley snorted angrily. "I think when he's barking at you about having a guy around *his* kids without any sort of provo-cation, that's a legit thing to be upset about."

"I just don't have the energy to have a big conversation about this and I don't have the patience to wait for him to figure it out." A twinge in her chest made her groan. "Ugh. I need to get home. Finn's probably getting hungry."

"Just remember that your number one priority is getting enough rest and protecting your health and recovery, not his stupid feelings. Call me tomorrow."

They ended the call and Chandler headed for home. While the garage door rolled up, she took some deep breaths. No, she and Oren didn't always see eye to eye on every little thing, but they'd never been so far off the same page. Heck, right now she didn't feel like they were even in the same book.

After she turned the car off and retrieved her bags, she took one last calming breath and went into the house. Everyone was in the living room. Maddie was in her pajamas, watching Princess Poppy for the zillionth time. Oren sat on the recliner, holding Finn, who was starting to fuss.

"He's getting hungry. Should I give him a bottle?"

"No, thanks. I can take him." She switched places with him, settling into the recliner and nestled Finn at her breast. "Oh, could you put the milk in the fridge? I left it on the table."

"Sure. How was Target?"

"Same old, same old."

He walked into the kitchen and Chandler frowned. She hadn't said anything about going to Target, and he couldn't have seen her come in with the bags. Lucky guess, maybe? The uneasy feeling multiplied when she scrolled through her phone and clicked into her email. There was an automated message from her service provider.

The message said: **Sign in from unrecognized device.**

Her heart pounded as she glanced through the message. Someone had signed into her email forty minutes earlier. She quickly logged into her account and changed her password. What a day.

Oren came back in and settled on the couch with Maddie.

"That's so weird."

"What?"

"I just checked my email and got a message that someone signed in from an unknown device. I hope I wasn't hacked. It seems like every time you turn around someone's accounts are being hacked."

"Huh."

"I don't think they could have gotten anything important." She groaned and let her head drop back against the chair. "Guess I'll have to change all the passwords for everything tomorrow. Not exactly how I wanted to spend my day. You should probably change your email password too, just in case."

"Yeah." He got his phone out and began tapping.

Finn finished his meal, so Chandler put him on her shoulder to burp him, then lay him on the floor to change his diaper.

"I'm sleepy," Maddie announced as soon as the credits began to roll on Princess Poppy.

"I got it," Oren said, and whisked her up the stairs with the requisite airplane noises.

Chandler finished getting Finn cleaned up and grabbed the remote. She settled back on the recliner with Finn and changed the channel. There was only so much Princess Poppy a person could stand.

She landed on a house hunting show and watched until the man's snide comments about tiny closets – when looking at walk-in closets the size of her living room – drove her too batty to keep watching. She flipped to a cooking show and let it play in the background while her mind wandered.

Finn cooed and gurgled happily.

"That's it, sweet boy, use up all that energy now so we can sleep through the night." She pretended to eat his feet. "Nom nom nom nom nom."

He grunted and stretched his legs straight out.

"Oh, no. You're not."

More grunts, and then the smell.

Chandler waved a hand in front of her face. "How can something so small make such a huge stench?"

He waved his arms and let out a happy screech.

"Yeah, I'm sure that does feel better, huh?" She took him upstairs.

Oren was just closing Maddie's door. "She's out like a light. Holy cow, is that him?" He scrunched up his face.

"Yup. We're going straight to the tub."

"I'll help."

Chandler put him on the changing pad they put on their dresser and they tag teamed getting his poop-covered clothes off, and then his supremely loaded diaper. As soon as she pulled the diaper off, he peed straight up into the air, a fire-hose blast that soaked the front of her shirt and pants. "Are you kidding me? I think you've been saving that up all day, little dude."

Oren popped a towel over Finn while Chandler stepped out of her clothes.

"Babies are disgusting," she grumbled.

"Can't argue with that." Oren wrapped him in the towel and headed for the bathroom.

Chandler threw an old t-shirt on and went in to bathe Finn.

"If you've got it under control, I'll grab the laundry," Oren offered.

"Thanks," she said over the running water.

Chapter Twenty-Six

Oren grabbed a laundry basket and threw in the nasty baby clothes, along with Chandler's pee-soaked clothes. He carried the basket down to the laundry room off the kitchen. As he picked Chandler's pants out of the basket, her phone fell out of her pocket. He grabbed it and set it on top of the washer while he started the load.

When the washer was running, he wiped her phone with a sanitizing wipe, just in case anything had gotten on it.

He tossed the wipe in the trash can and looked down at her phone in his hand. He already felt guilty for checking up on her location, even though they'd both willingly turned on their phones' location services years ago. And then logging into her email, where he found nothing. Which is probably what he'd find on her phone, right? Nothing.

But if there *was* something, where would it be? Obviously on her phone, right?

A quick peek at the call log and texts couldn't hurt. If anything, it would prove once and for all that his mother was just being a troublemaker and he could lay the whole thing to rest.

It would validate what he knew to be true. That his wife wasn't doing anything wrong.

He'd know for sure and he'd never have to check up on her again.

They – he – could start fresh knowing beyond a shadow of a doubt that they were solid.

Chandler would never have to know.

He swiped the face of her phone and entered her passcode. Her home screen with her most-used apps popped up. See? If she was hiding something, she would have changed the passcode.

A niggling voice in the back of his head insisted that this was a very, very bad idea, like the worst idea he had ever had, and he should turn off the phone right now, before he looked at anything.

Another voice egged him on. What could it hurt? Two seconds and she'd be completely absolved in his heart and mind. His mom could never sow a seed of doubt again.

He tapped on the phone icon and took a peek at her call log. Calls to and from him, her parents, Ashley, the pediatrician's office, and a few ignored incoming spam calls. Before he knew it, he'd scrolled back an entire year and saw nothing concerning.

See? He felt better already.

He tapped out of the call log and hesitated again before he tapped into her text app.

The washer jumped into a spin cycle.

The noise startled Oren. The little voice told him again that he'd seen all he needed to see and to stop looking before this went bad. He blew out a breath and scrolled down through the texts. Again, all the texts were back and forth with Ashley, him, her parents, Ingrid, Margo, a handful of other friends, and a bunch of reminder texts for doctor's appointments and upcoming bills.

He closed out of the messaging and did a quick swipe to see what apps she had installed. Social media, banking, games. No secret messaging apps or dating apps or anything that would cause any concern at all.

See? He'd been right to trust her, and stupid to listen to his mother.

Lesson learned.

He pressed the button to lock the phone and turned.

Chandler stood in the doorway, her face ashen. The corners of her mouth were turned down. Her eyes brimmed with tears. Her mouth opened, then snapped shut.

She held out her hand. It trembled.

Oren's arm felt like it wasn't attached to his body as he reached out to place her phone in her hand.

As soon as she touched it, she yanked it from his grasp.

"Chandler…"

"Don't." Her teeth clenched around the word as she bit it out.

He swallowed hard. This was *not* how this was supposed to go.

Chandler's mouth pinched in a hard line. She rapidly blinked away the unshed tears, and when she looked at him, he felt like slime.

"Chan…"

She whirled around and walked away.

Oren's heart pounded. It had seemed like a small thing, and it was only in hindsight he realized how very, very not small it was.

Heat spread up his neck.

Chandler had done nothing.

It had been him all along.

He'd been suspicious and jealous and unkind. He'd accused her of going behind his back. He'd accused her of violating his trust.

But it had been him.

He grasped the door jamb to steady himself. Spots swam in his vision.

He'd blamed her for burning down their marriage.

He'd blamed his mother.

But he was the one holding the match.

His stomach rolled. He'd been so concerned with making sure Chandler was trustworthy that he hadn't stopped to examine his own actions.

Until now.

When it was too late.

He slunk up the stairs, tail tucked between his legs, hoping she didn't slam the door in his face. How was he going to make up for this?

Finn slept peacefully in his crib. Chandler sat on the edge of the bed, rubbing lotion on her hands. She didn't look up when he came in.

Oren slowly crossed the room. He could feel the tension rolling off his wife, even though she was calmly rubbing her hands. He sat down beside her. Like a shot, she was up and moving into the bathroom. The door closed behind her with a quiet click, but it felt as loud as a gunshot.

He sat and waited. Five minutes. Ten. Twenty. Forty minutes later, Chandler came out of the bathroom. He looked up at her and wished he hadn't, because it made him feel guilty. Her cheeks were blotchy, her eyes red from crying.

"Chan…"

Her face hardened. She spoke low, so she didn't wake Finn. "Where are you sleeping?"

Maybe now was the time to make a stand. To sleep next to each other and regain some of the closeness they'd lost. He pointed to the bed. "Right here."

With a glare, she snatched her pillow from the bed and then yanked the comforter off the bed and carried them to the guest room.

Oren followed her. "Chan, can we talk about this?"

She shook the comforter over the bed, ignoring him.

He reached out and touched her elbow.

She jumped back as if he'd burned her. "Don't you touch me," she hissed. "You want to talk? Fine. Let's talk." She stalked around him and closed the door. "Let's start with why you were going through my phone. And then we can move onto why you logged into my email. Maybe then we can cover how you knew I went to Target before you even saw the bags." She crossed her arms over her chest.

Oren wasn't sure how to react to the pure fury radiating from her. He tried to organize his thoughts.

"Well? You wanted to talk so bad, spit it out. Let's talk about how you decided it was okay to start keeping tabs on me and tracking me like I'm an animal. How *dare* you."

"Chan…"

She snapped, "I know my name. Let's go. I want to hear it. Explain it all, Oren."

"Let's sit down." He was trying to buy a little time, so maybe she'd calm down, but clearly she wasn't having it.

"*Talk.*"

"First, I'm sorry."

She rolled her eyes, hard.

"I really am."

"Okay, what exactly are you sorry about?"

"Uh… I mean, for listening to my mom, first of all."

Her eyes narrowed. Clearly that had been the wrong thing

to say. Exasperated, he threw his hands up. "How am I supposed to make you understand when you won't even listen to me?"

Chandler's eyes met his with the coldest expression he'd ever seen. "I am listening. And I hear *everything you do*, loud and clear. What you *say* is irrelevant at this point."

"Then what's the point of having this conversation?"

She looked at him like he was stupid. Which is how he felt at the moment. She poked a finger in his direction. "*You* followed me in here. *You* insisted on talking. *You* had all these things to say and now, all of a sudden, you're acting pissy because you can't spit out any justification for the lousy selfish way you're treating me. I stood here and waited for you to say something – *anything* – that would make me want to listen to what you have to say, and all you can do is flounder and then act like *I'm* the one being unreasonable here. I'm tired and angry, and I am so done with this right now." She yanked the door open and pointed for him to leave.

He tried to make one last gesture before dropping it for the night. "I can sleep in here. You take the master."

"Get. Out."

"I'm just trying to be nice."

"I don't want you to be nice. I want you to leave me alone."

Oren edged toward the door. This was not how this was supposed to go at all. "I guess I'm just trying to understand why you're so mad. All I was doing was making sure you were being honest, and now I know for absolute certain that you were. I'd think you'd be glad I believe you and we can put this all behind us."

Instead of showing of any sort of understanding or gratitude, Chandler's face went red. Her lips parted and through her clenched, bared teeth, she spat, "Get. Out." She pushed on the door, effectively shoving him into the hallway.

The door closed and he heard the lock click into place. Okay, what he did was wrong, but she was definitely over-reacting.

Chapter Twenty-Seven

Tuesday morning found Chandler with a pounding headache and foul disposition. She put on a reasonable face while she made Maddie's breakfast.

"Good morning."

Oren came up behind her and she swore if he touched her, she'd stab him with the spatula in her hand. He kept his distance, but quietly said, "We'll talk tonight, okay?"

She poked at the eggs and ignored him.

"Okay, that's fine. I get that you don't want to talk to me."

She shoved the spatula under the eggs and lifted them onto a plate. Brushing past him, she set the plate in front of Maddie.

"Chepchup?"

"Sure." She got the ketchup from the fridge and squirted a small puddle on the plate. She personally thought ketchup on eggs was revolting, but it was an acquired taste Maddie had inherited from Oren.

"I'll see you tonight." Oren gave Maddie kisses.

Chandler went into the laundry room until she heard the door to the garage close behind him, then let out a long breath.

She was so distracted that when the doorbell chimed at nine, she nearly jumped out of her skin.

Maddie jumped up and down. "Jared!"

She pasted a smile on her face and let Jared and Isobel in. A few minutes later, Jared was playing Princess Poppy with Maddie while Finn watched from his swing.

"Ready?"

"I'm, like, so super excited. I was telling my mom about your sewing area and I hope you don't mind, but I showed her a picture of your space and she was like super jealous. I mean, not in a bad way, but she thought it was really awesome."

Chandler was glad for the distraction of Isobel's chatter. "Of course it's okay. If she wants to come over sometime, that's fine, too."

"Oooh, I'll let her know."

"Does she do much sewing?" She spread out the velvet fabric they'd been working on.

Isobel nodded, her blonde curls bouncing. "Yeah, she taught me the basics. I think she'd like to do more because she really enjoyed it. It was part of the homeschool curriculum that I had to learn different basic skills, like sewing and cooking and some household stuff."

Chandler nodded politely and made affirmative noises in the right places while Isobel talked. "Okay, now we'll sew the side hems on the outer panels. Then we'll hem the tops and add the loops for the curtain rods."

It was lunchtime when Jared came downstairs holding a fussing Finn, with Maddie close on his heels. "I think he's hungry. I changed his diaper, but he's still a little grumpy. Did you want me to give him a bottle or..." he trailed off, his cheeks turning pink.

"I'll take him, thanks." She reached out to take the baby. "Do you want to stay here for lunch? There's stuff in the fridge for sandwiches, and there's veggies already cut up in the crisper drawer."

"Sure. Mads, you want a sandwich and some veggies?"

"Yes!" Maddie grabbed Jared's hand and headed for the stairs.

Chandler chuckled. Her daughter, who wouldn't eat a vegetable to save her life, would probably scarf a whole plate of them down just to impress Jared.

"I'll be up when he's done." She settled onto the little couch and got Finn attached to her breast. He calmed immediately and slurped contentedly.

When he was done, she went upstairs. Maddie, Jared, and Isobel were at the table, their plates empty.

"I ate a WHOLE coocummer!"

"Wow, that's great. Did you like it?"

Maddie looked to Jared before declaring that cucumbers are her *favorite*.

Jared winked at Chandler. "I also like carrots a lot." He popped a baby carrot into his mouth.

"I try?"

"Sure." He pushed his plate to Maddie, and she took the smallest baby carrot.

She crunched on it and chewed, unsure.

"Mmm." Jared ate another carrot. "Is it good?"

"Yeah…" she said, but her scrunched up face said otherwise.

"You don't have to like it, but I'm really glad you tried it."

She swallowed the bit in her mouth and eyed the half still in her hand.

"You don't have to finish it," he said, and with that permission, she dropped it on her plate. "I like coocummers better."

He put another slice of cucumber on her plate.

A wisp of a thought ran through her mind – should she text

Oren that Jared and Isobel were here, just to avoid a repeat of yesterday's drama? Chandler fought a sudden sting of tears behind her eyes. Everything in this moment was perfectly normal. And everything in this moment was horribly wrong. Everything was falling apart. Including her. Especially her.

She passed Finn to Isobel. "I have to use the bathroom. I'll be right back."

"No problem." Isobel eagerly took the baby and immediately began talking to him. "How's my little buddy?"

Chandler got upstairs to the master bedroom and closed the door before rushing into the master bathroom, closing *that* door, and bursting into tears.

How dare he put her in the position of having the urge to "prove" what she's doing and who she's with just so she can have a little peace.

No. Not happening.

She took a minute to get herself together, used the toilet, then washed her hands and her face.

No more. She would not live like this.

Chapter Twenty-Eight

Oren picked at his lunch. He didn't have much of an appetite after last night. He felt bad about checking up on her, he really did. His phone vibrated with an incoming text. For a second, his hopes soared. Maybe it was Chandler sending another picture of her and the kids. He nearly dropped his phone, pulling it out of his pocket.

It was Elliott.

How's everything going?

He wasn't sure how to answer, so he said,

Do you have a minute to talk?

Sure.

Elliott picked up right away. "What's up?"

Oren looked around the courtyard to make sure there wasn't anyone close enough to overhear. "I screwed up. Big time. I'm not sure how to fix it."

"What happened?"

"I was told there was a guy at the house."

"By your mother," Elliott guessed drily.

"That's not important."

"It's more important than you want to admit, but anyway. Go on."

Oren's annoyance clicked up a notch. Why was everyone attacking his relationship with his mother? "Anyway. It turned out to be Jared, the kid from next door, so Chandler was mad at me for asking about it. Then she left the house to go to the grocery store and didn't come back for a while. So I... I, um..." He knew this part was going to sound bad, but he wasn't sure *how* bad. "I logged into the phone finder app and saw she was at Target instead of the grocery store."

"You tracked her phone? What were you thinking?"

"I don't know. It was stupid."

"Dang, you've got some serious making up to do."

Oren suddenly felt nauseous. If that alone was getting this reaction, he'd been way farther out of line than he'd thought. "It's worse than that."

Elliott blew out a long breath. "Okay, lay it on me."

"I logged into her email." He didn't even bother trying to justify it. "And that's not all. When she got home, the baby had a blowout all over her. She took him to get cleaned up and I took the laundry. Her, uh, her phone was still in her pocket."

After a long pause, Elliott said, "You didn't."

"I wiped it down and it was in my hand..."

"Oren, tell me you didn't go through her phone."

"It seemed like a good idea at the time. I knew, Elliott, I *knew* I wouldn't find anything, and I just wanted to prove myself right."

"Dude." Elliott's disappointment oozed through the phone.

"She came in the laundry room and saw me."

"Whoa."

"I didn't think it was that bad. I was right. There was nothing there. Now Chandler's not speaking to me. This morning she wouldn't even look at me."

"You're lucky she didn't set you on fire."

"I don't know how to make it right. I've never seen her this mad."

"Dude. You violated her privacy to make yourself feel better about something you shouldn't have been feeling in the first place."

Oren went on the defensive. "I can feel how I feel."

"Bullshit. You felt suspicious when you had zero reason to, ergo, your feelings were completely unjustified. And feelings aside, your actions… Dude."

"There were things that didn't add up," Oren said lamely.

"If you have any hope of saving your marriage, you need to stop. This entire situation is because you've been putting stock into the grenades your mom is throwing at your wife."

"I wish people would stop saying it's my mom's fault. It's mine."

"I wish you'd spend as much energy defending your wife as you do your mom. I'm not sure you truly understand what's at stake here."

The words landed right in his gut. Oren ran a hand down over his face. "I have no idea where I went so wrong."

"I don't know." Elliott's voice was sympathetic. "I hope you guys can come back from this."

Oren's blood ran cold. Surely this wasn't irreparable. Surely it could be fixed. Healed.

Surely.

The afternoon crawled by. He texted Chandler, asking how her day was. He checked his phone every few minutes to see if she had texted him back. She didn't.

It was almost quitting time when his phone vibrated.

He snatched the phone from beside his keyboard and was immediately filled with disappointment. And dread. It was Alan, letting him know he'd ordered the pizza for practice.

Oren had been so distracted by everything going on at home that he'd completely forgotten about play practice.

Great. One more reason for Chandler to be mad at him.

"Okay, everyone, that's a wrap. Good job. See you Thursday." Oren sat on the edge of the stage and made some notes on his clipboard. Gretchen and Alan came from the back of the stage. "I'm thinking we'll add some meet cute prompts and some breakup prompts," she said.

"Spilled coffee is always a romcom go-to you could use for the meet cute. Hey Oren, what are some breakup triggers we can use for the improv group?"

His mouth went dry. Might as well test out this scenario, right? "What if she catches him going through her phone?"

"Oh! Perfect." Gretchen nodded aggressively.

Alan agreed. "Put that on the list for sure."

Oh, crap. They were supposed to dismiss it as not even worthy of discussion. "You really think that justifies a breakup?"

Gretchen snorted like it was the stupidest question she'd ever heard. "Um, yeah, absolutely. It's not even so much the going through the phone as it is the complete disregard for a person's privacy and a blatant lack of trust or respect. It's gross." She gave a little wave and headed for the aisle. "See you Thursday."

Oren could only nod and force half a smile as she and Alan left the theater. After he'd talked to Elliott, he'd managed to convince himself that Ell was overstating how close to a deal breaker this might be.

Yes, it was wrong. He knew it was wrong. But to his mind, it was more of a two-weeks-on-the-couch kind of wrong. Apparently he was getting really good at being wrong these days.

He drove home slowly, dreading whatever might be waiting for him.

The dread only intensified when he walked in the door. Chandler sat at the kitchen table, her hands wrapped around a mug of tea.

"Kids in bed?" he asked.

She shot him a side-eye. "It's ten o'clock. Of course they're in bed."

"Sorry, theater ran late. That's where I was. The theater."

Her head turned and she faced him fully. "I assumed that's where you were, even though you couldn't even afford me the courtesy of a text to let me know. I suppose I could have tracked your phone, but that's not really my style."

"I didn't think you'd want to hear from me."

"You don't think, period." She waved her hand and closed her eyes. "It doesn't matter. We need to talk."

He swallowed hard. Those words never led anywhere good. "It's, uh, pretty late to have, uh, a big conversation."

"Whose fault is that?"

He slid into the chair across from hers. "Okay. What do we need to talk about?"

She looked into her cup, then firmly met his gaze. "Separation."

His brain worked to make sense of the word.

"I won't live like this," she continued. "You've already said you won't leave *your* house again, so I started looking for a place. I might have to leave my workshop here for a while. I'll come work while you're at work, but eventually I'll figure out a new space."

He opened his mouth, but nothing came out. He was afraid – legitimately afraid – of her dead calm and lack of tears.

"I will not be treated like I've done something wrong. I will not give up my agency and my right to privacy. I won't be checked up on. I won't live my life wondering if every place I go or person I interact with will make you suspicious. I will not be tracked like an animal."

Oren nodded vigorously and leaned in, spreading his hands, palms up. "I'll stop. I'm done. I saw what I needed to see. It won't happen again."

Her fingers tightened around the mug, to the point where her knuckles turned white. "We'll need to figure out when we'll each have the kids."

"Chan, we don't need to do this." He heard the desperation in his own voice, so he knew she had to hear it

"I need to do this. I can't live with someone I can't trust."

"But—"

"Someone so eager to believe the worst of me."

"Chan. I'm sorry. I'm so sorry."

She held up a hand. "You said that the first time, and the second time, so I'm not interested in your sorries. I'm exhausted and I don't have the energy or bandwidth or desire to deal with your manufactured insecurity."

"But—"

"I've made up my mind."

He could change her mind. Show her how deeply this was affecting him. "I don't feel—"

She was having none of it. "I frankly don't care how you feel right now. I've been tiptoeing around your feelings, been the victim of your feelings, and more concerned with your feelings than my own well-being. Understand, Oren, I'm not asking if you think this is what we should do. I'm telling you that I'm leaving, and the only back and forth is going to be about logistics."

He stared at the wood grain pattern on the table, wishing it could transport him back in time. To when? Maybe this afternoon so he could cancel practice and be home so she didn't have all this time to think? To yesterday morning, so he wouldn't track her or check her phone?

To last week, so he didn't call his mom for help? Looking back, he had other options that would have been better for her. He could have called Ashley or Margo or told Chandler's mom how bad the situation really was, but he'd taken the easy way out and called his mom. Had this really only been all the way off the rails for a week?

He couldn't understand how fast things had gone so bad. It was a snowball of bad decisions that turned into an avalanche without warning.

On the other hand, that gave him a little hope. Surely he could make up for a week of horrible decisions. They had a decade of good history. That had to have some weight, right?

Oren sat back in his chair. Surely she'd see the wisdom in taking it slow. This was a decision too big to rush into. "Can we just hold off on any major decisions until the weekend?"

"No." She didn't even hesitate.

So much for hope.

Chapter Twenty-Nine

Chandler couldn't make herself feel bad at Oren's stricken expression. She'd told him the truth. She simply didn't have the emotional bandwidth to deal with his feelings right now. He'd been warned. And warned. And warned. After all, they'd just had this nearly identical conversation three or four days ago. At some point, he needed to get it through his head that this was not how they were going to live.

"It's late," she said, to break the oppressive silence.

"Yeah."

"I'm figuring on getting things finalized over the next couple of days. Hopefully, I'll have a place ironed out by the weekend." She stood up and Oren jumped to his feet as well.

When she walked past, he reached out and grabbed her hand.

"Chan, it doesn't make sense for you to find a place, especially when you work out of the house. I'll…" he swallowed hard. "I'll find a place."

She gently extracted her hand from his grasp. "I appreciate what you're saying, but this can't be a delay tactic."

"I know."

"Do you want me to search for places?"

"Do I *want* you to? No. I don't want to do this at all."

She pulled in a long breath.

"But if you could help me, that'd be great." He stood straight and finally met her eyes with determination. "Just make sure it's a short-term situation, because I will fix this, Chandler."

She had her doubts.

Wednesday morning was just another day. Chandler had the kids in her workshop. Finn was in his swing while Maddie laid on the floor watching Princess Poppy on the iPad. Chandler traced a corset pattern onto black leather with a chalk pencil. A repeat customer had requested a significant rush order for an upcoming burlesque show she was performing. Luckily, Chandler already had her measurements on file, so it was much easier than doing a rush order from scratch. And thanks to Ingrid's generosity, she had everything on hand.

Focusing on the project helped keep her mind off her dumpster fire of a personal life.

She took a break mid-morning to take the kids to the park and let Maddie run off some energy. Hopefully she'd nap after lunch so Chandler could finish cutting the pieces for the corset order.

At the park, Maddie ran off to play in the sandbox with another little girl from the neighborhood. The mom was nearby reading a book, so Chandler took advantage of the opportunity to make laps with Finn's stroller and get some exercise herself. And call Ashley while she was out of Maddie's earshot.

"Am I doing the right thing?"

"Absolutely." Ashley didn't even hesitate. "We'll get the basement ready when Ell gets home so he has a place to stay. No sense being hasty and laying out a security deposit and all that money when he can stay here for as long as you guys need to figure things out."

"Thank you, but I don't know if he'll want to stay with you guys."

"What are his other options? A hotel? Finding a crappy apartment? Going to his mother's house? Ick."

"You're right, but I know he'll balk at imposing on you guys."

"I'll have Ell call him. He'll know what to say without calling him a stupid idiot."

Chandler had to laugh at that.

"Hey, we both know that's how I'd start, sooooo, probably best I'm not the one to reach out to him."

"Probably not." Chandler glanced over to see Maddie and the little girl giggling. "I feel like I'm doing something wrong."

"That's because the whole situation is wrong, honey. Everything about this is wrong. It was never supposed to be this way, so of course you feel like this. But the truth is, you're doing everything right. This is hard and it sucks. It sucks so bad, but it's the only way anything will change."

"I know."

"Trust yourself. And if you can't trust yourself, trust me. Trust Ell. We've got both of your best interests at heart."

Chandler blinked back tears. It felt so good to have someone to lean on. "I love you."

"I love you, too. This is all going to work out. No matter what, you're going to be fine."

She sniffled and nodded, even though Ash couldn't see her. "Okay."

"I'll text Ell and have him call Oren right away."

"Okay. Thank you."

"We'll get through this. I got you, boo."

Chandler smiled through her tears. "Okay, boo."

She disconnected the call and wiped her face. She walked slowly around the park to where Maddie was and sat on the bench beside the other mom. "Shannon, right?"

"Yeah." She looked a little uncertain.

"Chandler. We live right down this street."

Recognition dawned in Shannon's eyes. "Oh yeah, sorry. I knew that. We live over on Maple."

"Are there other kids on your block?"

"None Kinsley's age. Lots of older kids, though."

Chandler nodded. "I think Maddie's the only one on our street. All the other kids are teenagers."

"Maybe we could schedule some playdates?"

"That'd be great." She didn't actually think it would be great. Something about Shannon just felt off, but she couldn't put her finger on it.

"Who's this little guy?"

Chandler picked the baby out of the stroller. He was wide awake, taking everything in. "This is Finn. He's ten weeks old."

"Aww, he's so sweet."

After a few more minutes of small talk, they exchanged phone numbers and promised to set up a playdate but didn't actually set a date.

"I'm hungry," Maddie announced.

"That's my cue," Chandler said.

Shannon agreed. "I'm glad she said it. I was thinking it, but the girls were having such a good time I didn't want to pull Kinsley away."

Chandler settled Finn back in the stroller and said, "See you later."

"I'll text you about that playdate. Let's go, sweetie."

"Bye!" Kinsley yelled with a wave to Maddie.

Maddie waved, but was already heading toward the edge of the park. Food was always her number one priority.

"Slow down," Chandler warned as they got closer to the street and sidewalk. Again, she looked at the broken fence. She should probably at least pick up the broken sticks before the grass got too high.

Maddie stopped and jumped back and forth from one foot to the other until her mom caught up with her. "Can we have pizzas?"

"Sure." She was glad Maddie wasn't a picky eater.

A few minutes later, Maddie stood on her stool at the kitchen counter, helping spread pizza sauce on slices of toast, then sprinkling them with cheese and adding too many mini-pepperonis.

Chandler popped them into the oven. She'd just started nursing Finn when someone knocked at the door.

Maddie hollered, "It's Jared and Isobel!"

"I'm right here, you don't have to yell." She pulled the door open and let them in.

"Sorry, is this a bad time?" Isobel asked as they followed her to the living room.

"Not at all. I wasn't expecting to see you today."

"Yeah, sorry," Isobel said. "We both had interviews at General Custard's."

"Cool. Do you think you'll get the jobs?"

Isobel nodded. "They hired both of us. It's only weekends, though, so we're still available if you want some babysitting done." She hunched her shoulders and looked shyly up at Jared. "And, um, I'd, like, really like to learn more stuff with the costuming. If that's okay."

"Of course. In fact, I'm getting ready to put boning in a corset."

Isobel's eyes went wide. She clasped her hands under her chin, excitement on her face. "You make corsets? Those are *so cool.*"

"Yup. My client does burlesque shows, and she placed a rush order. I cut the first layer this morning, but there's plenty left to do."

"Awesome."

Jared said, "Maybe since I have zero interest in sewing, I should do the babysitting and Isobel can be your apprentice, or whatever it's called."

Chandler settled back in her recliner while the kids sat on the couch. Maddie scrambled onto Jared's lap. "You really want to officially babysit?"

"Yay!" Maddie shrieked.

Jared chuckled. "It's fun."

"I can't pay much," Chandler warned. She gave him a number.

"That's not bad when you figure the commute is pretty sweet."

They all laughed.

"Honestly," he said, "General Custard's isn't paying much more than that."

Chandler moved the baby to her shoulder. "And Isobel, I can't pay you anything at all. I can't afford to hire two people."

Isobel nodded. "Yeah, I already thought of that. Technically, I'd be interning or apprenticing to learn the ropes, right? I was hoping maybe you could teach me some of the business stuff, too." She hesitated, then pushed on. "I was thinking that if it goes good you'd be willing to write me a letter of recommendation when I need one."

"Absolutely." Chandler was impressed. She'd have to work out the math, but maybe instead of an hourly rate, she could pay Isobel a percentage of the projects she helped with. In any event, she felt more settled than she had in what felt like forever.

A reliable, trustworthy babysitter. An eager apprentice. Jobs coming in. Big, well-paying jobs.

Pride bloomed in her chest.

She could do this on her own after all.

Chapter Thirty

Oren couldn't wait to get home. Maybe after a good night's sleep and the day to think, Chandler had changed her mind. He'd texted her that he was bringing pizza home, so hopefully they could talk instead of cooking and cleaning up.

He pulled into the garage and sat, clenching the steering wheel. He hated feeling like a stranger in his own home.

He hated that Chandler wanted him out.

More than that, he hated that he'd hurt her so badly she wanted him out. It hadn't seemed like such a big deal at the time. Certainly not a big enough deal to separate.

Separate.

Even *thinking* the word made him nauseous.

He pulled himself together and walked into the house.

"Daddy!" Maddie came careening around the corner from the living room and hurled herself at his legs.

"Hey, pumpkin. Let me set these down."

"Pizza!" She clapped her hands and jumped up and down.

Chandler carried Finn into the kitchen.

"Hey." Oren asked, "Do you want me to take him, or should I get the pizza ready?"

"You can take him."

Oren took the baby and watched Chandler move around the kitchen, getting plates and napkins and the pizza cutter to cut Maddie's slice into bite-sized pieces. "One is loaded veggie, no onion, one is pepperoni, and one is just cheese."

"Three pizzas?"

"I figured that'd give us leftovers for lunch.'

She nodded once, but focused on cutting Maddie's pizza. "Okay, up into your seat."

Maddie scrambled up and began inhaling her pizza.

Oren sat down, holding Finn with one arm and a slice of pizza with the other. "How was your day?" Nice, safe topic.

"Great. Isobel wants to learn how to do costuming, and Jared offered to babysit a few hours a week."

"Jared's babysitting me and Finn," Maddie said around a full mouth.

"I thought Isobel was interested in babysitting."

Chandler shrugged. "Doesn't really matter to me. Jared's great with the kids and Isobel's really eager to learn. It's nice to be mentoring her."

"Isn't it kind of weird he'd want to babysit, though? Seems odd for a teenage boy." It was the last job on Earth he would have taken at that age.

"Mannies are a thing, you know."

Oren felt the irritation building in her tight tone. "I just meant he might not want to keep doing it all summer."

"Even if he only helps me out for two weeks, that's a huge load off my shoulders."

"I suppose." He didn't point out that asking him to leave was what put the load onto her shoulders in the first place.

Her eyes cut to him. "You suppose?"

Holy cow, he did not want to fight, especially about something like this. Apparently, he couldn't say or do anything right anymore. "Never mind. If you think it'll work out, that's great."

"It is great." She rolled her eyes and tossed her pizza crust into the box. "Did you want another piece?" she asked Maddie.

Maddie's pigtails bounced as she nodded. Pizza sauce coated her fingers and ringed her mouth. She announced, "We had pizza FOUR times today."

Chandler gently corrected, "Two times." She held up two fingers. "Lunch and dinner. One, two."

"Oh, yeah. We had pizza TWO times today."

For some reason, that annoyed Oren. Pizza multiple times a day wasn't exactly healthy. "You could have told me that. I would have gotten subs or something."

"It's fine. We made bread pizzas for lunch. It's not like we went out and got pizza."

"Still, pizza twice in one day?"

Her eyes fired daggers. "Do you have a point?"

Crap, he'd done it again. "I just figured you'd be sick of pizza if you had it twice. No big deal."

Is this how it was going to be now? Snipping over every little thing? Getting on each other's nerves for nothing? Was she going to hear every word he said through the filter of how badly he'd screwed up? Maybe a few days apart was a good thing. Give her heart time to grow fonder.

He handed Finn to her and cleared the table. He divided the remaining pizza into plastic containers and put them in the fridge.

Maddie skipped off to the living room.

"How's this going to work? Do you want me to give Maddie her bath and put her to bed, or do you want me to leave now? Or should I just stay in the guest room and we'll work through this here?"

"You can put Maddie to bed and then go."

Wow, she didn't even entertain the notion of him staying. That stung.

He took Maddie upstairs and went through her bath and bedtime routine. She must have done some serious activity in the afternoon, because she was out like a light before he'd even started reading her bedtime story. He put the book on the nightstand and went back downstairs.

Chandler sat on the couch, folding towels while Finn sat in his swing playing with his bare feet.

He didn't want to bring it up, but he had to. "So, um, I guess you know Elliott called me."

"Yeah."

"You really want me to go?" His voice hitched on the last word.

She dropped the towel into the basket beside her feet. "Want? Not necessarily. Need? Yes. Please stop acting as though if you badger me enough I'll change my mind."

"I just want to make sure."

Instead of answering, she let out a heavy sigh. "Remember to take your pizza for lunch."

"Okay. Can I come over after work tomorrow and see the kids?"

"Don't you have practice Thursdays?" she countered.

"Oh." This was going to be more complicated than he'd imagined.

"I have to get Finn to bed. You should go."

Ouch. Being dismissed stung.

At eight thirty, he pulled into Elliott and Ashley's driveway. He felt like a complete schmuck walking up to the house with his duffel bag and lunch cooler. On the front porch, he stopped and almost turned around, but the door opened.

"Come on in," Elliott said.

Oren walked in and wasn't sure what to think. Ashley, Margo, and Connor sat in the living room. He managed an awkward laugh. "Is this an intervention?"

Ashley said, "Yes. Sit down."

He swallowed hard. He'd been joking. She clearly was not.

Elliott took the spot on the couch next to Ashley. He leaned forward, his elbows on his knees.

Oren sat in the chair across from Connor. "Okay?"

Connor and Elliott exchanged a look before Elliott said, "Look. We're here because we care about you and we want to help you fix your marriage. We're not here to judge you or beat up on you."

He wasn't so sure Ashley wouldn't like the chance to beat up on him. Literally.

Connor added, "We're here for you, man. Whatever we need to do to help, we'll do it."

Oren shook his head. "Make my wife understand where I'm coming from?"

"Where would that be?" Ashley asked.

"Um…" He looked to Elliott for help.

Elliott shrugged. "Valid question. How can we help her understand your position if we don't?"

"You guys seriously don't understand my position at all? I know I screwed up big time. But I don't think I did anything that warrants kicking me out." Their collective attitude was a curve ball. He couldn't possibly be *this* wrong. Could he?

"How did you screw up?" Connor asked.

"Oh, come on. You guys already know the whole story."

Connor gently clarified. "I want to hear it from your

perspective. You want us to understand where you're coming from, so help us get there."

This whole setup thumped on his last nerve. He felt attacked, especially with Ashley sitting there, carefully managing her expressions, because he knew she was mad at him. "Forget it."

Margo spoke softly. "Oren. I imagine it feels like we're ganging up on you, but I promise we're not. If you want to save your marriage, though, you're going to have to suck it up and get uncomfortable."

He knew she was right, but that didn't make it feel any better. "You're all going to attack my mother, and I'm not going to listen to that."

Ashley snorted.

Elliott elbowed her.

"See? You want to blame all of this on my mom."

"No." Ashley's eyes blazed. "I think your mother is meddling and ridiculous and would love to get Chandler out of your life, and you know it too because she's always been that way. So trust me when I tell you that I lay all of the blame entirely at your feet and not hers."

"Ash," Elliott said, nudging her again.

"No. I'm not going to coddle him. It's not about his mother. It's about him treating Chandler like dirt and pretending he doesn't understand why she needs space."

The muscle in Oren's jaw twitched as he clenched his teeth. "So what, you support her breaking up our family?" His fingers gripped the arms of the chair.

"Her?! I support you recognizing what went wrong and fixing it. Why do you think we offered you our basement?"

"So I could get out faster," he shot back.

She leapt to her feet and pointed at him. She yelled, "No, dumbass, it's because we didn't want either of you making any permanent steps, like taking out a lease for an apartment. We want you guys to fix this and get back together and get past it, but that's going to require you to actually grasp what you've done instead of hand-waving with some whiny generic 'I know I messed up' crap. I'm furious at you right now, but if you think for one second that I want you guys to get a divorce, then you're dumber than a box of rocks."

As much as he hated her words, and as much as he wasn't too fond of her in this moment, he knew it was the truth. Ashley was fighting for Chandler's happiness. She had Chandler's back, come hell or high water. Wasn't that supposed to be his place? Were they right? They couldn't all be wrong, could they?

Elliott put his hand on her arm. "Ash."

She dragged her hands down her face. "Sorry. I knew I shouldn't be part of this because I can't sit here and be quiet."

He tugged her arm and she sat down, blinking away angry tears.

Elliott looked at Oren. "We've got your back. And if that means saying things you don't want to hear, that's what we're going to do in order to help you. This isn't about your feelings, man, it's about your *life*."

Oren felt himself deflate. "I don't know what to do. I don't know how I got here."

Margo's voice was kind. "When is the first time you felt things were off?"

He didn't want to say it out loud, but didn't feel like he had much choice. "The morning I called my mom." He held a hand up. "Not because of my mom, but that was when I realized Chandler was in a bad place and I hadn't noticed her sinking that far."

Ashley nodded. "I didn't know, either. I figured she was busy, so I was giving her space."

Connor said, "I guess I don't understand how that ended up being a red flag that made you not trust her."

Oren wasn't sure either. "I think maybe it was such a shock that things were so bad that it wasn't so much of a stretch to think things were bad in other areas, too. I don't know. I really don't."

Margo shifted in her seat. "I guess it just feels really unfair that Chandler never actually did anything to raise suspicion. You never would have thought anything bad about her if the idea hadn't been presented to you. I'm trying so hard to see it from your perspective, but all I can think of is that Chandler's not only dealing with postpartum issues, a sick baby, and a toddler, now she's got a vindictive mother-in-law and a troubled marriage, and it seems like it's all for nothing."

Oren blinked back tears. "It is. For nothing All of this. I've wrecked everything for no reason." The weight of the situation settled squarely on his shoulders, and it was the heaviest thing he'd ever felt.

Ashley said, "It's not unfixable."

Coming from Ashley, it meant a lot. If anyone had a bead on Chandler, it was her best friend. The first tear fell, and he was afraid it would unleash a torrent. "Can you… can you talk to her?"

It was Elliott who answered. "No. We're here to support you, but you've got to do the work. You know we had all kinds of issues with Ash's stepmom when we first got married. We almost broke up, but we decided to try a few counseling sessions and see if we could work through it instead."

Ashley nodded and put her hand on Elliott's knee.

He covered her hand with his. "The pastor we saw gave us some amazing advice that we really took to heart. He said we needed to treat our marriage like a garden, and one of the most important things is to put a fence around it. If there's no fence, anyone can walk in and plant seeds. Rabbits and deer will walk right in and take everything down to the ground. If there's a fence, we can control what comes in and out and make sure the only things growing are the things we planted."

Ashley jumped in. "He said the gate on the fence should have two locks – one we each control, so we have to agree on what comes in and what goes out. Maybe we let a neighbor come in and help themselves to some extra tomatoes, and we both agree that's okay, but we can't let the whole neighborhood come in and trample the crops and take all the veggies and crops we've worked so hard to grow. Does that make sense?"

"Sort of. I'm not really into gardening metaphors, I guess, but yeah, I get what you're saying. I just… how can I put up a fence to keep my own mother out?"

Elliott said, "You're not building a fortress. Think of it like a picket fence. You can see your mom, you can talk to her and share whatever you like with her, but she can't reach in and take all the peppers you're saving."

"Boundaries," Connor said. "It's all about boundaries, not about cutting her off and not having a relationship with her. It's about making Chandler your number one priority and protecting her."

That made him feel even worse. Not only had he not been protecting her, he'd been the one attacking her. And for what? For nothing.

No wonder she'd asked him to leave.

Elliott said, "Another thing we learned in counseling is that trust is like water. It's earned in cups and lost in buckets. Right now your bucked is knocked over and you have to refill it cup by cup. It's going to take time, but you have a solid history. You'll get there."

"How?" Oren sat forward and put his head in his hands. "It's so far off the rails I don't even know where to start."

"Remind her why she fell in love with you in the first place," Margo said. "Start small. Take her on a date."

"Yeah. We can take the kids tomorrow night," Connor offered.

"I have practice tomorrow night. How about Friday?"

His four friends exchanged a look. Uh oh, what did that mean?

"No problem. We can watch them Friday," Elliott said.

Now he just had to convince Chandler to go out with him.

Chapter Thirty-One

Chandler stood in the bathroom, brushing her teeth, when she heard her phone ding. She finished, turned off the light, and climbed into bed before picking up her phone.

Oren had texted her.

Just wanted to say good night. Sleep well.

You too. Good night

Finn stirred in his crib, then settled. She put her phone on the nightstand and fell into a dreamless sleep.

Thursday was another busy day. It slowed her down a little, showing Isobel how to sew boning into the corset, but Isobel was a fast learner and so enthusiastic that it was a joy to teach her. It helped that it also got Chandler out of her own head for a while. They overlaid the leather with a deep purple lace.

"This is so pretty," Isobel said, fingering the delicate fabric. "Is this from the inventory you got from Ingrid?"

"No, I actually had this in stock from my last order for this same client. It was so pretty I bought extra."

"Isn't burlesque like stripping?"

Chandler shrugged. "I mean, I think it can be similar, but it's more about a performance and putting on a show than getting dollar bills stuffed in a g-string."

"My friend's mom teaches pole dancing classes. I tried it once, but I don't have the upper body strength to be any good at it."

Chandler hoped her eyes didn't bug out of her head at the thought of Isobel pole dancing. "Yeah, I think they have to be really athletic and practice a lot."

"Is this high enough?"

Chandler checked the boning and shook her head. "It has to go all the way up here." She pointed to the place she wanted it to go. "You're doing great."

"It's really tight." Isobel pushed at the boning.

"It has to be, so it doesn't slip."

"That makes sense. Do you do a lot of burlesque costumes?"

"I wouldn't say a lot. They're really expensive, so most of my customers just get the cheaper outfits to wear to the RenFaire."

She moved to let Chandler inspect the garment. "Do you get a lot of orders around Halloween?"

"I do." Chandler held the corset up. "Perfect."

"You should totally market Halloween costumes."

"Not a bad idea."

Her phone vibrated.

> I'm thinking about you. Hope you're having a good day. Is Isobel helping you today?

She debated whether to ignore him or not. At least he was trying. So she typed back,

Yes we're working now.

She wasn't sure how she felt about having a conversation with him, but it felt so weird and empty when they weren't in contact throughout the day.

Late in the afternoon, after Isobel and Jared left and she had Maddie conked out on the couch and Finn nursing, she used her free hand to scroll through the pictures on her phone. Was it really only weeks ago that she was in the hospital having Finn? Well, technically she'd had him in the theater. Her own face and Oren's beamed at the camera as Finn lay nestled against her chest. Then, pictures of Maddie's first time holding her brother. And a shot of Maddie scowling and outraged after Finn spit up on Princess Giraffe.

She wished she had a time machine and could go back to that moment. Before Finn was sick, before she'd exhausted herself so deeply she couldn't get out, before Janice had planted poison seeds in Oren's mind.

While she scrolled, she wracked her brain for ways she might possibly have contributed to the situation, but even with the benefit of hindsight, she came up empty. No, she wasn't perfect. She was a little anal retentive about a lot of things. She tended to see things in black and white and could maybe be inflexible at times.

Sure, she'd made a mistake transferring the money for Ingrid from the wrong account. But that was an honest, easily fixed error. She should have asked for help instead of trying to handle everything on her own. Beyond that, this was all on his shoulders.

All she could do was be open to allowing him the opportunity to rebuild the trust he'd broken. The trick would be being open to it while still maintaining her boundaries.

She never thought she'd have to put boundaries between

her and Oren. It sucked, and it hurt, but in the calmness, now that she'd had time to relax and think, she was optimistic that they might be able to put their life back together.

She was looking at pictures of Maddie's fourth birthday party when a message popped up.

Heading in to practice. I'll call you after.

Okay

was all she typed back.

The evening was like any other evening Oren was away for practice. She got Maddie her bath and got the kids to bed. It was nearly nine when his call came in.

"Hi."

"Hey," he said.

"Did you have a good practice?" She worked at loading the dishwasher as she talked.

"It was good right up until the point we thought Wes was having a heart attack."

She froze, holding a dirty plate in midair. "What?"

"He tripped off the edge of the stage and then couldn't speak. He was wheezing and holding his chest. Gretchen called the ambulance, but after a minute or two he came around and said he just had the wind knocked out of him. The EMTs checked him out and took his blood pressure and everything and he was fine."

"Goodness."

"Yeah. Gave us quite the scare. How was your evening?"

"Same old, same old."

"Sorry I had practice tonight and couldn't help with the kids."

She didn't answer, and it felt like he had something else to say, so she just waited.

"If you haven't talked to Ashley, they volunteered to watch the kids tomorrow night. I was hoping…" he cleared his throat. "I was hoping, uh, you might, um, well, I was hoping you might be willing to have dinner with me."

"Oh."

"I thought we might go to Holy Guacamole since we haven't been there yet."

Wow, he was pulling out all the stops. The new restaurant had opened while she was pregnant and couldn't handle the spicy foods she loved, and since then… well, there just hadn't been time. "Okay."

"Great! I was thinking I'll pick you and the kids up, drop them with Ashley and Ell, and we can go from there? If that works?"

She couldn't think of a reason to disagree, but she did anyway. "No, I'll drop the kids off and pick you up there." That would give him no chance to make up an excuse to stay at the house.

"Sure."

After a few awkward attempts at stilted conversation, they ended the call. Chandler lay in bed, staring up at the dark ceiling. Emotions swirled around her, but she wasn't sure what she should be feeling. She wanted everything to get back to normal, but normal couldn't mean waiting around on eggshells to see if Oren slipped back into the comfort zone of not standing up to his mother.

She turned and fluffed the pillow, being as quiet as possible so she didn't wake Finn, and stared over at the empty side of the bed. Maybe they'd both gotten complacent. Comfortable. She could admit she hadn't been putting him first on her list, but at least her excuse was a sick newborn and not a meddling adult. She tried to imagine a scenario in which her parents accused Oren of cheating or neglecting their children or making bad financial decisions for the family. She knew there was no way she would accept their word without finding out for herself.

She thought over their decade together. They'd always been a team, right up until last week. Why couldn't they just go back and erase the past week and make different decisions?

Slipping into sleep, she decided that the ten good years they'd shared outweighed the last ten bad days. That didn't mean she was compromising her position. It just meant she would move forward with an open mind.

Finn sounded the alarm in the wee hours.

Chandler rolled out of bed and hurried to the bathroom before getting him settled in for his breakfast. She rocked him while she scrolled through social media. Isobel had posted some pictures on Chandler's page and they'd garnered a few clicks through to her online store and even a new sale.

"Mama," Maddie said sleepily from the doorway.

"Yes, pumpkin?"

"Where's Daddy?"

Ugh. Nothing like starting the day off with a heavy conversation. She went with the first explanation she could think of. "He had a sleepover with Elliott."

Maddie scowled. "Why?"

"Because they're friends." She had the brilliant idea to deflect. "Guess what."

Maddie eyed her suspiciously. "What?"

"You and Finn are going to see Olivia and Hannah tonight."

"We do?" That perked her up.

"Yup. You get to play with Hannah while Daddy and I have some grownup time."

"Can I take Princess Giraffe?"

"Sure."

"Can Finn stay here?"

She bit back a laugh. "Nope. Why would you want that?"

"He's boring." She flounced over and scrambled onto the bed. "He don't *do* anything."

"He's a baby. When you were a baby, this is pretty much what you did all day."

Maddie scowled and flopped back onto the pillows. "Nuh uh."

"Yes huh. All babies start out boring, but then they get a little bigger and do a little more and soon they're big kids like you and can do lots of things."

"I can do this," Maddie said. She stuck her legs up in the air and over her head until her toes touched the headboard. "See?"

"I see you."

"I can do this." She rolled onto her hands and knees and let out an emphatic, "MOOO! I can be a cow!"

Chandler laughed. "A cow?"

"Cows are fun."

"Did you know cows eat grass? So they kind of eat salads all day."

Maddie's face scrunched into disgust. "I hate salad."

"Cows love salad. And you know who else loves salad."

"Who?"

"Jared."

Ah, the magic word. Maddie beamed. "I like salad." She flopped back onto the pillows.

"Maybe I'll make salad for breakfast."

Maddie stared up at the ceiling, contemplating this unfortunate turn of events. "Can we have smiley waffles instead?"

"Sure."

"I hafta pee," she announced before scrambling off the bed and going into the bathroom.

"Do you need help?"

"Nuh uh."

Chandler listened for the scrape of the stool across the floor and a minute later heard the unmistakable tinkling, followed a few minutes later by a flush. Another scrape across the floor, and running water in the sink, along with Maddie humming the Princess Poppy theme song.

Then Maddie reappeared, holding her hands up. "I put the smelly soap on."

"Good job." She adjusted Finn and rose. "Let's get some breakfast."

Maddie skipped ahead to her room to grab Princess Giraffe before making her way down the stairs.

After breakfast was over, it was another long day of getting the corset order done.

Isobel was excited when they finished. She held the corset up by the French doors and traced the stitching with her finger. "It's so good! It looks like it came from a store." She immediately gasped. "I mean, uh, I meant that, um—"

Chandler chuckled. "I know exactly what you mean. When I first started sewing, I was always amazed when things turned out looking professionally done. I always felt like everything would look homemade."

Isobel nodded. "That's what I was afraid of."

"You did an amazing job."

She blushed. "Thank you. And, like, thanks for teaching me." She took a bunch of photos to post online.

"Hold off on posting those until the corset gets delivered. Speaking of which, I'll show you how I package my orders." She opened a cupboard and took out a flat box and a pack of tissue paper. She had Isobel fold the box while she wrote out a quick thank you card.

They wrapped the corset in black tissue paper, which really set off the purple lace, then secured the tissue with a heart-shaped "thank you" sticker. Chandler put an extra set of corset lacing and the card on top and added a sheet of bubble wrap before closing the box.

"Do you always send more string?"

"Only for my best customers." She taped the box shut.

"How do you decide who gets the string and a card?"

"Well, I give pretty much everyone a thank you card, unless they were particularly difficult to work with."

"Do you get lots of difficult people?"

Chandler finished writing the customer's address on the package. "Not often, thank goodness. The last bad one I had ordered a full gown and accessories and then charged back the payment saying she never ordered the items. It took three months to get it resolved. Then she had the nerve to try placing another order with me. Needless to say, I rejected the order."

"That's, like, so ridiculous."

Chandler double checked the seams were taped. "I'm really glad you worked with me on this."

Isobel beamed. "Me, too. I learned a lot." She shifted and cocked her head. "So, you, like, don't have any separate social media for your costumes? Like business accounts?"

"Nope, just personal. Those pictures you posted brought in an order, by the way."

Her eyes widened. "That's awesome. You know, you'd get a lot more business and traffic to your webstore if you did some videos. I could totally help getting you set up on all the different platforms."

"It's definitely something we can work on." Chandler

tapped the package. "But right now I need to get this to the post office."

Isobel went up the stairs ahead of her.

Jared sat on the living room floor, a peacock feather tiara perched on his head, holding Finn and watching a Princess Poppy movie. Maddie was conked out in the middle of the room.

Chandler raised an eyebrow at the television. "Good movie?" she asked quietly.

Jared blushed and tried not to laugh.

"I have to run to the post office." She sighed and took a step toward Maddie. She hated waking her.

Jared waved his hand. "You don't have to get her up. We're fine."

"You sure you don't mind?"

A bright grin split his face. "I have to see how this ends."

"I'll only be gone fifteen or twenty minutes."

It felt weird, leaving the kids at home with Jared and Isobel. When she was in the car heading to the post office, she realized it was the first time she'd left them with someone who wasn't family, aside from Ashley and Elliott.

At the post office, she startled walking up the steps, terrified for a split second that she'd forgotten the kids in the car. She knew she hadn't, but hurried back to the car to double check anyway.

Inside, she waited in line behind a customer who was mailing what looked like a thousand envelopes and just had to block the window to affix stamps to each one. The clerk gave her an apologetic look over the man's shoulder.

Chandler read the posters and gave the Most Wanted mugshot a look to see if she recognized the person. She didn't. A little smile played at her lips. She and Oren had a game where they'd try to decide who among their acquaintances would be the most likely to end up on an FBI wanted list, and for what.

The man finally left and she gave the package to the clerk. "Priority, please."

"Sure."

A few minutes later, she slipped the tracking slip and receipt into her wallet and headed out. She pushed the door open just as another person pulled it from the outside.

"Oh, sorr—" Chandler froze.

Janice raised her eyebrows and bobbed her head as she theatrically looked for the kids. "You're alone?"

"Hello, Janice." Chandler's chest tightened.

"Where are the kids?"

"Home." She regretted answering before the word was even fully spoken.

"Home? Oh, you mean the house my son pays for that you threw him out of?"

A couple stepped behind Janice, trying to get into the post office. Janice moved aside to let them in, and Chandler took advantage of the commotion to scoot out around their other side.

"Chandler," Janice snapped.

Chandler ignored her and speed-walked to her car. She jumped in and locked the doors. Thankfully, Janice had abandoned her chase, so Chandler drove away. Stopped at a red light, her fingers ached. She loosened them from the steering wheel and took a few deep breaths.

She had not been prepared to run into her mother-in-law. It might have been cowardly to flee, but there was no way that situation was going to go well.

This called for caffeine. She swung into the parking lot of Caretti's Coffee Shop.

At the counter, she ignored the delicious-looking baked

goods in the glass case and said, "Hi, Jody. I need something with a kick."

"Rough day?"

Chandler groaned. "Rough week. Rough month."

"How much of a kick do you need?" Jody turned and pointed to the decorative chalkboard menu board. "We have a brand new jalapeño coconut iced coffee. Kick from caffeine and spice both." She took out a tiny plastic cup and poured a sip into it. "Here. See what you think."

"Jalapeño coffee?" Skeptical, Chandler drank the sample and savored it for half a second. "Take. My. Money. This is fabulous. Largest one you've got, please."

Jody grinned. "I know, right? Another one of Eric's weird flavor combos that turns out to be amazing." She filled the cup and handed it to Chandler.

"I hope you're keeping this on the menu." She swiped her card. "Thanks a bunch."

She sipped the coffee on her way back to the car. The pepper gave it quite a kick. It was a good warm up to tonight's dinner, where she planned to indulge in the spiciest food Holy Guacamole had to offer.

Dread sent an icy finger up her spine. She'd actually been looking forward to this evening. But now that there had been a run-in with Janice, she wasn't sure it was a good idea. Surely by now Janice had called Oren and told him who-knows-what about her abandoned and neglected children.

She drove back home and texted Ashley before she went into the house.

Should I just cancel??

The reply was almost immediate.

NO!!!!!

Three dots appeared and blinked forever. Chandler knew she was in for a lengthy message. She went in the house. Maddie was awake, her hair a rat's nest as she sat on the couch with a plate balanced on her knees.

"Sorry," Jared said. "I didn't know if food was allowed in the living room."

Chandler blinked in surprise. Her daughter, who supposedly hated vegetables, had a plate of cauliflower, cucumbers, cherry tomatoes, green pepper slices, and a puddle of ranch dressing. She was happily snacking on everything. "Not a problem." She pointed to the plate. "How did you manage this?"

He reached over and took a piece of cauliflower to pop into his mouth. Maddie imitated him, crunching on her own bit of cauliflower. "Monkey see, monkey do."

"I have a monkey," Maddie added.

Isobel sat in the recliner, rocking Finn. "He was really fussing, so I gave him a bottle and changed his diaper."

"Wow, you guys are amazing." Chandler hated to think of them both leaving for college in under two months. Hopefully by then… nope, not even going to entertain what the future might hold.

Her phone vibrated.

She's a wanker. Don't let her get you down and don't assume the worst of Oren. He's trying. I think tonight will be really good for you guys to sit and talk without the kids and remember what it was like to date each other. Give him a chance, and if it doesn't go well, I'll personally kick his ass when he gets back tonight.

Chandler had to laugh at that. She texted back,

Got it. Thank you.

She ended the message with a string of heart face emojis.

Ashley was right. She had to give him a chance because it wasn't going to do their marriage any good for *either* of them to make assumptions and jump to conclusions.

Jared stood and took Maddie's empty plate to the kitchen. When he came back, he said, "If you don't need anything else, we'll get going."

"Nope, that's it. Thank you so much." She pointed to his head. "Looks great, but you might want to leave that here."

"Oh!" He pulled the tiara off and set it on the end table.

Isobel put Finn in his swing. "See you Monday!"

After they were gone, Chandler got Maddie a bath and then got herself dressed. She agonized over what to wear and what to do with her hair. In the end, she picked her favorite jeans, a flowered top, and a ponytail.

She swiped on some eyeliner and lip gloss. Deep breath, then she got the kids and Princess Giraffe situated in the car.

"You look pretty, Mommy."

"Aww, thanks, pumpkin." She glanced in the rearview mirror. "You're going to have so much fun with Livvie and Hannah."

Maddie sighed contentedly and hummed the Princess Poppy theme song.

Chandler wished she felt as calm as her daughter. Instead, her stomach was tied in knots. It felt like this date was a precipice. A do or die. A new beginning.

Or the official beginning of the end.

Chapter Thirty-Two

"Bro, you're going to wear holes in the carpet." Elliott sat on the basement sofa.

Oren stopped pacing, then started right back up again. "I think Holy Guacamole was a bad idea. Anything spicy is going to go straight through me because I'm so nervous. That's all I need. Try to impress her and end up with diarrhea in a restaurant bathroom. I think I'm gonna puke."

"Breathe."

He stopped and bent over, pressing his hands to his knees. "Seriously, why am I so nervous? It feels like a first date, only way worse."

"Try to relax. She's probably not going to stab you."

"She might. I've been awful to her. There's so much riding on this."

"Hey." Elliott patted his shoulder. "Just be genuine. Listen to her and don't do anything stupid."

"That's the part I'm worried about!" Oren flailed his arms and resumed pacing. "Everything I do lately is wrong. Everything I say or do. All of it."

"All you have to do is think before you speak. That's it.

Every time you want to say something, take a breath before you talk. It'll be fine."

Ashley called down the stairs, "They're here!"

Oren froze. "Okay. Here we go." He ran his hands down the front of his shirt – his blue button-down that was one of Chandler's favorites.

"You got this. It's gonna be great."

He swallowed hard, then climbed the stairs. He came into the kitchen just as Chandler and the kids came through the door.

"Maddie!" Hannah jumped up and down.

Maddie joined her and they raced off toward the living room.

Chandler handed Finn to Ashley. "You sure you're up for extra kids?"

"Been looking forward to getting my baby fix all day."

Oren's heart pounded. "Hey."

"Hey." Her blue eyes fixed on his. The corners crinkled as she smiled.

He noticed she'd even put on some makeup. "You look great."

A faint blush colored her cheeks. "Thanks."

"You kids should get going," Ashley said, nudging them toward the door. "Oh! Before you go, I found this." She turned to the kitchen counter and turned back with a book in her hands. "Read this. Seriously. The counselor we saw wrote it. It's so good."

Chandler took the book and read the cover. "*Mending Fences: Building, Maintaining, and Fixing Boundaries.* Thanks."

"It's super good, I promise." She waved her hand. "Sorry, I'm holding you up. Go, go, go."

Oren's palms were slick with sweat. He wiped them on his jeans. "Yeah. Shall we?" He gestured to the door.

Chandler turned to Ashley. "Finn just ate, so he should be good for a while. If not, there's a bottle—"

Ashley flicked her hand, dismissing Chandler's directions. "Blah blah blah. Go. Have fun."

Oren caught the look that the women exchanged. It gave him a little boost to realize Chandler was nervous, too. That felt like it leveled the playing field just a little.

They walked outside and he pulled the door shut. "My car or yours?"

"Either one is fine."

"Okay." He led her to his car and opened the door for her to get in. He wiped his palms on his pants again as he rounded the front of the car to get in the driver's seat. "I, uh, I've heard good things about this place."

"Me, too. I probably should have looked the menu up online to see what they have, but I didn't have time."

Oren eased the car out of the driveway. "I asked Seth about it today. I guess they've been there quite a few times and really like it. He said there's lots of spicy stuff on the menu."

"Good. I've been craving something spicy. It feels like I've been eating bland food forever. I mean, I guess it's actually been almost a year, well, not quite. More like nine or ten months. It's all Finn's fault." She gave a nervous laugh.

She was talking fast and kind of loud, another solid clue that she was as nervous as he was about tonight. "Yeah, I think Seth eats a lot of spicy stuff, too."

"You'll have to send him over to Caretti's Coffee Shop. I stopped there today and got a jalapeño coconut iced coffee. It was actually amazing. Spicy and smooth. Weird combination, but it worked."

"Sounds like something he'd like. I'll stick with regular coffee." He put his turn signal on and drove into the parking lot of the restaurant.

"I can't believe it's this close and this is the first time we've been here." Chandler unfastened her seatbelt and stared up at the huge neon sign. The restaurant's name was massive, flanked on each side by smiling cartoon bowls of guacamole with gold halos. She hopped out of the car before he could get out and open her door.

On the sidewalk, he wiped his hands again. More to keep himself from grabbing her hand than to wipe his palms this time. He wanted nothing more than to reach over and touch his wife.

"This place is packed." Chandler pulled the door open and the sounds of laughter and conversation spilled out over them.

After a brutally awkward ten minute wait, the hostess led them to a small table along the back wall and handed them two huge laminated menus. "Your server will be right with you."

"Thanks," they answered in unison.

"You getting a margarita?" he asked.

"No, I don't think it would mix well with this jalapeño coffee. I'm going to stick with tea tonight. You?"

"Same." He looked at the menu, but nothing was clicking in his brain. He was more focused on the woman across from him. So familiar, but so unfamiliar and distant right now.

"What are you getting?"

Her voice snapped him back to the present. He said, "I'm not sure. You?"

"Taco sampler. Of course." She smiled at him over the menus. "They have carne asada."

"Perfect." She'd thought of him and what he'd like. A warm feeling flowed through him.

Their server came a few minutes later, looking rather harried. "Sorry for the wait. We had three people call off and we're scrambling to make sure all the tables are covered."

"No problem," Oren said.

"Oh. Darn. I'm Dakota and I'll be taking care of you this evening. I'm supposed to say that first. Sorry."

The poor kid looked like he might burst into tears. Oren repeated, "No problem. We're ready to order whenever you're ready."

Dakota took a breath and readied his electronic order taking device. "Ready."

Chandler said, "I'd like the grande taco sampler."

"That comes with spicy sour cream, our homemade pico de gallo, and creamy cilantro lime dressing. Are those okay? We can substitute for any of the sauces along the side here." He pointed to a block of sauce options on the menu.

"That sounds perfect, thank you."

"And for you, sir?"

"I'll have the carne asada."

"Great. Can I start you with an appetizer? The guacamole with chips and salsa is to die for, seriously."

"Yes," Chandler answered without any hesitation.

They gave the server their drink orders, and he walked away.

"Five dollars says you're going to have enough leftovers to feed yourself all weekend." Mexican food was definitely one of the things that made Chandler's short list of acceptable leftovers.

She laughed and the sound warmed his heart. It felt like forever since he'd heard her laugh. "I don't know. I might be able to inhale all of it. Look how amazing this food looks." She sat up straighter and looked around at the food on the tables around them.

Instead of looking at the plates of food, he looked at her. "Yeah."

Her blonde ponytail swished across her shoulders. Oren

wanted to touch it like he normally did when they sat on the couch together and he had his arm across her shoulders and would stroke her hair and twirl it around his fingers.

"How's the corset order coming along?"

Chandler finished her sip of tea and set the glass down. "Fantastic. I thought it would be a lot slower going since I was teaching Isobel how to do it, but it went really well. I finished it up and got it shipped out this afternoon."

"That's great. Do you have a bunch of other projects in the queue?"

"I got an order from the pictures Isobel posted online. I'm hoping to finish the theater curtains on Monday or Tuesday, and I'm kind of holding on the project with Nate and Kim to see if the production is going to happen."

"Is there a chance it might not?"

"Kim said there's some conflict with the scriptwriters and to be honest, most of what she was telling me was so far out of my wheelhouse that I didn't pay a lot of attention to half of what she said. Isn't that awful?"

Oren chuckled. "No, makes sense to me."

The server sidled up to the table with a big tray balanced in one hand and a folding tray stand in the other. He opened the stand and set the loaded tray on top of it. "Who had the carne asada?"

"Over here," Oren said, and leaned away from the table to give him room to set the plate down.

"And the taco sampler." He set the platter in front of Chandler, then gave her the sauces.

"Thank you. This looks amazing."

Oren had to smile at the expression on her face. She looked ready to dive onto the plate and inhale everything in front of her.

"Anything else right now?"

"Could I get more tea, please?"

"Of course. I'll be right back with that."

He left, and Oren leaned forward to get a better look at her massive plate. "What is all that?"

She pointed to each set of two tacos in turn. "Fish, shrimp, chicken, beef, and pulled pork."

"What's your strategy?"

She considered. "I can do the chicken, beef, and pork as leftovers, so I'm definitely eating both fish and both shrimp tacos. Then I'll just start with one of the other ones and see how far I get. Yours looks good, too."

"It smells amazing." Truth be told, Oren would probably be happy eating shredded paper towels if it meant having a nice, calm, relaxed, normal moment like this with Chandler. He scooped a forkful of the beans and rice. It was seasoned perfectly. The Mexican street corn was also delicious. Then he tackled the perfectly cooked and seasoned beef. It practically melted in his mouth.

When he finished sampling his food, he said, "How is it?"

Chandler paused mid-bite and used her middle finger to wipe cilantro lime dressing from her lip. "Ohhhhh my goodness, this is the best fish taco I've ever eaten." She shoved the last bit in her mouth.

The noise around them prevented much conversation, so they ate the rest of their meals in a comfortable, happy silence. Oren felt better about their relationship than he had since this whole thing blew up.

Dakota appeared with fresh tea. He set the glasses down, cleared the empty glasses, and said, "Did you save room for dessert?"

Oren deferred to Chandler. She looked down at her plate, then up at the waiter. "Can I get a box for this, and then I'd like to try the traditional flan, please."

"Of course."

Oren put his hand up. "None for me, thanks."

"Two forks, please," she said.

His heart nearly stopped in his chest. Sharing a dessert? That had to be a good sign, right?

Dakota left and came back a few minutes later with a box, fresh sauces, and a plate with the round flan flanked by two forks.

Chandler arranged her uneaten tacos in the box and wedged the cups of sauces in before closing the lid. "I think you'll owe me five dollars. I ate almost half, and I'll have the other half for lunch. It will definitely not last me all weekend."

"Impressive."

She took her fork and had a bite of the flan. Her eyes drifted shut. "This is amazing."

Oren took a bite, and it was good, but it could have been dirt and it would have been delicious as long as he was sharing it with her.

Dakota brought the bill. "I'll take that when you're ready. How was everything?"

"Wonderful." He meant more than the food.

Her mouth full, Chandler bobbed her head and gave a thumbs up.

"Great. There's a survey at the bottom of your slip. Fill it out and you'll be entered for a chance at a $100 gift card."

"Awesome." Oren pulled out his wallet and quickly scanned the bill. "You can take this now if you're ready."

"Great." Dakota took the slip and his card and left.

"Did you want me to get—"

"No, of course not."

She shrugged. "Okay. Thanks for dinner."

"Thanks for coming."

Their eyes finally met and he held her gaze. The moment

was shattered when Dakota reappeared with the slip and Oren's card. "Sign the top copy, bottom copy is yours. You folks have a great weekend."

"You, too," they answered in unison.

Oren filled out the slip, leaving a generous tip. As they stood, he pointed. "Don't forget your box."

Chandler snatched it up. "Not a chance."

They wound their way through tables and into the now-packed lobby. Oren heard the hostess tell a newcomer that there was a ninety-minute wait for a table. Chandler pushed through the door ahead of him. When they reached the side-walk, he said, "Sounds like we came at the right time."

"I know! Ninety minutes for a table? I mean, I'd wait. Totally worth it."

"I'm glad we did this. We should make it a point to go out more. Just the two of us." *If we stay together*, his mind added.

"Definitely. It was so nice to only worry about my own food for a change."

"So you'd rate the food a ten out of ten?"

"Twelve out of ten. Amazing."

He gently nudged her arm with his elbow. "What about the company?"

She pretended to consider. "I'll give the company a solid six."

"Six? That's it?"

She grabbed his hand and grinned at him. "I still haven't forgiven you, so I had to dock some points."

He swallowed hard. She was holding his hand. This was progress, no matter how you sliced it. He gave her fingers a squeeze. "That's fair. I'll get those points back, Chan, I promise."

Her expression turned serious as she looked up into his eyes. "I hope so."

"Thank you for giving me the chance."

They walked slowly toward the car, holding hands.

"Well, well. Isn't *this* cozy?"

Oren's throat tightened. Seriously?

Janice stepped onto the sidewalk in front of them, followed by his dad.

"Hi," was all Oren could manage.

Janice cast a pointed look at their joined hands. "I see—"

"Stop." Oren found his voice. "Just stop. We're not doing this. *You're* not doing this."

His mom turned her attention to Chandler. "A whole day without the children. Must be delightful for you to feel single and free again."

He felt Chandler tense and pull her hand from his under the guise of adjusting her box of leftovers. He could feel her slipping away, and the thought alone was devastating. It spurred him to find his backbone. "You have a choice. You can apologize now, or you can live knowing you've cut off your son and grandchildren because you can't control your mouth."

She blinked at him.

"I'm serious. I've told you more than once. I've had it. This is it. I'm done."

"She threw you out! I'm on your side!"

Oren shook his head. This. Right here. This is what everyone had been trying to make him see. "There aren't any sides. We're a team."

Janice snorted. "A team? She threw you out. What if she actually divorces you? You'll regret the choice you're making then, won't you?"

He slowly shook his head. "No. No matter what happens, I will never regret choosing Chandler. Do you understand me? Never."

"Hey, now," Theo said.

Oren ignored him. "I'm not having this conversation with you again. Until you can behave with a minimum of decency, I have nothing to say to you."

Janice's eyes narrowed. "You'll come crawling back as soon as you need something." She jabbed a finger toward Chandler. "*You* can't even handle your own children without help."

Oren stepped in front of Chandler. This was it. He was making his stand. He meant what he'd said. Even if their marriage ended, he'd forever regret not taking her side. He would never, as long as he'd live, regret going to bat for her. "I'm sorry this is the choice you're making. I'd hoped you would be reasonable and decent." He shook his head sadly.

"What are you saying?" For the first time, Janice seemed uncertain.

Theo grumbled, "This is ridiculous."

"Mom, I love you. But no one can treat my wife this way and stay in my life. Not even you."

Her mouth gaped, then snapped shut. "You'll regret this." She shoved past Oren and stepped into the grass to give Chandler a wide berth.

Theo shook his head and followed his wife toward the restaurant.

Oren was afraid to look at Chandler. Had he said the right things? Had he said enough of the right things?

She nudged him toward the car. They walked again, slowly, and he couldn't help but notice she didn't take his hand.

His stomach dropped.

Was this it?

Chapter Thirty-Three

Chandler wasn't sure what to say. She couldn't have imagined a more awkward and uncomfortable encounter. She was glad Oren had stood up to his mother, but it didn't feel good. It was never her intention to get him to cut his mother off. All she wanted was to be treated with respect and a modicum of politeness.

Oren stepped off the sidewalk and opened her door. She slid in, holding her box of leftovers like a shield in front of her.

Once they were buckled up, he started the car but didn't back out of the space.

"I'm sorry," he said. "I hate that that just happened."

"Me, too." She picked at the corner of the box with her fingernail. "Are you okay?"

"Yeah. I'm good. I know the past couple of weeks have been tough, and I've made some big mistakes, but you gotta believe that there was never a question of who I'd choose."

She bristled a little. "I never asked you to choose."

"I know. And I know you never would."

"I don't want you to cut off your mother on my account. I'm

not shouldering that responsibility. I don't want you to ever blame me for coming between you and your family."

He turned in his seat and gingerly reached over to touch her arm. "You're my family. You and Maddie and Finn are my family. You're a part of me. You're my number one priority. I hope Mom comes around and we can have a relationship. But Chan, I'm not wasting my time with anyone who treats my family – my heart and soul – like garbage. I'm not choosing between you and my mother. I see that now. I'm choosing between protecting my family or allowing my family be hurt. And that's no choice at all."

Chandler blinked back tears that stung the backs of her eyes. She couldn't answer, so she nodded.

Oren backed out of the parking space and a few minutes later they were headed back to Ashley and Elliott's house.

Inside, the kids were camped around the television watching a Princess Poppy movie. Olivia was far more inter-ested in coloring in her coloring book, but Maddie and Hannah were glued to the screen.

Ashley sat on the couch with Elliott, who was holding Finn. She looked up and smiled. "How was your date?"

"Good," Chandler answered. "The food was beyond amazing."

"Had a little run-in afterwards that no one expected," Oren added.

Ashley jumped to her feet and pulled Chandler into the kitchen. "What happened?"

Chandler grabbed a bottle of water from the fridge and settled on a kitchen chair. She sighed. "Everything was going great. Great food, great conversation, everything was really nice. And when we were leaving, his parents were coming in. Janice decided to run her mouth right there on the sidewalk."

"Oh, no. What did Oren do?"

"He told her he was done with her nonsense and if she couldn't be a decent person, he didn't want to have a relationship with her."

Ashley's jaw dropped. "Whoa. What are you thinking?"

"I told him I didn't want him to choose between me and his mother because I don't want that kind of responsibility." She couldn't help the shy smile that played across her lips or the warm feeling in her chest. "He said he wasn't choosing between me and his mom. He was choosing whether or not to protect his family, and whoever was on the other side didn't matter."

"Good answer."

"I thought so." She let out a long breath. "I don't want him to cut his parents off. I just want to be treated like a human being."

"I don't think you can have both of those things right now. And for what it's worth, I agree with him. He has to decide whether or not he's going to stand up and protect his family." Ashley reached over and squeezed Chandler's arm. "It's a good start toward making amends, isn't it?"

"For sure. I just have to get over feeling like I'm responsible for creating a rift between Oren and his parents."

"The only person responsible for that Grand Canyon-sized rift is his mom and her big mouth."

"I know that in my head. I just have to make my gut believe it."

Oren came into the kitchen. "Sorry to interrupt. Maddie's fast asleep. Do you want me to keep her tonight?"

Chandler looked to Ashley. "Is it okay with you?"

"Of course."

"I should probably head home."

"Sure," Oren said, nodding. "I'll get Finn."

The awkwardness was back and she hated it. It felt wrong

to be leaving him at their friends' house, but it didn't feel any more right to let him come home.

A few minutes later, she hugged Ashley at the door. "Thanks for watching the kids."

"No problem. I'll talk to you later."

Oren carried Finn and his diaper bag out to the car. He strapped Finn in the car seat and closed the door.

"So—" they both started at the same time.

Chandler gave a little nervous laugh. "Will you bring her over in the morning or should I come get her?"

"I'll bring her home on my way to practice."

"You're going to three days a week?"

"It looks like it. Is that… is that not okay?"

Her emotions tangled. It felt like him going to practice three days a week meant there was only half a week left for him to arrange to see his kids, which meant zero days to work on their marriage. "It's nothing new, right? It just feels like that gives us less time to… work on things."

Oren shoved his hands in his pockets and stared down at the concrete driveway. "I mean, it's always a tough schedule, but we'll figure it out."

"Sure." She wasn't sure at all.

Oren opened her door.

Before she slid into the driver's seat, she reached over and gave him a hug. It was stiff and weird and didn't help ease her mind at all. "See you tomorrow."

"Drive safe." He pushed the door shut and waved as she backed out of the driveway.

She drove home and sat in the garage for a while. This evening had started off awkward, become wonderful, turned sour, and ended back at awkward.

Finn stirred, pulling her from her thoughts. She took him into the house and got them both ready for bed. When he was fed, changed, and secure in his crib, Chandler sat down at the kitchen table with the baby monitor and a notebook.

She opened it to a fresh page and wrote the number one on the first line. She started listing all the things she loved about Oren and their life together, and easily filled two pages. Then she started the second list. Her mother-in-law topped that one, followed by Oren's recent failure to maintain boundaries with number one.

When she finished that much, much shorter list, she began a third. Things she could do to make everything better. Number one? Have patience and an open mind.

This was *not* going to be easy.

Chapter Thirty-Four

Oren woke up Saturday morning to Maddie's foot mashed painfully into the side of his neck. He twisted out of the way and slid off the pull-out sofa. Maddie had snuck downstairs sometime after he'd fallen asleep, because she had been put to bed with Hannah.

While he was grateful to have a warm, safe, free place to stay, he missed his house. The tiny guest bathroom was a wonderful amenity, but he much preferred the upgraded shower he and Chandler had put into their own bathroom.

He arched his back until it cracked. He also missed his bed. His nice, expensive, ergonomic, personalized softness bed. More than that, he missed waking up to Chandler's warmth and soft breathing next to him. He ached to touch her. It felt like it had been forever since they'd shared any intimacy. The last part of her pregnancy had been hard on her, and with Finn's constant infections and their lack of sleep… well, it had been a while, and he missed her.

Her.

Not just the physical part. He missed the light touches as

they passed in the hallway, the quick kisses on his way out the door…

He froze in the middle of brushing his teeth.

Well, now. That was part of the current problem, wasn't it? He was always on his way out the door, and somewhere along the way he'd gotten into too much of a rush to take two seconds to give his wife a smile or a touch or a kiss.

Ugh. Nothing was more humbling than facing the consequences of one's own actions.

He got dressed and came out to find an empty room. He folded the bed back into a sofa and put his things out of sight. He followed the sound of voices upstairs to the kitchen.

Ashley poured pancake batter onto a griddle while Elliott poured orange juice for the three girls. "Juice?" he asked.

"Sure. Thanks. Can I help?"

Ashley said, "Would you grab the syrup out of the fridge? It's in the door."

Oren pulled out the bottles and set them on the dining room table.

Once Ashley and Elliott were finished with their breakfast, Oren followed them to the kitchen. In a low voice, he said, "I think I've made a decision."

Both of them looked at him expectantly.

"I'm going to quit the theater."

"What?!" Ashley demanded.

"It hit me this morning. She's always at home doing the heavy lifting and I'm working and doing the theater and I'm hardly ever home. So if I give it up, I'll be home more. She knows how much I love doing theater, so I think it'll show her how serious I am."

"That's a great idea," Elliott said at the exact time Ashley said, "That's a terrible idea."

They both stared at Ashley.

Elliott said, "No, it's a great idea. It can be his big grand gesture that shows her how much she means to him."

"Nope," she answered. "She already feels like she's making you give up a relationship with your mother. Now you want to make her feel like she's forcing you to give up the theater, too?"

"Of course not."

"That's how she'll see it."

"I think you're wrong."

Ashley crossed her arms and raised an eyebrow. "Suit yourself."

Oren shrugged. Ashley might be Chandler's best friend, but surely he knew his wife better than that.

Elliott suggested a compromise. "Maybe tell her that's what you plan to do before you do it and see how she reacts?"

"Fine. I'll tell her first, but I've made up my mind."

He got Maddie into the car, and they headed for home. Should he still be calling it home? He pulled into the driveway and watched Maddie race across the front lawn to the porch, where she unceremoniously pounded on the door.

Oren reached the porch just as Chandler opened the door.

"My goodness, no need to beat a hole in the door, princess."

Maddie yelled, "I hafta poop!" and made a beeline for the bathroom.

Oren lifted his hands at his wife's expression. "I promise she went right before we left."

"Did you have breakfast?"

"Yeah."

She glanced at her watch. "Do you have to leave for practice right away?"

"In a minute. I wanted to talk to you about that."

"About practice?" She looked confused as she glanced at him while she situated Finn in his swing.

"Yeah. About the whole theater."

She straightened. "Okay?"

He pulled in a big breath and smiled. "I'm going to give up the theater."

"What?"

"We need time together, right? And between shuffling the kids and work, something's got to give. So I'm willing to let the theater go and prove to you I'm committed to making this work."

Her eyes narrowed.

Crap, was Ashley right about this?

"I... thought you'd be happy?"

"Happy? Why would I be happy about this? Of course, it sounds good in theory, but it's not. You've already decided to press pause on your relationship with your mother, and who knows what that's going to look like in the long run. Now you're going to quit the theater, too? Why? To be here with me? And you think that's not going to start eating at you and make you resentful and angry? Maybe not today or tomorrow, but eventually you'll make a mental list of everything you've 'given up' for me." She made air quotes around the last bit.

Okay, yup, Ashley had nailed it. Great.

Chandler pinched the bridge of her nose and squeezed her eyes shut. "I appreciate the intention behind what you're saying. I do. But that's not a solution. Neither of us can give up things that feed our souls, Oren. You need the theater like I need to sketch and create."

He blurted out, "What about therapy?" He actually hadn't thought much about it, but Elliott had been open about how much a few counseling sessions had helped them early on in their marriage.

She froze. "Are you serious? You'd go?"

"Of course I'd go."

"Okay."

"I'll take care of everything. I'll get the info from Elliott and schedule an appointment." *This* decision actually made him feel empowered. Like he was really doing something positive to move them forward. And it made a lot more sense than quitting the theater.

"Okay. Great."

"I have to run, but can I come over this evening?"

"Sure."

"I'll bring supper."

That earned him a smile. "Perfect. I'll be polishing off my leftover tacos for lunch."

As he drove to the theater, his mind ping ponged back and forth between what he could do to make things better at home, and what needed done for the *Hamlet* production.

There were already three cars in the parking lot when he arrived. Inside, Gretchen teased, "You're three minutes late. We were ready to send out a search party."

Alan laughed. "I think that's the first time you haven't beaten us here."

"Sorry, guys." Wow. More people he was letting down.

"We're just teasing." Gretchen looked down at him from her place on the stage where she and Alan were setting up the large table the cast would be sitting around to go over the script. "You okay?"

Alan stopped moving chairs and came to stand beside Gretchen. "Oh, no, is Finn sick again? You look tired."

Oren opened his mouth to protest and insist everything was fine, but nothing came out. He shook his head. "No, the baby's fine. Just a lot going on." He took a deep breath. "Chandler and I are going through some stuff right now. It's a lot with that and the kids and gearing up for this production. I offered to quit the theater, but that just pissed her off."

Gretchen rolled her eyes. "Of course it did."

Seriously? Was this some woman thing that they could see but men couldn't?

She continued. "I'm sure she doesn't want you to give it up, but use your head. It's not all or nothing. I mean, you could take a step back from being production manager. It's not like no one else here has the experience. *Ahem*."

"I know, but it's kind of a lot."

"You did not just say that." Her eyes narrowed, clearly offended.

"Dude," Alan added.

Oren sat on the edge of the stage, his legs dangling. Gretchen and Alan joined him, sitting on either side of him. "I wasn't implying you couldn't handle it. I know you've managed bigger productions and have the experience. I just meant I didn't want to impose on your time like that."

"Oren, let's be real for a minute, okay? You've got a brand new baby. Maddie's what, four? You have a full-time job, and a wife on top of this production. You can't do it all well, so you're going to be half-assing something. Or everything. No matter how much of an anal retentive control freak you are, something's gonna give. Or you can let go a little bit and let us handle *Hamlet* so you have the energy to handle the most important things in your life."

Oren looked at Gretchen. He wanted to argue and insist he could handle it all, but every word she said was true. He also noticed she only said to let go and let them handle *Hamlet*. This didn't have to be forever. He surprised himself by saying, "Okay."

"Okay?" Gretchen looked past him to Alan.

Alan's bushy eyebrows climbed to the middle of his forehead. "Did you say 'Okay'?"

"Yeah." He laughed. It felt like a thousand pounds had lifted from his shoulders. "Yeah, I did."

The rest of the actors filed in and gathered around the theater.

When everyone had taken their spots at the table, Oren stood up. "Hey, everyone, I have an announcement."

Fifteen pairs of eyes focused on him.

"Effective immediately, Gretchen will be managing the play. I will also step back from my role as King Claudius and take on some bit parts instead. With the baby and… other things, I just need a little break."

Wes raised his hand.

"Yes?"

"What about the spring production?"

Oren held up a hand. "Let's get through *Hamlet* before we worry about *Macbeth*. To be clear, I'm not quitting or leaving. I'm just taking a step back. Gretchen?" He sat down.

Gretchen tapped her script. "Okay, with that taken care of, let's dig into the scripts and see who wants to be the king."

While everyone got their scripts out, Oren pulled his notebook and clipboard from his messenger bag and slid it to Gretchen. "All my notes are in here. I think I'm going to go." He was almost giddy at the thought of skipping a practice, something he hadn't done in the thirteen years he'd been involved in the theater, except that one time he had food poisoning and the hospital refused to release him.

"Go. I'll text you later with whatever bit part you end up with. We've got this."

"I know you do. Thanks." He took his bag and hopped off the stage and headed for home.

He knew exactly what he was going to do when he got there, too.

Twenty minutes later, he pulled into the driveway. Instead of going into the house, he went into the garage and put gas in the chainsaw.

Chapter Thirty-Five

Chandler heard the buzzing noise of the saw from her workshop where she was pinning the last panels of the theater curtains. Maddie happily colored in her Princess Poppy coloring book while Finn dozed.

She looked out the French doors across the lawn. Oren was outside, sawing the smaller branches off the huge branch that had come off the tree. To be honest, she'd forgotten about the mess in the side yard.

"What's that?" Maddie asked.

"Daddy's cutting the tree that fell."

"Daddy?" She perked up and rushed over to the door. She put her hands on the glass and watched him.

"Yeah, he must have gotten done early at the theater." She couldn't imagine why he was here and not there. Saturday practices were always more in-depth than weeknights.

Movement from the corner of her eye caught her attention. A pickup truck backed across the lawn to where Oren worked. She watched Oren straighten and start talking as Rowan jumped out of the cab and pulled on a pair of gloves.

The two men worked together to load the smaller sticks

into the back of Rowan's truck. When they were done with that, Rowan produced his own chainsaw, a much larger model than Oren's, and cut up the biggest branch, which was the size of a whole tree on its own.

Chandler went back to her work. A while later, Oren tapped on the French doors. Maddie ran over to open the door for him.

"Sorry," Chandler said. "I didn't realize it was locked."

He poked his thumb over his shoulder. "We got the tree cut up and Rowan's hauling it away. He said he can use a lot of it for projects, and he'll season the rest to use in his woodstove."

"Great. I'm glad it's not just going to waste."

"Do you mind if I grab a shower?"

"Of course not."

He leaned down and gave Maddie her kisses, then disappeared up the stairs.

Maddie was itching to follow, so Chandler took the kids upstairs and made Maddie a sandwich for lunch. She heated her tacos in the air fryer to get them crispy.

Oren bounded into the kitchen. "Something smells amazing."

She handed him a glass of water. "It's either Maddie's ham sandwich and peanut butter apple slices, or my leftover tacos."

"Definitely the tacos."

The air fryer chimed to announce it was done.

"How come you're not at the theater?" Chandler asked as she opened the fryer. She was afraid of the answer.

"I'm taking a step back."

Her shoulders slumped. "I thought we talked about this." She steeled herself against his reasoning for ignoring what she'd said.

"Yes. We did. And you were completely right. I'm not quitting. I just stepped down as stage manager for *Hamlet*, and instead of King Claudius, I'm going to take one of the smaller parts. Maybe a soldier or something. We'll reevaluate when we start working on *Macbeth*."

Chandler blinked. A reasonable compromise? Wow. She divided the tacos onto two plates. "Are you sure about this?"

"One hundred percent. Besides, Gretchen has been wanting to be in charge, so it's a win-win."

She handed him a plate, and his eyes widened.

"Are you seriously sharing your leftover tacos with me?"

She shrugged one shoulder. "Yes, but that means you have to take me back to Holy Guacamole so I can get more."

"Any time you want." His voice was soft, and she knew her offhanded comment had suggested something bigger than just getting more tacos.

She supposed it did.

He asked, "Did you start reading that book Ashley gave us?"

"No, I think I left it in your car."

"Elliott said there were workbooks they got that went with it. I checked, and the bookstore has them in stock. I reserved two."

This. This is what she'd been needing to see from him. A real desire to get back on track even if it made him uncomfortable. "Really?"

"Yeah. I mean, if you wanted to do that. Ell said it might take a while to get an actual appointment since he's booked pretty solid. Maybe we can get a head start?"

"Did you want to get them today?" She was surprised – in a very good way – at the way he was taking the initiative.

"If you're not too busy."

"No, I was just working on the curtains, but they don't have to be done today."

Oren finished his first taco. "You weren't kidding. These are fantastic."

"Told you so."

"Even as dreaded leftovers."

Chandler snickered behind her hand. "I can't help that I'm too precious for most leftovers."

"Precious? You mean snooty."

"What's snooty?" Maddie asked.

Chandler looked at Oren. He said it, he could explain it.

"Uh, it kind of means fancy."

"Is Mommy fancy?"

"She sure is."

Maddie scrunched up her face like she couldn't quite believe him. "Princess Poppy is fancy."

"She's very fancy."

Apparently fancy was a more interesting word than snooty, because Maddie said it at least five more times in the next two sentences about Princess Poppy.

Chandler watched Oren and Maddie go back and forth about the princess, and she had a hard time remembering why she'd asked him to leave.

"—now?"

She blinked. "I'm sorry, what?"

"I was just asking if you wanted to go now. Maybe we can bring P-I-Z-Z-A home?"

Chandler licked the last of the sauce off her fingers and wiggled her eyebrows. "Or more T-A-C-O-S?"

Oren laughed. "I've created a monster."

She loved the way the corners of his eyes crinkled when he laughed. She got up to put the plates in the dishwasher. "Potty breaks for everyone, then we can head out."

Oren took Maddie's hand without hesitating. "Let's go potty, then we're going to the bookstore."

"Yay!" Maddie skipped to the stairs and held Oren's hand as she jumped up every single step.

Chandler walked behind them, wishing she had as much energy as her daughter. A little while later, they were on the highway. Oren nudged her arm and jerked his head toward the back seat.

She peeked and smiled at Maddie, fast asleep in her car seat, with her arm stretched out to hold her little brother's hand.

"Do you think you'll regret stepping back at the theater?"

Oren glanced over, then put his eyes back on the road. "No. It's something I should have done anyway, at least for this production, with Finn being so little. I'd thought about it, but never *really* considered it, if you know what I mean."

"Yeah."

"Have you heard any more on the show for Nate and Kim?"

"Since last night? No."

He scrunched up his nose like he did when he was embarrassed. "I guess we did talk about that at dinner, didn't we?"

"Briefly. Honestly, I'm not disappointed about having a delay. I had more Ren Faire orders come in this morning, so I'll work on those next week. It's for some of the dresses I already have listed, so the orders are pretty much done except for some alterations and accessories. Should be an easy job. I think a lot of it is from Isobel doing social media for me."

"That's great."

"We'll have to go through the theater costumes and see what needs fixed or replaced. We should do that within the next couple of weeks, so I have time to take care of it before dress rehearsals start."

"Maybe next Tuesday? See if Jared can babysit and you can go through the costumes with Gretchen and see what she wants done."

"Sounds like a plan." She noted the way he talked about Jared babysitting without batting an eye. One more point in his favor.

The drive went by quickly and they were soon at the strip mall where the bookstore was, nestled between an office supply store and a grocery outlet. Oren found a parking space a little distance from the bookstore entrance, so they had room to get the stroller out without dinging anyone's car. Oren wrestled with the stroller and Finn while Chandler woke Maddie up.

"Hey pumpkin, we're here."

Maddie blinked sleepily, but her eyes widened when she saw the bookstore. She wriggled as Chandler tried to unfasten her car seat straps and jumped out of the car. She was so excited she didn't even grab Princess Giraffe.

"Whoa, slow down. There's cars that can't see you. Hold my hand or hand on the stroller."

Maddie grabbed the stroller handle and walked alongside Oren.

Inside, a huge cardboard cutout of Princess Poppy heralded the release of a brand new Poppy book.

"Daddy! Look!"

"I see. Use your inside voice, pumpkin." He looked at Chandler. "I'll take Maddie back to the kids' section." He grimaced. "Go look around. I'll be fine."

Chandler laughed, but she didn't need to be told twice. She browsed through aisles and shelves alone, touching the book spines and enjoying the unique bookstore smell. She picked out a new novel by one of her favorite authors and moseyed into the nonfiction section. She wasn't sure what she was looking for until she found herself standing in the Relationships aisle, scanning the shelves. She found the *Mending Fences* book, which she picked up so they'd each have a copy to read, and close to it was a book called *Drama Llamas* by a renowned psychologist with a bunch of letters after her name. Chandler pulled it out and read the back. It was about not getting caught up in other people's dramatic behavior, but leafing through it, it seemed to be a bunch of buzzwords and cheerleading with little substance.

She put it back on the shelf and made her way toward the children's section to save her husband. Oren was sitting on an uncomfortable-looking plastic child-sized chair. "You already have that one." He looked up and mouthed, "Save me."

Maddie was in her glory, surrounded by a Princess Poppy display and shelves of Princess Poppy books and merchandise.

"How are you holding up?" Chandler asked with a smile.

"Fine, but one of us needs to hit the lottery if they're going to keep making all this crap."

Maddie held another book out to Oren. "This one."

"You have this one, too."

With a weary sigh only a four-year-old girl can manage, she clapped her hand to her forehead. "You say I have them *all*, Daddy."

"That's because you do. Except this one." He tapped the copy of the newly released book that was on the table beside him.

Chandler muttered, "How many adventures can one princess even have?"

"Right?" He glanced at the books in her hand. "Find something?"

"Yeah. Did you want to go look around?"

He stood up.

Chandler touched his arm. "Don't leave me here long. I already feel myself breaking into Poppy hives."

He smiled. "Pretty sure there's a line of overpriced licensed Princess Poppy ointments for that."

"Undoubtedly."

In the end, he found a mystery novel by one of his favorite authors. "I'll take the kids out while you check out?"

"Perfect."

As she stood in line, she checked out the row of impulse-buy items and grabbed a pair of socks for Oren. They were bright green with "To Be or Not To Be" written all over them, with polka dots that were actually little cartoon skulls. Perfect.

She gave Oren's name and got the workbooks, then paid for their items and went out to the car. Maddie was in her seat, impatiently waiting for her new Princess Poppy book. Chandler gave it to her and stowed the bag in the back with the stroller.

She hopped in her seat and buckled up.

"Where to?"

"What are the options?"

"We could go to the P-A-R-K and then pick up P-I-Z-Z-A?"

"Sounds G-O-O-D to M-E," she answered with a laugh.

Chapter Thirty-Six

Oren couldn't have asked for a better day. Finally, the black cloud of tension that had been hanging over him and Chandler seemed to have dissipated, or at least moved off into the distance.

At the park, he helped Chandler settle on a bench in the shade to nurse Finn, then he took Maddie to the swings. He pushed her and a voice at his side said, "Hi, Oren."

He turned his head, keeping his hands out so Maddie didn't swing back and knock him over. "Hi… sorry?"

"Shannon."

"Right. Sorry. And this is Kresley?" He nodded toward the girl playing with a ball several yards away.

"Kinsley."

"Sorry."

She laughed, a melodic but forced sound. "It's okay. You were close."

"Yeah."

"I hear you and your wife are separated."

Wow, she wasn't beating around the bush, was she? "Is that right?"

"Sorry, I guess it's just a rumor then?"

He pushed Maddie, hoping she'd tire of the swings. Like now would be good. "Not sure how it's any of your concern."

Undeterred, she said, "Can I get your number? We can arrange playdates with Kinsley and Maggie."

"Maddie." He didn't know why he bothered to correct her.

"Right. Maddie. They get along so well. It'll be fun."

"Can't help you. Chandler handles the schedule for the kids."

"It's so nice to see dads at the park with their kids."

He stopped pushing Maddie so the swing slowed. "We're actually here as a family."

Her face froze for a moment. "Oh. Well. You could always take my number anyway. In case you ever need a couch to crash on."

"I'll pass." Who *was* this woman?

He scooped Maddie off the swing. "Let's do the slides over by Mommy."

"Okay," Maddie sing-songed and skipped away, oblivious to… whatever this was.

"Gosh, I didn't realize your wife was here."

Oren was glad she was. This woman was kind of scary in a predatory sort of way.

She continued. "So you're not separated?"

Rude or not, he decided to just ignore her and walk away. No good could come from continuing to engage. He escaped back over to Chandler. She'd gotten Finn settled in the stroller and was standing near the slide, watching Maddie scramble up the ladder like a spider monkey.

"That was weird."

"Hmm?"

"That woman. Shannon? I think she was hitting on me." He suppressed a shudder.

Chandler's eyebrow rose. "Oh?"

"Yeah. She asked for my number so we could arrange play-dates. After she asked me like six times if we were separated."

"Wow. Rumor mill moves fast, doesn't it?"

"It's creepy." He glanced over his shoulder. Shannon was at the merry-go-round with Kinsley, but she smiled when he looked over. "Can we go now?"

Chandler must have caught the look, because she said, "Yeah. Let's go," in the dry tone she used when she was annoyed.

On the one hand, he didn't like feeling like a slab of meat thrown into a tiger cage, but on the other hand, he was glad to see his wife giving off some jealous vibes. Maybe not *jealous*, exactly, but definitely territorial.

He bit the inside of his cheek to keep from grinning. Things were looking up.

Chapter Thirty-Seven

Okay, she'd never admit it, but that whole thing with Shannon ticked her off. What kind of sleazy hag goes up to a guy – *when his wife is right there!* – and tries to get his number using some lame playdate cover excuse. No wonder she got a bad vibe from her when they'd seen each other at the playground. Ugh.

And then it annoyed her all over again because she never for one second thought Oren was doing anything wrong, but his mother says boo and he's all suspicious of her. It wasn't fair. In fact, it was aggravating and irritating.

She buckled her seatbelt as Oren climbed into the driver's seat.

They drove home in silence while she stewed. After they unloaded the kids and got inside, Oren said, "I'll call to order the P-I-Z-Z-A, okay?"

"Fine."

He paused, clearly knowing something was up. "Chan?"

"No mushroom. I'm going to the bathroom." She left him standing there, a confused look on his face.

Upstairs, she stared into the mirror. Is this how it was going to be forever? Everything is coasting along, just fine, and then *boom*, something comes out of left field and brings up her hurt feelings again?

She splashed cold water on her face. It didn't do anything except annoy her and get her wet. Why was that so popular in movies? She yanked the hand towel off the rack and wiped her face. One deep breath, then another, and she started to calm down.

To be honest, she wasn't even sure what she was agitated about, which annoyed her even more.

She looked into her own eyes. "It's fine. You're fine. It's only been a few days. It's perfectly natural to be on edge." She imagined that Ashley would tell her much the same thing, and that helped, too.

They'd been on top of a mountain of crap. It was only natural that climbing down would entail some stench and yuck. She grimaced. What a horrible metaphor. Where did she come up with that? Hmm. Maybe because she was standing in the bathroom.

Downstairs, Maddie had clearly overheard Oren placing the food order, because she was jumping around the room chanting, "Piz-za! Piz-za! Piz-za!" Princess Giraffe flopped helplessly in her arms.

"Somebody approves of our dinner plans," Chandler said as she came back into the kitchen.

"No kidding." He spoke just a little louder. 'Wait until she finds out I ordered her a salad."

Maddie stopped short. "What?"

"I ordered you a salad."

Chandler had to laugh at Maddie's outraged expression, and her tiny fists planted on her hips.

"Daddy!"

Oren laughed, too. "But Jared said you like veggies now." At Maddie's stunned expression, he confessed, "I'm teasing."

She still looked suspicious.

"I ordered pizza. With pepperoni. No salad or veggies."

"Piz-za!" She resumed jumping across the room, into the hall, and headed for the living room.

"Do you want to start reading the first chapter? Maybe we can read and talk about it?" Oren asked.

"Yeah. I actually bought a copy so we can both read at our own speed."

"Good idea." He brought the bag of books to the kitchen table and handed her the book and workbook. He took his own workbook and Ashley's copy of the book and sat down.

"Oh. Wait." Chandler got up and got a sticky note out of the junk drawer. She wrote "Ash & Ell" on it and stuck it to the book Oren had. "So we don't get them mixed up."

"You're so smart."

"Yeah, I am," she joked.

He regarded her for a moment, then opened the book.

Chandler opened her book and read through the introduction. It was hard to concentrate on the book when Oren was next to her. Maddie was doing who-knows-what in the living room, and it would soon be time to feed Finn.

She'd barely read two pages when the pizza delivery arrived.

After they ate, Chandler said, "Maybe we should read through the first chapter separately and talk about it tomorrow? I'll be able to concentrate better after the kids are in bed."

"Sure."

"I don't want to disappoint you." The last thing she wanted to do was shut down his enthusiasm.

"You never have."

Maddie's blood-curdling scream had them running into the living room. She stood in the middle of the room, crying and pointing at the wall with one hand while the other squeezed Princess Giraffe in a death grip.

A big black spider crawled up the wall, unbothered by the commotion he was creating.

"Eeeew," Oren said. "I guess I'm on spider duty, huh?"

"It ain't gonna be me," Chandler said. She picked Maddie up. "Okay, shhh. It's easier to catch spiders when it's quiet, okay?"

Maddie's crying turned down to a sobbing whimper. She clutched Chandler's shoulders and refused to look away from the spider.

"He's not so scary. He's just looking for a bug to eat."

"He eat bugs?" Maddie asked tearfully.

"Yup. Spiders eat those nasty mosquitoes and they eat flies."

"Flies are yucky." She wiped her eyes.

Oren found a box lid. He opened the window and reached up to poke the spider with the box. It fell into the box lid and Oren flicked it out the window.

"See? Now he's back outside so he can find a nice juicy bug for supper."

"Okay."

Finn wailed in the kitchen.

Chandler tried to set Maddie down, but she clung tightly.

"I got it," Oren said. He went into the kitchen and came back, bouncing Finn on his shoulder.

"Here, pumpkin, you go to Daddy so I can feed the baby, okay?"

Maddie's chin quivered.

"The spider's gone. He won't come back in.'

Maddie let Chandler set her down, and immediately clutched Oren's leg.

Chandler took Finn and settled on the recliner to nurse.

Oren said, "Let's get your bath and put your jammies on. Then we can read your new Princess Poppy book."

Maddie nodded.

Chandler listened to them go up the stairs and relaxed back against the chair. At some point, she dozed until the clomping footsteps came back down the stairs.

Finn had fallen off her breast, fast asleep, so she covered up and rocked him while Oren and Maddie cuddled on the couch and he read her new book.

After he closed the book, Maddie insisted he read it again.

"It's bedtime, so I'll read it again after you're tucked in."

Chandler followed them up the stairs and took Finn into the master bedroom. She got him changed and ready for bed. She'd just laid him in the crib when Oren came into the room.

"She's asleep."

"So's he."

He hesitated. "I guess I should head out. I don't want to make noise when Ashley and Elliott are getting the kids to bed."

"Yeah."

"I'll see you tomorrow."

Chandler smiled. "Sounds good."

Oren leaned over and kissed her cheek. "Good night."

"Night."

After he left, she went downstairs and settled on the recliner with the book. The first chapter began with the author explaining how he viewed boundaries as fences.

He talked about how important it is for couples to decide on the right kind of fence to put up. Are they both comfortable with a decorative fence that doesn't keep anything out, a brick wall that doesn't let anything in, or something in the middle?

Then he talked about the importance of maintaining the fence and not letting it fall into disrepair.

Chandler closed the book and stared across the room. Is that what they'd done? Gotten busy and comfortable – or complacent – and their marriage had slowly been needing maintenance? Ouch.

If she really thought about it, maybe she didn't need to be so angry with Oren. He'd said some stupid, hurtful things, but she believed that if he'd have taken a minute to step back and think, he wouldn't have really thought she was doing anything wrong. If he had taken that minute, they wouldn't be in this situation.

Which meant that maybe their fence had already been crushed and that's why his mom was able to wiggle in and sow discord. Just like the picket fence in the side yard. Sure, it was largely decorative, but it kept the deer out of the garden. Well, it used to, but now it had been on the ground for almost a week, ignored and keeping nothing out.

Her mind followed that track. She hadn't checked the garden for ages. They'd scaled way back this year because of the baby, but there were probably rotten tomatoes and bitter cucumbers by now. She made a mental note to check the garden in the morning.

Just one more thing that was being neglected.

Her tired brain reminded her that she was also neglecting sleep, and it was time for bed.

Chapter Thirty-Eight

"Okay, so you were right. She totally saw it as me choosing between her and the theater. At practice today, though, I decided to step back. Gretchen is going to manage it all, and I'm taking a bit part for *Hamlet*. I'll reevaluate in the spring and see if I want to do more for *Macbeth*, but I felt really good about limiting my responsibilities with it right now."

"See?" Ashley grinned. "It doesn't have to be all or nothing."

A good lesson he wished he'd figured out long ago. "I was thinking of taking her to Duck Park tomorrow. It's where we had our first official date. We didn't have any money back then. We did a picnic and walked the trail along the creek and fed the ducks. Is that too cheesy?"

She shook her head enthusiastically. "It's the perfect amount of cheesy. We'll babysit."

Oren winced. "I feel like I'm taking advantage of you. You're giving me a place to stay, and you've watched the kids a lot."

Elliott said, "You guys would do it for us in a heartbeat."

"I know, but—"

"No buts. We'll take the kids. You can return the favor later. Seriously."

"I appreciate it."

"We know you do," Elliott said.

"Okay. I had another idea that I want to run past you." Oren pulled out his phone and opened a screenshot he'd taken. He passed his phone to Ashley.

She gasped. "That's beautiful."

"It's similar to the engagement ring I had originally gotten her, but upgraded a little bit."

"Oh, she'll love it."

Elliott peered at the screen. "Does she want an upgrade?"

"Her original one was lost on vacation one year. We'd just had Maddie, so she didn't want to spend the money to replace it."

"Well then, I say go for it. It's a really nice ring."

Ashley was still staring at it. "Oren, she will absolutely love this."

He took his phone back and let out a little laugh. "I think I'm more nervous now than I was the first time around."

Elliott clapped his shoulder. "It's all going to work out. You're talking and that's the most important thing. Just keep showing her she's your number one priority, and everything will fall back into place."

"Thanks. Both of you. Now I'm going to go start reading that book you gave us."

Ashley nodded. "It's a little cheesy, and he carries the fence thing *way* too far sometimes, but it helped us so much."

"It really did," Elliott agreed.

Oren headed down to the basement, feeling better than he had since everything blew up. He still hated that he wasn't home, but for the first time, he was confident this was just temporary. And let's be honest. Ashley was no longer breathing fire and that had to be a sign he was on the right track.

Oren woke up on Sunday with the book still tented over his chest. Even though the fences in the book were metaphorical, it was a good reminder that their real fence still needed to be fixed.

He jumped out of bed and took a quick shower. His plan? Stop by the house, see what's needed to fix the fence, then go shopping for that and the picnic items. He pulled on a pair of shorts and a t-shirt and headed out the door.

He moved the broken pickets and was relieved to see there was less damage than he'd imagined. He'd only have to replace one top rail and half a dozen pickets. The support posts and bottom rail were fine.

"Hey." Chandler crossed the lawn.

"Hey. I'm just stopping to see what I need to fix the fence."

She snort-laughed. "I have a feeling we're both taking that book too literally."

"I mean, it couldn't be better timing, could it?"

"I suppose not. I was coming out to check the garden."

"I'm not seeing a lot of color from here."

They walked to the back corner of the property where the garden lay decimated. The cucumber plants had been chewed to the ground, and the tomato plants were bare.

"Wow. I feel like there's a lesson in this," Chandler said drily.

"Yup."

She sighed. "Well, that's disappointing. I was hoping there'd at least be a few tomatoes left. I could eat a good tomato sandwich."

"We can fix the garden after I fix the fence." He leaned over and kissed her cheek. "I'll be back in a bit."

Inspired, he hopped in his car and headed to Hannigan's Hardware. He bought the pickets and screws to fix the fence, then drove to the Hickory Hollow Nursery and bought some mature tomato plants and a couple of cucumber plants. Since he was on such a roll, he also bought hanging baskets of flowers for the front porch since they hadn't gotten around to putting any up this year, and a few fresh tomatoes from the farm stand next to the nursery.

His car was packed to the gills, but he also stopped at the market to buy some picnic food. Pre-made sandwiches, cut up veggies with dip, and whoopie pies for dessert. A couple bottles of water, and lunch was taken care of.

He also grabbed two big bags of peas to feed the ducks, since it was the safest thing to give them.

He headed back to the house, feeling pretty darn proud of himself. Barely ten o'clock and it had already been a productive day.

He and Chandler worked together, lining up the new pickets and screwing them into the rails. Maddie played in the yard while Finn hung out in his stroller in the shade, his bright eyes taking everything in. They talked as they worked. No big topics, just normal, everyday, regular stuff. All the stuff he'd missed so much. All the stuff he'd almost lost.

By noon, the fence was good as new, sturdy and strong. All that was left was a few coats of paint. He was equal parts glad and annoyed. Glad it was done, and annoyed he'd been putting it off because it looked like a bigger job than it was.

There was probably a lesson in that, too.

They dropped the kids off with Ashley and Elliott.

"Where are we going?"

"You'll see."

"Why can't you tell me?"

Oren laughed. "You're as bad as Maddie. You'll see in a few minutes."

She made an impatient growling noise and he laughed again.

"Almost there." He put on his turn signal and turned.

"Duck Park? We're going to the park?"

He was afraid for a second that she'd be disappointed, but the feeling didn't last long.

"Aww, you remembered this is where we had our first official date." Her voice was soft.

"I did." He parked the car and paused at the back to retrieve his backpack with the picnic gear before opening her door. "Milady."

"Milord." She curtseyed.

He led the way across a small bridge to a pavilion with picnic tables, where he spread a cheap plastic tablecloth he'd gotten at the dollar store. He laid out the food and plastic silverware and napkins.

"You've thought of everything." She clapped her hands in delight. "You even remembered the whoopie pies."

"I remember everything about that day." A soft smile played at his lips. "You were wearing a yellow dress with little white polka dots, and your hair was dark. Almost black."

She squeezed her eyes shut. "A huge misunderstanding between me and Miss Clairol."

"You had these silver dangly earrings that matched the bracelet you had on." He saw it clearly in his mind's eye. He'd been so tongue tied and nervous and excited.

"Wow."

"You only ate half your sandwich."

"I was so nervous I thought I'd barf. I wasn't sure if you'd like me or not."

"When we went over to feed the ducks, you slipped and I thought for sure you were going down the bank and into the water."

"I have no idea how I caught myself. I was so awkward."

"You were perfect. And you still are."

Chapter Thirty-Nine

Well, what do you say to *that*? Chandler felt her cheeks heat and knew they were bright red. It felt like a first date all over again. Uncertain about what the future holds, hoping it's good, trying not to be awkward, trying to make a good impression.

After they finished eating, Oren cleaned up their trash and put it in the trash can. "There's one thing that's different this time."

"Only one?" she quipped.

He pulled a bag of peas out of his backpack. "Since bread's bad for the ducks, I brought peas."

"Nice."

The paved walking trail wound out around the pavilion and into a wooded area. It met up with the creek and ran alongside it for about a quarter of a mile. They strolled along the busy trail. At the creek, mallards waited patiently for the next group of humans to come through with food.

"There's a whole flock of them." Chandler loved seeing the ducks. They were so colorful up close, with the sun shining on their feathers. Even the dull-colored females who looked plain brown from a distance shimmered with blue and gold in the light.

"Did you know that a group of ducks on the ground is called a sord? When they're in flight, they're a flock."

Chandler tossed a handful of peas and the gentle quacks got louder as the ducks surrounded the treats. "I had no idea. Is that a fun fact you learned so you could impress me today?"

She could tell from the way he smiled and turned his face away that was exactly what he'd done.

"What else you got?"

He cleared his throat and laughed. "Did you know these guys – mallards – can fly fifty-five miles per hour? That's faster than the average waterfowl. Also, mallards have the biggest duck population in the world. They can live up to twenty years, although the average lifespan is three to five years."

"That's quite impressive."

"Then I did my job." He was still blushing.

She held out her hand for more peas. "I appreciate the effort. And I appreciate you fixing the fence. And getting the workbooks. I hate the way this has been for the last few weeks, and I'm really happy to be getting back on the same page. I think… I finally feel like the dark cloud is moving away and I'm feeling optimistic. I was truly worried it wouldn't ever get better."

"Me, too."

She recognized the regret in his eyes. They finished doling out the peas in comfortable silence. Oren put the empty bag in his backpack and slung it over his shoulder.

Chandler watched the ducks for a few more minutes, just enjoying their soft quacks and the way the ones in the water dove with their fluffy butts sticking up in the air. "We'll have to bring Maddie here soon."

They started back on the trail. A woodpecker flew across in front of them and landed on a tree. It immediately began hammering against the bark.

"How do they not get headaches?" Oren said.

She reached over and slipped her hand in his. "That can be your next fun fact project. Impress me with your knowledge of woodpeckers."

"I'm sensing a bird theme."

"Nah, you can do something different after that."

"Okay, what animal should I learn fun facts about?"

"How about chickens?" She realized what she said as soon as she'd said it, and they both started laughing until they wheezed. She took a step, then had to stop because tears blurred her vision from laughing so hard.

As soon as Oren could breathe, he teased, "When did chickens get declassified as birds?"

"I think it was the same time Pluto got declassified as a planet."

A small, bright yellow bird darted across the path.

Oren squeezed her hand. "That's also a bird."

She started laughing again. "What about that?" She pointed to a squirrel.

"Not a bird."

"That?" She pointed at a goose out on the creek.

"Bird."

She looked around and settled on a dog that was being walked. "That?"

"Not a bird."

"Are you sure?"

"Like eighty percent sure."

"That's pretty high."

The trail looped back around to the parking lot. Oren tossed his backpack into the trunk and opened Chandler's door.

She leaned back in her seat, content with the day.

"Having a good time?"

She smiled over at him. "The best."

"It's about to get even better."

Sitting up straight, she said, "Oh?"

"Yup." He drove to Caretti's Coffee Shop. "Thought you might like some caffeine."

"You're pulling out the big guns, aren't you?"

"Whatever I need to do."

They walked inside, and Oren made a beeline for the case of baked goods.

"We just had whoopie pies."

"So?" He tapped the glass. "I'm getting a piece of that."

Chandler came alongside him and rested her chin on his shoulder as she looked at the desserts. "Ooooooh, that looks amazing."

"Can I help you?" Samantha, the owners' oldest daughter, manned the counter.

"Two slices of the strawberry lemon cheesecake, please." Oren ordered for them.

"Oh my gosh, good choice. It's amazing. Ruth made it as an exclusive recipe. *So* good." She boxed the two slices of cheesecake. "Anything else?"

"A large jalapeño coconut iced coffee."

Oren added, "And a large vanilla coffee."

"You got it." Samantha turned away to make their coffees.

"I was thinking I'll take you home and help you get the plants in the ground, then I can entertain the kids until bedtime so you have time to do whatever."

He really *was* pulling out all the stops today. "That'd be great. Thanks."

Chandler pushed sweaty hair off her face as she sat back onto her heels. Her gardening glove undoubtedly left a streak of dirt across her forehead, but the new tomato and cucumber plants were in the ground and all the weeds were pulled and in a pile. "I'd say we've earned that cheesecake."

"For sure." Oren handed her his half-full bottle of water.

She drained it in two swallows. "There's more cold water in the garage fridge."

Oren got to his feet and held his hands down to pull her up.

"I'm going to feel this tomorrow, but it looks amazing, doesn't it?"

He nodded, surveying the garden plot. "Teamwork."

She held up her hand for a high five. "Makes the dream work."

Oren scooped the weeds into the wheelbarrow. "I'll dump these in the compost and grab a shower."

"I'll get water and put it in the kitchen for you." She jogged around the house to the garage and grabbed two bottles of water. She sat at the kitchen table and downed one of them. She was refilling it with water from the fridge dispenser when Oren came in. "Go ahead and take your shower, then I'll get mine."

After he took his shower and left to pick up the kids, Chandler took a long bath. It was nice to have time to pamper herself a bit. She shampooed and conditioned her hair and then just leaned back and relaxed. Her mind wandered over the day's events. They'd been productive in so many ways – not just getting the fence and the garden fixed, but she could feel in her heart they'd done some major repairs on their relationship, too.

She rinsed the conditioner out of her hair and wrapped herself in her favorite fuzzy towel. It was only seven o'clock, but she put on the yoga pants and tank top she'd wear to bed instead of bothering with "real" clothes.

More relaxed than she'd been in forever, Chandler settled onto the recliner and dug into the workbook while she pumped her milk. She was just finishing up when she heard the garage door opening.

Maddie trudged into the living room and yawned, a huge, soul-deep yawn. "Love you, Mama," she said, then slowly lumbered up the stairs.

Oren came in and handed Finn to her.

"Big day?"

"Elliott said they took all the kids to the park and then out for ice cream. Kept them outside and running all day long."

"Brilliant. We should take notes."

"Done." He leaned down and kissed her forehead.

She smoothed Finn's fine hair. "Did he eat?"

"Yeah, I fed him right before we came home. He'll probably need changed, though. Do you want me to do that or put Maddie to bed?"

"You can have diaper duty. I'll go up with her." She passed Finn back to him and went upstairs.

Maddie crashed on her bed, fully dressed, face-down.

Chandler tugged her boots off and set them on the floor, then rolled Maddie onto her back. She promptly rolled onto her side, never waking up.

She ran a hand over Maddie's tangled hair and had to smile at the streak of dirt across her forehead. Apparently Monday would be laundry day for the bedding. She removed Maddie's tutu and pulled the blanket up to her shoulder before kissing her cheek and tucking Princess Giraffe in beside her.

She gently closed the bedroom door and padded back

downstairs. Oren had put Finn in his swing. "I figured he'd probably need to eat again before going to bed for the night."

"Probably." She sat cross-legged on the couch with her book, workbook, and a pen. "Ready?"

"Almost." He disappeared into the hallway, then reappeared a minute later with the slices of cheesecake and two forks. "Our reward for all the work we got done today."

"Ooooh, it looks amazing." She took her plate and fork and leaned back. "Did you get a chance to read the first chapter?"

"Yeah, but I didn't do much with the workbook."

"I started, but didn't get too far."

He sat on the opposite end of the couch and flipped his workbook open.

Chandler watched his eyes skim the pages.

"It looks like our first fun activity is to draw a fence or find a picture of our ideal fence and paste the picture in here. What's the point of that?"

Chandler swallowed her bite of cheesecake. "First of all, this is the best cheesecake I've ever had in my life. I'm glad Ruth is still baking, even though she retired from the bakery. Second of all, it makes sense to me, if we're going all in on the whole fence analogy. I think it's so you can see if you both end up choosing the same type of fence so you can see if you're starting out on the same page."

"I guess." He sounded skeptical.

"Do you want to draw or paste? I have some magazines we can cut pictures from if you want."

"Nah, I'll wing it."

They went silent, eating their cheesecake and sketching their fences. Chandler finished her cheesecake and put the finishing touches on her picket fence. She was drawing in a few sprays of grass when Oren said, "Done?"

"Yup. Reveal on the count of three." She held her workbook facing herself and prepared to turn it around. "One. Two."

Oren said, "Three."

They both flipped their notebooks and started to laugh.

They'd both drawn picket fences.

Maybe they were on the same page after all.

Chapter Forty

It was weird how much happiness it gave him to see that he and Chandler had drawn the same kind of fence. He asked, "What does a picket fence mean to you?"

She leaned back and stretched her legs out toward him. "It means comfortable and homey to me. It's not isolating because you can see in and out, but it does keep a visible barrier around the property and it requires effort to come in and out. You?"

"Probably the same. It's welcoming. Like we're not trying to keep people out, but it's clear where the property lines are." He still thought the fence metaphor was a little much, but he had to admit it made sense in this context.

"In my mind, it's also easy. It's easy to maintain and keep up. It's not a ton of work and effort, but it does need repainted every once in a while."

"And it's not indestructible. Sometimes there's a downed tree that breaks part of the fence. So it's probably a good idea to walk the perimeter on a regular basis to check for weak spots."

"What do you think we can do to check in on our fence?"

He looked down at his drawing. "Well, for starters, I can stop letting my busyness get in the way of making sure my wife is getting everything she needs to be healthy."

She blinked a few times. "And I can ask for help."

He reached over and rested his hand on her leg. "I'm sorry I didn't see how much of a hard time you were having. It shouldn't be your sole responsibility to let me know when you need help."

"I appreciate that so much. I thought about reaching out to Ashley a few times, but it was so hard to just put one foot in front of the other I couldn't even pick up the phone."

"Maybe we should put it on the calendar to check in with each other once a week or once a month or something."

"That's a great idea." The best part of the idea? It meant she was looking forward. Together. With him. "And not just checking in, but really talking. And having intentional date nights."

Finn stirred and fussed in the bassinet.

"Want me to get him?"

"Thanks, but I'll take him upstairs and nurse him so I can get him right in the crib when he's done." She stretched and got up to get the baby. "I'm thinking it's time to move him to his nursery."

"Sure." He didn't love the idea, but realistically, the monitor stayed right beside the bed, and he wasn't far away. And to be fair, Chandler had kids hanging off her or crawling on her all day, every day, so having the master bedroom back as an adult space would probably be a good thing for her.

"I also might not nurse him as long as I did Maddie."

Oren's brows rose. "Oh?"

She bounced Finn. "I want my body back. I was thinking of cutting back and just doing bedtime and maybe morning. But I haven't decided anything for sure. We'll see."

Oren got up and rubbed Finn's back, and kissed his head. "Whatever you decide, I support you." He meant it. Sure, he had an opinion on breastfeeding, he thought it was wonderful, but it wasn't his body, and as long as the baby was fed and healthy, what did it really matter?

The way her eyes lit up with surprise and pleasure told him he'd said exactly the right thing.

"I'm going to head out. I'll see you tomorrow after work?"

"Sounds good." He leaned in and gave her a quick kiss on the lips. She smiled and erased the second guessing about whether it had been a good idea. "Sweet dreams."

"You, too. Text me when you get there."

The whole way to Ashley and Elliott's, he sang along with the radio. He tiptoed into the house and heard noises from upstairs. He assumed everyone was getting ready for bed, so he locked the doors and went to the basement.

His phone vibrated with an incoming call. He smiled, thinking it might be Chandler.

Nope. His smile vanished.

He hesitated, but swiped to answer the call. "Hi, Mom."

"Oren. Your grandfather's birthday is Wednesday. He wants us all to go to DiMaggio's for dinner Wednesday evening." Her tone was brusque.

"I'll check with Chandler and see if we can make it."

She gave a rude snort. "She let you back in the house?"

He closed his eyes and imagined his picket fence. "I'm not discussing that with you."

"Oh, so she's still keeping you out." Somehow, she sounded victorious. Like she'd won something.

How sick was it that she'd consider his broken marriage a win? He'd been so, so, so blind. Never again. Fences. Boundaries. They went up now. "What time Wednesday?"

She changed tactics. "You need to be able to talk about

these things. It's not good to hold those negative feelings inside."

Oof. She certainly didn't hold anything negative inside when it came to Chandler, did she? "What time Wednesday?" he repeated.

"I only want what's best for you."

"Time."

"Six thirty," she snapped.

"I'll text you tomorrow and let you know if we can come."

"Well, it's for your side of the family, so I assume you'll magically have plans."

Fence, fence, fence. They'd missed one get-together five years ago to go to Chandler's cousin's wedding, and that somehow turned into them "always" blowing off his family's gatherings.

"I'll let you know. Good night."

The line went dead.

He pulled in a deep breath and blew it out. His phone vibrated with an incoming text.

Elliott.

You home?

Yeah, I locked the front door. Night.

Elliott texted back a thumbs up emoji.

Oren swiped over to the text thread with Chandler and typed,

Got home. Birthday party for Pappy Tom Wednesday at DiMaggio's. They reed head count.

The three dots blinked a few times, then her message popped up.

Ok. You're in charge of getting a card.

His shoulders sagged. Ugh. He was kind of hoping she'd have a reason they couldn't go. Oh, well.

Ok. Sweet dreams. Love you.

Love you too.

He couldn't stop the grin from spreading across his face. Right there. He'd endure a million books about fence metaphors and making changes to his schedule for that. It was the most important thing in the world.

Chapter Forty-One

Chandler woke up early Monday morning and got a head start on stripping her sheets and the sheets on Finn's crib. As soon as Maddie woke up, she stripped her bed and took the load to the laundry room.

"Breakfast first or bath first?"

Maddie scowled. "I don't want a bath."

"Too bad. You're still sweaty and dirty from yesterday."

She crossed her arms. "I like sweaty."

"You also like taking baths."

"No."

"What if I let you use Mommy's big tub?"

Maddie surrendered that battle. "FINE."

As Chandler suspected, Maddie was perfectly happy once she got in the big garden tub. She played with her Princess Poppy bath toys while Princess Giraffe sat on the counter and supervised.

Finn was fed and changed and content in his bouncy seat while Chandler sat on the edge of the tub and tapped out a to do list on her phone.

"Is Jared coming today?"

Chandler checked the time. "Yup. He'll be here at nine, so you have a little while to play."

Maddie beamed. Whatever bad mood she was in earlier seemed to vanish.

At nine on the dot, Isobel and Jared came to the front door. Jared took the kids while Chandler and Isobel went downstairs. By noon, the curtains for the theater were almost done.

"We'll finish these hems after lunch and then I'll see if Oren can go to the theater tonight and we'll start hanging them."

"Can we go see them tomorrow?"

"Sure." She felt bad she hadn't thought to include Isobel. Duh, it only made sense she'd want to see the finished product she'd had a hand in making. An idea took shape. "Do you think you and Jared could come along to the theater tomorrow evening? Oren has practice, but I need to go through the costumes and props. If Jared could entertain the kids while you help me go through the stuff, that would be amazing."

Isobel's eyes were wide. "That would be fun to see all the behind-the-scenes stuff. The one homeschool group I was in put on a play, but we moved right before tryouts so I didn't get to participate. And then after we moved here none of the groups did a play."

"There are homeschool groups? I kind of assumed homeschool families kind of stayed to themselves?" It made sense, but she'd never given it any thought.

"Not at all." Isobel shook her head. "I mean, sure, some do, but there are groups that do all kinds of things. Some groups go on field trips, or there's a really cool science nature group that works on conservation stuff, and there's art groups. My parents had a religious studies group since they're both missionaries. It was pretty cool."

Learn something new every day, right? "Maybe you should

mention this to Gretchen. We're always looking for volunteers, and there are tons of learning opportunities in the theater."

Isobel nodded enthusiastically. "I bet like carpentry for sets would be popular."

"That's a great idea, Isobel." Chandler made a mental note to talk to Rowan. He was a master carpenter and did a lot of volunteer work for the theater. He might have some ideas for projects a younger group could manage.

They went upstairs. Chandler opened a bowl of macaroni salad and set out bread and sandwich ingredients on the counter. She made Maddie's ham and cheese sandwich and cut it diagonally, then put a scoop of macaroni salad on her plate and set it on the table.

Jared popped her up in the air and into her booster seat. "Yum, your lunch looks delicious. I'm going to have the same thing."

Maddie beamed and dug into her macaroni salad.

Chandler made her own plate, then sat with Finn in one arm while the other was free so she could eat.

"So we're going to the theater tomorrow night," Isobel told Jared. She launched into a monologue about the curtains.

When she was finished, Jared simply said, "Okay."

Chandler hid a smile behind her sandwich. They were adorable together. Now nineteen and heading off to college soon, she wondered if their relationship would last. They'd been best friends since they were fourteen, and dating since sixteen. So young, but they'd both had enough life experiences – good and bad – to rival any thirty year old.

When lunch was over, she told Jared, "We should be done with these curtains in half an hour. Then we'll fold them up and if you could help put them in the back of my car, that'd be great."

"Sure." He took Finn from her and said to Maddie, "Want to do some sidewalk chalk?"

"Yeah!" Maddie ran off to get the plastic bucket with chunky pieces of colorful chalk.

Chandler couldn't help but marvel at how good Jared was with the kids. She couldn't have asked for a better babysitter. It would stink when he left for college.

Back downstairs, she hovered behind Isobel as she carefully fed the curtains into the sewing machine. The heavy fabric didn't move easily, so she helped keep it in a manageable position so Isobel could focus on keeping the hem straight.

When Isobel was done sewing, she glanced up over her shoulder. "Is that good?"

"Perfect. Now snip the threads right at the fabric. Yes, right there. Great." She lifted the panel up and took it to the main island, then took the final panel over to the sewing machine. "Last one."

Isobel finished the last hem and snipped the thread. "I can't wait to see them up."

"Me, either." She pulled a plastic bin out from under her work table. "These are the rope ties I mentioned. They'll be perfect." She laid one of the golden ropes against the velvet fabric.

"Oooooh, yeah, I like that a lot." Isobel held one of the ropes up. "Some of the fringes are kind of sad, though."

"Good catch. Let's trim the odd ones off."

Ten minutes later, the rope fringes were once again uniform and back in the bin. Chandler and Isobel worked together to fold the curtains. When all the panels were neatly piled, Chandler went into the storage room to find large plastic tubs to put them in.

"Good work, Isobel. I'm really proud of you."

Isobel blushed. "Thanks. You're a good teacher."

After Jared loaded the curtains into the car, he and Isobel left.

Pleased with a super productive day's work, Chandler tossed the wet sheets into the dryer and had Maddie help her gather a load of towels to wash. After that, she loaded Finn into the stroller and took the kids to the park to enjoy the perfect weather. Hot, but not too hot. Nice breeze, just enough puffy clouds to keep the sun from being too harsh. She smiled as she glanced into the back yard, where the fence was fixed and the broken branches no longer littered the ground.

A handful of neighborhood kids ran around as their moms stood around or occupied the benches. Maddie took off to join Kinsley at the merry-go-round. Ugh. That meant Shannon was nearby.

Chandler smiled around gritted teeth as Shannon waved at her. She waved back, then busied herself getting Finn strapped into the baby carrier so he could look around.

"Chandler! It's so nice to see you out and about."

What the heck was she talking about? "Excuse me?"

Shannon sat on the bench beside Grace, another neighborhood mom whose twins, Rupert and Ellis, played in the sandbox. "I just meant that I heard you were unwell. I'm glad you seem to be doing better."

Grace looked surprised. "Oh, were you sick?"

Chandler's brow creased. "Not at all."

"Really?"

Shannon was poking her last nerve. Chandler shook her head and said, "I'm not sure what you're talking about. Especially since we just saw each other here last week, and then again over at the big park on Saturday, where you asked my husband for his number." She wasn't in the mood to tiptoe around this woman's nonsense.

Grace gasped.

"Just to coordinate playdates." Shannon rolled her eyes. "But you guys are separated anyway, so if you don't want him, what does it matter?"

Grace's jaw dropped. "Shannon!"

"You know what, Shannon? Piss off." She turned and walked toward the merry-go-round and sat on the bench at the far side of the park, seething.

She was furious at Shannon, and then furious at Oren, because in her imagination, he wouldn't react properly if the roles were reversed. She pulled out her phone and scrolled angrily through social media, which only made her feel worse. Bad news interspersed with picture-perfect photos from perfect families. It was a recipe for a bad mood, so she closed the app and opened her camera instead.

She snapped several photos of Maddie, spinning around and around, her hair flowing, laughing, exuding pure joy at the moment. That's exactly what she needed to focus on.

She texted one of the photos to Oren, who immediately responded with a heart emoji. Then she texted him that the curtains were finished and asked if they could hang them that evening.

Sure. Can't wait to see you.

It took the edge off her annoyance at Imaginary Oren. It wasn't fair to be mad at him for how he may or may not hypothetically behave. Of course, it hadn't been fair for him to be mad at her for real — she took a deep breath and cut off that train of thought. There would be no moving forward if she kept beating the same dead horse. She glanced over at Shannon. Maybe she could beat her instead. Okay, not really, but holy cow was that woman something else.

She tapped into her phone.

Ashley picked up on the third ring and listened to the entire story. "She *what*?"

"I know, right? What kind of nasty bridge troll acts like that?"

"I wonder where she's getting her information. That's so weird." Ashley made a gasping noise like she'd just thought of something. "I half wonder if she knows Janice, since it sounds like the crap she'd say. Hang on."

Chandler waited. Was that even possible?

A minute later, Ashley said, "Yup. Shannon's mom and Janice are like BFFs or something."

"What? How do you know?"

"Facebook."

"You're a genius." She'd unfollowed Janice so long ago it didn't even occur to her to check there.

"It's why you love me."

"One reason among too many to count."

"Should I send her a message? Tell her to stop being a sleazy skank? I'll do it," Ashley offered sincerely.

"No!" Chandler laughed. "I appreciate the support, though." A throat clearing drew her attention, so she ended the call.

Grace stood nearby and gave an uncomfortable smile. "Hi. Chandler. I'm so sorry about all that." She waved her hand to encompass the situation. "I just wanted to tell you I had nothing to do with any of it. I try to stay away from the drama and gossip, but I feel like I was kind of caught in it here."

"No, it's okay."

Grace continued carefully. "This is none of my business, but since it was kind of thrown out there, if it's true that you're having health struggles, or if you and Oren are having problems and you need someone to talk to, my door is always open. Chuck and I separated for a while last year. We got through it."

"Thank you. I appreciate that. My health is fine, and we're working through some issues right now, but we're definitely moving in a positive direction."

"Good. I'll keep you in our prayers."

"Thanks." She appreciated the sentiment. Usually when she heard that, it seemed rote or forced, but Grace was genuine.

"Well, I have to get the boys and head home, but the offer stands. If you ever need to talk, I'm a ready ear."

"Thank you, Grace."

Grace bent down and gave Finn a big smile. "Bye, handsome guy."

Finn rewarded her with a giant, toothless smile.

"I love that age. See you later."

"Bye."

Maddie had moved on from the merry-go-round to the swings. She'd gotten on the seat and was furiously pumping her legs, trying to get some movement.

Kinsley was nowhere to be seen, and neither was her mother. Good. Hopefully, they'd gone home and would stay there. Or even better, maybe they went home to pack for a move to Timbuktu.

Chandler walked over and pushed Maddie on the swing a few times. "Okay, let's head home and get cleaned up before Daddy gets home."

Chapter Forty-Two

After dinner, Oren drove them to the theater.

Chandler wrung her hands the whole way over. "I'm so anxious to make sure everything is the right size and hangs the way it's supposed to."

"I'm sure they're perfect." He'd be shocked if the curtains had a single flaw. Chandler was meticulous about her work, and she'd have been even more careful since she was teaching Isobel.

While Chandler wrangled the kids, Oren schlepped the heavy plastic bins inside. "This everything?"

"Yeah."

"I'll get the ladder." He went to the back and brought the ladder out. He held it while Chandler climbed up to the scaffolding catwalk where she could access the hooks for the curtains.

"Okay, send the first one up," she called down.

Oren put the first tote on the dumbwaiter and used the heavy rope to hoist it to the platform. He kept an eye on Maddie, who was sitting in the front row coloring next to Finn's stroller. Soon, all the curtains were up with Chandler.

She called down, "Clear the area. I'm going to start dropping these."

"Got it." Oren hopped off the stage and sat with Maddie.

"Mommy's up high."

"Yup. Keep watching. The curtains are going to start falling down."

"Why?"

"So Mommy can hang the new ones she just made."

"Oh." Maddie went back to coloring.

The first heavy velvet curtain landed in a puddle on the stage with a soft *whump* and a plume of dust.

Chandler worked her way across the catwalk, releasing all of the panels.

"Holy cow, these things are dusty," Oren called up to her.

"Well, when's the last time we had them cleaned? That was probably four years ago." She crossed back to the other side of the catwalk. "Moment of truth."

Oren watched her clip the curtains onto the hooks and rods. She steadily worked her way across the stage.

"Okay, don't look."

He put his hand up to block his view of the stage and instead looked at Maddie's coloring book. "Not looking," he called.

"Why aren't you looking?"

"Mommy wants to put all the curtains where they belong before she shows them to me." He heard the flutter of falling fabric, but resisted the urge to peek.

"Coming down."

"Be careful," Oren warned.

A moment later, he heard footsteps on the stage.

"Almost ready. Don't look yet."

"Okay." He heard her scrambling back and forth across the

stage, then saw her feet as she came down the steps and walked into the aisle.

"I think that's about as good as it gets," she said.

"Can I look?"

"I hope you're happy with them."

"Can I look?"

"Yeah, go ahead."

He stood up and shuffled to the aisle, his hand still covering his view. "Ready?"

"Yup. Look."

He moved his hand and stared up at the stage. There were no words to properly convey his awe. Chandler had made a new backdrop curtain, the curtains that would open and close during performances, and a stationery set of decorative drapes at the sides of the stage that were gathered with gold ropes.

"What do you think?"

"I think you're amazing. These look fantastic." They really did. The deep red velvet was much richer and more luxurious than the old faded curtains she'd just taken down. "You outdid yourself, honey. It's just incredible."

"I feel like I should have gathered them more over there." She pointed.

He grabbed her hand and pressed a kiss to her fingers. "Nope. They're perfect. I mean it."

"Princess Giraffe says the curtains are pretty, Mommy."

Chandler scooped Maddie up and hugged her. "Well, thank you, Princess Giraffe. What does Princess Maddie think?"

She nodded vigorously. "Pretty."

Oren snapped a few pictures with his phone. "I should have taken before pictures, but I didn't even think of it."

"Oh, darn, neither did I."

He teased, "Why don't you put the old ones back up so we can get pictures? Then we'll put these back up."

"Ha, ha. Very funny. Speaking of the old curtains, help me get them folded up. We'll put them in those bins… oh, darn."

"Left the bins up top, didn't you?"

"Yep."

Oren watched the ladder while Chandler climbed back up to the catwalk and put the empty bins onto the dumbwaiter. He lowered the platform while she climbed back down. They folded the dusty curtains and got them into the bins. "Are we taking these along home?"

"Yeah. I'll put them in the storage room until I can figure out where to get them cleaned."

He put the bins in the back of the car, then loaded Finn's stroller in the little bit of space that was left while Chandler buckled both kids in their seats.

Back home, they got the kids in bed and settled onto the couch.

Oren said, "I was reading ahead, and I found something that I can't stop thinking about."

"Oh?" Chandler shifted toward him.

It had been on his mind for days. "There's a thing he called 'overshadowing' and it really jumped out at me."

"I didn't read any more yet. What's overshadowing?"

"It's basically when one person does something so outrageously bad that it overshadows anything the other person does, even if they're also doing something bad. Like the difference between stealing a candy bar versus robbing a bank."

"Oh. That makes sense. But why is it sticking with you?"

"Well, I know this book emphasizes how both parties contribute to the positives and the negatives of every relationship, and I think overall, that's true. But what got us here, what brought this all to the boiling point… that was all me. What I did by acting like a jerk about the money and by even suggesting there was a boyfriend – which I absolutely never actually thought for a second and I don't know why I ever said that – and basically attacking your integrity was so egregious and over the top that it overshadows anything you might have done to contribute. I just want you to know I recognize that and I acknowledge it and I'm sorry."

She reached over and took his hand. "I appreciate that. And I've thought a lot about all the things leading up to the boiling point, and I guess I agree with you. We both have work to do with mending our fences, but I've been feeling really defensive because there's nothing I could, would, or should have done differently in all those blowups. So yeah, I accept that we both have some maintenance to do on our fence, but you were the tree that knocked over a chunk of it. And your mom was probably the gust of wind."

He swallowed hard and managed a half-smirk. "Are you calling my mother a windbag?"

Chandler laughed. "Hey. If the shoe fits, right?" She slowly grew serious. "I don't think you can understand how much it means to me that you've accepted that responsibility. It makes it a lot easier to forgive and believe it won't happen again."

"Good. Because it won't." He reached over and tucked a strand of hair behind her ear. The way her eyes drifted shut at his touch made him ache with impatience for getting them back to normal.

Tuesday dragged and it took forever before he picked up Chandler and the kids. Jared and Isobel followed them to the theater.

Isobel's voice echoed throughout the theater. "OH MY GOSH! They look so good!"

Chandler agreed. "You did a great job."

"You did all the hard stuff."

"Still, you were a huge help."

The door creaked open, then slammed shut. Gretchen and Alan bustled into the theater.

Gretchen's gasp filled the air. "Look at that! You did those?"

Chandler shrugged. "Isobel and I made them. Then Oren and I came in last night and hung them."

Gretchen grabbed her in a big hug.

Alan whistled. "Those look fantastic."

"Thanks."

Oren couldn't be more proud of his wife. He knew she was talented, but it was always nice when other people recognized it.

She said to Gretchen, "Isobel's going to help me go through the costumes and props and see what needs fixed and whatnot."

"Awesome. The rhinestones on the queen's costume are pretty loose, and one of the crowns is in pretty rough shape."

"Okay. I'll pull them out. And if you have a few minutes, Isobel had some thoughts about involving some local home-school groups in the theater."

"Oh? Let's go chat while I get my stuff organized." Gretchen led Isobel down the aisle and up onto the stage where the table and chairs were set up.

Oren put his arm around Chandler's waist. "Told you they'd love the curtains."

"I'm glad."

The rest of the troupe filtered in over the next few minutes.

"I'm going to head back to the costumes." She pulled a notebook and pen out of her bag and headed backstage.

Gretchen showed Isobel where to go, then sat at the head of the table. "Oren, I cast you as Marcellus. Is that okay?"

He nodded. "Perfect. Thank you." He was relieved. He'd assumed Gretchen would give him a tiny bit part, but Marcellus was significant, although a much smaller part than King Claudius. In other words, the perfect compromise.

Chapter Forty-Three

Chandler and Isobel finished going through the costumes and props and ended up with a bin full of things that needed fixed or replaced.

"You about finished?" Oren popped his head into the prop room.

"Yep, we're done. Can you take this to the car, please?"

Oren took the bin while Chandler pushed the stroller, Isobel carried Finn, and Jared walked with Maddie.

"Thanks for coming tonight. You were both such a huge help."

"No problem," Jared said.

"See you Thursday," Isobel said as she climbed into Jared's car.

Oren slid into the driver's seat. "She's not helping you out tomorrow?"

"They're both working at General Custard's tomorrow while a bunch of people are out for some food vendor thing or something." She couldn't exactly remember what Isobel had told her because she was talking *really* fast. "On the upside, it'll give me the whole day to mentally prepare for dinner with your family."

"Yeah, I'm not looking forward to it much myself."

"It'll be nice to see Pappy Tom. We haven't seen him since Easter." She tried to find the bright side.

"Definitely."

She yawned and leaned back against her seat. It had been a busy day, and she was ready for bed.

Wednesday crawled by. Probably because each passing moment added to the dread in Chandler's gut. By the time Oren came to pick her and the kids up, she felt like she wanted to barf. Janice had undoubtedly shared her opinions and lies about Chandler to the whole family, so she had no idea what sort of vipers nest she'd be walking into.

They pulled into the DiMaggio's parking lot and unloaded the kids. Chandler carried Finn, holding him like a shield in front of her.

Oren's hand on her back gave her some comfort, but that small voice in her head wondered if he was going to end up leaving her to fend for herself at some point.

The hostess led them to the private room where most of the family was already seated.

Oren's aunt Cindy immediately reached for Finn. "Oh, you're such a big boy, aren't you?"

"Happy birthday, Pappy," Oren said.

"Good to see you." Tom's warm smile included Chandler.

Janice and Theo were the last to arrive. Thankfully, they were seated at the far end of the table. Janice refused to even look in their direction.

The waitress brought baskets of bread and took everyone's drink orders.

Pappy Tom announced, "Everyone get whatever you want. This is on me."

"That's silly," Janice snapped. "You should get what you want on your birthday, not buy for everyone else."

"What I want is for everyone to enjoy a good meal as my treat. I won't hear anything else about it."

Chandler hid a smile behind her brown leather menu. It wasn't often Janice was put in her place. It was nice to see Theo's dad wasn't putting up with any nonsense.

The waitress came back with drinks and took the food orders. Chandler picked the seafood lasagna. Not the cheapest thing on the menu, but not one of the most expensive, either. Once they were relieved of their menus, Oren reached under the table and squeezed her hand.

She squeezed back.

Cindy said, "Oh, my, somebody needs a diaper change. Here. Hand me the diaper bag. I'll take him to the restroom."

"I'll get him," Chandler said, standing.

"Don't be silly. Give me the bag."

Reluctantly, Chandler gave Cindy the diaper bag.

Janice muttered, "I don't think she ever changes her own baby."

Theo let out a heavy sigh. "Can you not?"

From the corner of her eye, Chandler saw Oren was talking with his uncle Rick and most likely hadn't heard anything.

She squeezed her hands together on her lap, sitting straight and willing the time to speed up.

It didn't.

A few minutes later, Cindy came back with Finn, who was starting to get fussy. "I think he's getting hungry."

Chandler took the baby and smiled at Cindy. "Me, too."

She'd specifically worn her most discreet nursing top that let absolutely nothing get exposed as she attached Finn.

"At the table!" Janice mock-whispered. "It's indecent."

Oren definitely heard that one. He shook his head. "Uh-uh. We're not doing this."

Cindy and Rick looked back and forth between Oren and Janice. Chandler tried to disappear into the background.

Maddie held up her placemat. "I drawed Pappy Tom."

"Wow, Maddie, this looks just like me." Tom beamed at the purple circle with randomly placed green lines like it was a Monet. "I'm going to put this on my fridge."

Maddie grinned.

The waitress came in with appetizers, so Oren asked for another placemat.

Janice scowled disapprovingly.

Chandler decided to avert her eyes and just not even look at that side of the table.

"Is Maddie starting preschool in the fall?" Cindy asked.

"We haven't decided yet. She barely hits the birthday cutoff, so we're considering waiting until next fall."

Janice said, "She'll fall behind."

Cindy, completely unaware of the tension, shook her head. "I think she'll be fine either way. Her little brain is learning so much right now whether she's at home or if she goes to preschool for a few hours a week."

Chandler saw Janice's eyes widen, then narrow. She did not appreciate being contradicted, especially about something that landed in Chandler's favor, no matter how petty. "Well. I've read the research and children – especially girls – Madelyn's age should begin getting a formal education so they can have good careers and not just stay home and pop out babies."

Still oblivious, Cindy made a face. "What? Nobody does

that. Besides, Chandler used to work with little ones, I think she'd know what's best."

"Hmm."

Oren opened his mouth, but the waitress and a second server came into the room and placed the entrees in front of everyone. He leaned over and said, "If you want to go, we can go. We don't have to tolerate this."

"Hopefully she'll focus on her food and we can eat in peace." She doubted it, but the lasagna smelled amazing.

He took Finn from her arms. "You can eat with both hands for a change," he said with a wink.

Surprisingly, the meal passed with general conversation about the food. Everything was fine until Theo said, "Dad? You okay?"

Chandler looked at Tom, whose eyes bulged. His face was an alarming shade of red. "He's choking!" She jumped to her feet. Her chair fell to the floor behind her and she ran around the table. Behind Tom, she said, "Stand up if you can."

He struggled to his feet, one frail fist pounding the table, the other clawing at his own throat.

Chandler gripped him, planting her fist in his sternum, and jerked back and upwards. His arms flailed. She used every ounce of her strength and heaved her fists up under his ribcage once, twice, three times.

The third time, something flew across the room and Tom sucked in a labored breath. His knees buckled, and he went to the floor, pulling Chandler with him. Slowly, the surroundings filtered back into her consciousness. Oren, Rick, and Theo pulled the table back and crowded around. Cindy was on the phone with 9-1-1.

Chandler was partially under Tom, who was struggling to get up. "Stay still, it's okay." She gripped his shoulders and extracted her leg from under him, then eased him to the ground. "Take it easy."

He grabbed her arm. Tears slipped out of the corners of his eyes. "Chandler—"

"Shh, don't try to talk. Just breathe for a minute."

"Dad?" Cindy kneeled behind Chandler and rested a hand on her shoulder to peer at her dad. "The ambulance is on the way." Her voice was thick.

"Bah. Get me up," he rasped.

Theo and Rick helped him up to sit in his chair.

Chandler stood up.

Tom grimaced and put a hand on his middle. "You've got a grip."

"Sorry."

"What did you do?" Janice demanded.

Cindy yelled, "She saved his life is what she did!" and burst into tears.

Rick came over and pulled his wife into his arms.

All eyes were on Chandler.

She was grateful when the EMTs rushed into the room.

"I don't need to go to no hospital," Tom argued weakly.

"Yes, you do," Theo said. "You need to get checked out."

Rick and Cindy agreed wholeheartedly.

Chandler felt awful. She'd felt something give with that last thrust, and she was afraid she'd broken one of Tom's ribs. Judging from the way he complied with the EMTs loading him onto the stretcher, she figured he was in a great deal of pain.

An oxygen mask was placed over his face, and they wheeled him out. Theo said, "We'll follow him to the hospital." He and Janice walked out alongside him.

As soon as the stretcher was out of the room, the waitress came back with a concerned smile. "Is there anything I can do?"

Rick gestured to the table. "Can we get this boxed up, please?"

"Of course." She hurried from the room and came back a minute later with takeout containers.

Cindy asked, "Do you have a pen?"

"Sure." The waitress handed her one.

As they boxed up the food, Cindy wrote names on the lids.

The waitress left again and came back with bags to put the containers in. "Um, this is super awkward, but who gets the check?"

Rick held out his hand. "I'll take it, thank you." He stuck his card in the folder and handed it back.

Chandler packed up Maddie's crayons while Oren held her. She wasn't crying, but she looked upset.

"Are you going to the hospital?" Oren asked.

Cindy nodded. "Yeah. We'll head right over." She gripped Chandler's arms. Tears filled her eyes again. "Thank you."

Chandler hugged her, but she was glad when Cindy let go and she and Rick left. She took one more glance around the room to make sure nothing was left behind. Maddie's placemat drawing lay on the floor under Tom's chair. She picked it up and put it in the diaper bag.

Chapter Forty-Four

Oren was worried about Chandler. She hadn't said a word the whole way home. When they pulled in the driveway, she pasted what he knew was a fake smile on her face and got Maddie out of her seat.

Inside, he encouraged Chandler to go change and get comfortable before he headed to the hospital. He put Finn in his crib and when Chandler was cuddled up reading to Maddie, he left.

There was an unsettling, nervous energy that filled the waiting room. His parents and aunt and uncle sat huddled in one corner of the room. His mother looked up. "I'm not surprised you came alone."

"What?"

"She shattered two of his ribs! They just came out and told us he needs more x-rays to make sure nothing else was damaged."

Cindy's face reddened. "Stop it, Janice."

"Don't defend her. She probably hurt him on purpose."

Cindy went to her feet. "Shut up."

Janice stood and faced her sister-in-law. "I will not." She turned to Oren. "She never should have been there tonight. If she hadn't come, your grandfather's ribs wouldn't be crushed."

"She saved his life!" Cindy yelled for the second time that evening.

"He's going to be worse off with broken bones at his age. She should have left him alone!"

The crack of Cindy's hand across Janice's face brought an abrupt halt to everything. Oren froze. Theo and Rick both froze.

"Get out." Cindy's voice was dead calm.

"How *dare*—"

Theo yanked Janice's arm and pulled her away.

Oren didn't know what to say or do.

Eventually, Rick cleared his throat. "Probably shouldn't have slapped her."

Cindy rubbed her palm. "I suppose not, but all I heard was her saying Dad would be better off dead than with cracked ribs."

"That's not what she meant, sweetheart." Rick pulled her against him and rubbed her back.

Cindy sniffled. "You know what? I've spent four decades giving her the benefit of the doubt and excusing the hateful things she says. No more." She turned to Oren. "I'm sorry. I know that's your mother, but she's not a very nice person. Don't let her poison that precious family of yours."

Oren's throat thickened. His jaw tightened, and before he knew it, tears streamed down his face.

Cindy grabbed him in a hug, and Rick squeezed his shoulder.

Words spilled like an overturned bucket. Everything she – and then he – had done over the past few weeks tumbled out.

When he was done, they didn't look surprised. Rick was the first to speak. "We're here to support you any way we can."

Cindy patted his cheek. "It'll work out. I saw the way you two looked at each other tonight."

He wanted to believe she was right.

Chapter Forty-Five

Chandler's phone dinged close to midnight. It was a text from Oren.

> Rick & Cindy taking Pappy Tom home.
> Cracked rib, nothing serious.

> That's wonderful news!!

She still felt horribly guilty about injuring him. She'd spent all evening second guessing herself. If her hands had been properly placed, his ribs shouldn't have cracked. It was a lot harder to perform the maneuver perfectly on a real, moving, panicking person, but she still had trouble giving herself grace.

She eventually fell into a fitful sleep until Finn's squawking through the monitor woke her somewhere around four. She sleepily made her way to the nursery and slumped in the rocking chair to nurse. When he'd had his fill, he grunted, balled up his fists, and stretched his little legs out. His beet-red face terrified her for a second, so similar to Tom's last night.

"He's just pooping. He's just pooping," she whispered to herself. A few seconds later, the awful stench confirmed it.

Finn relaxed, pleased with his output, while Chandler set to the task of getting him cleaned up and changed and back into the crib.

She wasn't sure if the smell still clinging to her was just stuck in her nose, or if she was wearing some of it. So there, at four thirty in the morning, she crawled in the shower instead of back into bed.

She wrapped her hair in a towel and pulled her favorite big towel around her body, then sat in the comfy reading chair in her bedroom and read through the next chapter in their book. Just as Oren had said, it covered overshadowing behavior. The next chapter covered abuse and infidelity, so she skimmed through it. Thankfully, their problems weren't in that realm.

The next chapter was about rediscovery. She read with interest about ways to rediscover each other, and essentially rediscover the buried treasure of your relationship's foundation. Here, the fence analogies got a little silly, but she appreciated the concept. Each chunk of foundation should be "fenced" – by which he meant protected and valued. It was an idea Chandler could get behind, but Ashley had been right. He went a little too far with his theme, but his perspective was spot on.

She must have dozed at some point, because she woke with a start. The book was on the floor and Finn cooed through the monitor. She rubbed her eyes. The clock said six thirty, but it still felt way too early to get up.

Maddie disagreed.

Chandler heard her in her little bathroom, singing the Princess Poppy theme song.

Ready or not, the day had dawned.

It was an uneventful day that just rolled along at a lazy pace. The weather was dreary and warm. There was a brief break in the drizzly rain after lunch, so Chandler sat on the porch with Finn while Maddie ran off a bazillion watts of energy, getting herself good and muddy in the process.

Oren stopped by that evening after practice to get the kids to bed. They sat on the couch together. Chandler scooched over against him and rested her head on his shoulder while his arm went around her.

"I talked to Pappy Tom this afternoon," he said.

"Is he okay? Really? I feel so bad. I must have been in the wrong position because I shouldn't have cracked his ribs."

Oren squeezed her shoulder. "Chan. You saved his life. Believe me, he's not upset about a cracked rib."

"I know, but it has to be painful. And ribs take forever to heal, especially at his age."

"Stop it," he chided gently. "He's *alive* because you didn't hesitate. A cracked rib is nothing compared to the alternative."

"Come back home," she suddenly said.

He tensed a little beside her and shifted to meet her eyes. "Are you sure?"

"I'm sure."

"I didn't even get to bring out my secret Friday night weapon that was guaranteed to make you forgive me."

"What was that?"

"I was going to take you to Holy Guacamole again."

Chandler giggled. "Again? You really are all in, aren't you?"

"Maybe that'll be our new Friday night tradition. We'll get a sitter and go to Holy Guacamole every Friday."

"Oooh, yes. I like this plan. Then I can get different taco platters every Friday. Mmmm. Or maybe the enchiladas. And one of the specialty margaritas I haven't tried yet."

He snuggled closer. "We'll put a fence around our date nights."

"Tacos? That fence is going to be a brick wall. Ten feet high."

"You got it." He inched closer.

She could feel him hesitate, waiting to see if she approved. She wrapped her fingers in his hair and pulled his mouth to hers.

Sometime later, she snuggled against his shirt, listening to his heart thumping. "Oren?"

"Yeah?"

"I don't want you to stay in the guest room.'

Chapter Forty-Six

Three days later
Sunday, July 4

"Where are we going?" Chandler demanded. "It's almost bedtime."

Oren simply hummed and tapped the steering wheel. He couldn't wait to show her, but he didn't want to spoil it.

Maddie's feet kicked against the seat. "Where are we, Daddy?"

"You'll see in a minute. It's not far."

Chandler pointed out the window. "Are we going to the C-A-M-P-G-R-O-U-N-D?"

Instead of answering her, he turned onto the lane and followed the little dirt road to the Hickory Hollow Campground's already full parking lot.

"We're going to see the big fireworks show," he finally admitted. He parked the car and got Finn's stroller out of the back while Chandler got Maddie out of her seat.

They walked up the sidewalk toward the huge lodge house.

"You're here!" Bonnie Taylor, one of the campground's owners, flung open the front door and rushed across the porch to give Chandler a massive hug. Her husband, Doug, the other owner, followed close behind. He shook Oren's hand. "Glad to see you. It's been a long time."

"Too long," Oren agreed. He played their last trip here in his mind. Their honeymoon, where they'd met Margo and Connor and Ashley and Elliott.

"We've got you all set up."

Chandler looked at him and raised an eyebrow. She looked even more suspicious when she saw Ashley and Elliott come around the side of the lodge.

"What's going on?"

Ashley was all innocence. "Just here for the fireworks." She reached for Maddie's hand. "Livvie and Hannah are waiting for you."

Maddie took off without so much as a backwards glance.

Elliott nudged Oren away from the stroller. "I've got this."

"What's going on?" she asked.

Bonnie couldn't contain her grin. "Right this way, please." She and Doug led them inside the house and up the stairs, through a small storage room, and up another set of stairs to an overhead door. Doug pushed it up and gestured for them to go out onto the lodge's small widow's walk.

Up on the roof, the tiny widow's walk had been outfitted with thick blankets and huge throw pillows. There was a bottle of wine and two glasses and a plate of fruit and cheese.

"Come down the same way after the fireworks. Just pull this door shut." Bonnie winked and lowered the door into place.

Oren adjusted the pillows and motioned for Chandler to join him. They got situated and she laughed.

"What's so funny?"

She touched a finger to the top of the rail. "The railing around the widow's walk. It looks like a fence."

Oren looked at the wrought iron railing. "I totally planned it that way."

Chandler nudged his side. "Did not."

The sky quickly fell dark, the inky blackness dotted with millions of stars. Beyond the lodge, they could see the stage area where campers and Hickory Hollow residents were gathered. A band played country music.

Oren poured them each a glass of wine and they polished off the snacks as they listened to the music. After the song finished, Doug's voice echoed across the campground. "And now if you'll all turn your attention that way towards the river, we'll get started."

A moment later, the stage lights went off and the first burst of fireworks boomed and sprayed across the sky.

Chandler gasped and leaned closer to him.

He caught the scent of her shampoo and knew beyond the shadow of a doubt that he was the luckiest man alive.

The fireworks bloomed and exploded, lighting up her face. Her fingers laced with his, holding his hand tight.

As the explosions slowed, she relaxed back against him. "Our honeymoon was the best trip ever. We need to come back here soon for a whole week. I bet Ash and Ell and Margo and Connor would, too. We could swap kid duty so we all get some fun time."

"That's a great idea." He didn't tell her yet that he and the guys were already planning that exact trip for September.

The fireworks finale set off. Boom after boom after boom with spray after spray after spray of colorful lights filled the sky, followed by a cloud of smoke that hung in the humid summer air.

"Before we go down, I have one more surprise for you." He shoved his hand deep in his pocket and pulled out a small velvet box.

"What is this?"

"Open it." He put the box in her hand.

She popped the lid open and gasped. "It's like my first one!"

Oren took the ring out of the box. "I hope you still like it."

"I love it."

"And I hope you still like me." He shifted until he knelt on one knee. His heart hammered relentlessly. "Chandler Marie Nelson Turner, will you still be my wife?"

She nodded and managed to say, "Yes," through tears.

He slipped the ring on her finger.

The stage lights flipped back on, ending the moment. They took the pillows and blanket down and left them in the storage room, then headed out to the stage, where the band had vacated in favor of karaoke.

They made their way to the blankets where their friends were.

"Did you see the lights!" Maddie was still wound up from the experience.

"We did. Did you like them?"

She nodded her head vigorously.

Finn slept through the whole thing.

Oren waited until Chandler was occupied with showing off her ring to Margo and Ashley before he slipped away.

Doug clapped his back, and when the song was over, handed Oren the microphone. He went to the center of the stage, more nervous than he was on an opening night of a play.

"Well, I can't sing to save my life, so I won't subject you all to that."

Laughter rippled through the crowd.

"Even though I don't have a song, I still wanted to get up and embarrass myself in front of the woman of my dreams. So. Without further ado, Chandler, this is for you." He cleared his throat.

"How do I love thee? Let me count the ways.
I love thee to the depth and breadth and height
My soul can reach, when feeling out of sight
For the ends of being and ideal grace.
I love thee to the level of every day's
Most quiet need, by sun and candle-light.
I love thee freely, as men strive for right.
I love thee purely, as they turn from praise.
I love thee with the passion put to use
In my old griefs, and with my childhood's faith.
I love thee with a love I seemed to lose
With my lost saints. I love thee with the breath,
Smiles, tears, of all my life; and, if God choose,
I shall but love thee better after death."

"That's Elizabeth Barrett Browning, and I know my beautiful wife is probably confused because I'm usually quoting Shakespeare. I wouldn't want to disappoint, so here's this line from *Hamlet*: '*Doubt thou the stars are fire; Doubt that the sun doth move; Doubt truth to be a liar; But never doubt I love.*'"

He exited the stage to applause and made his way back to the blanket. Chandler jumped to her feet and threw her arms around him.

He held her tight. *This has to be the best moment of my life.*

Chandler kissed him, and he thought, *Nope, this one is.*

And after getting so close losing those moments, he knew he'd never let them go.

Epilogue

Nine Months Later
  Sunday, April 10

"Blow, Finny, like this." Maddie pursed her lips and blew out the candle on Finn's cupcake.

Squealing with delight, Finn slapped his palms against the tray of his high chair and the cupcake bounced. Chandler scooped the cupcake away and relit the candle while Megan snapped photos from a short distance away.

"You try," Maddie encouraged.

Finn huffed out a breath and the tiny flame flickered.

Chandler recognized the signs of impatience as his attention wandered. "You help him blow it out."

Maddie counted, "3… 2… 1… blow!" Finn "helped" his sister, which resulted in some rather unsanitary conditions spraying over the top of the cupcake.

Chandler snatched the candle before Finn's curious fingers could touch it. "You can eat it now."

Janice conceded, "You were right. Having cupcakes was a much better idea than a regular cake."

Chandler took the comment as a win. It had been a long, hard road, but they'd gotten to a good place. Janice still wasn't thrilled with having limited contact, but she'd eventually learned to control herself. It had been horribly awkward at first. The Labor Day picnic had been a complete nightmare, Thanksgiving was marginally better, Christmas was tolerable, and now Janice finally seemed to understand that she no longer had a starring role in Oren's life. Important, yes, of course. But if she wanted to be a significant part of it, the toxic behavior had to go. And for the most part, it had.

"I'm just glad it's warm enough to be outside," Chandler said.

Lisa agreed. "Much better to have the mess out here. And the noise."

Ashley made a face. "So. Much. Noise."

Kids ran around the yard, yelling and burning off a ton of energy. Jared and Isobel helped wrangle them all, keeping a watchful eye to make sure no one ran toward the road.

Oren and the guys, including Pappy Tom, healed and healthy, were stationed around the grill. The original plan had been cupcakes and chips, but since it was so nice out, it had evolved into a full-blown cookout with their families, friends, and people from the neighborhood, including Grace and her husband and twins.

No one had been disappointed when Shannon and Kinsley moved away last fall, and the rumor mill was quite robust with speculation about the reasons why.

Gretchen and Alan came around the side of the house. "Sorry we're late," she said, handing off a brightly wrapped package to Alan and pointing to the table laden with gifts.

"I was hoping you'd come. It didn't seem right to have

Finn's first birthday without you." Chandler gave her a hug and explained to Grace, "She actually delivered Finn right on the theater stage after the last performance of *Much Ado About Nothing*."

Grace's mouth dropped open. "You had him on stage?"

"Not by choice," Chandler laughed. "This year's closing night was much less dramatic."

The night before had been the theater's final performance of *Macbeth*. This play had ended with a standing ovation – and no births.

Oren rather enjoyed his smaller role at the theater, and was content to assist Gretchen and Alan wherever they wanted his help. He'd used some of his newfound free time to help Chandler with her thriving business. For a multitude of reasons, Isobel had opted to live at home and do her college courses online. With the business her social media skills brought in, they were able to officially hire her as a part time assistant.

Finn watched the children playing for a few minutes, then fussed to be let down.

"I'll take him," Janice offered. She walked him around in the grass, holding his hands while he toddled around. It wouldn't be long before he took his first independent steps.

Oren came over and slipped his arms around Chandler's waist. "We're going to set up the volleyball net. You need me to do anything?"

She leaned back into him. "Nope, it's all under control until time to clean up."

He snapped his fingers. "Trash bags. I'll grab those heavy duty trash bags out of the garage since I'm headed there anyway."

"Good idea."

The afternoon went by in a flurry of activity and food and

laughter and at one point, a tornado of shredded wrapping paper.

The grand finale of the event was when Oren and the guys got a little rambunctious while playing volleyball. The ball sailed up in the air and headed out of bounds. Oren dove, whacked the ball before it hit the ground, and tumbled into the fence, breaking through one of the pickets with his foot.

Chandler folded her arms and shook her head as Oren sheepishly went into the garage and fished out a picket.

"Good thing we got extras," he grumbled.

The guys paused their game and helped Oren fix the fence. As good friends do.

Enjoyed this visit to Hickory Hollow? Keep going and take a little side trip to Ireland in Book 7 of the series, Two Tickets to Paradise.

When the Hickory Hollow Ladies' Society offers Becky Reed an all-expense-paid trip to Ireland, it seems like the perfect distraction from her ex-husband's wedding. One catch — it's a trip for two and the Ladies are crossing their fingers that the Emerald Isle will inspire love between Becky and her travel companion, Noah. But for Becky, the only kissing will be between her and the Blarney Stone. No matter how sweet — and kissable — Noah is.

Hickory Hollow. Get comfy, stay a while!

You don't want to miss news of upcoming books, events, and behind-the-scenes sneak peeks! Sign up for my newsletter today at carriejacobs.com!

Acknowledgments

Author's Note

Dear Reader,

I'll just head the question off at the pass: NO, I do not have an awful mother-in-law! My MIL is a lovely woman who I get along with very well. It was super fun to write Janice for just that reason – it's fiction, where awful people are a great deal of fun to write. In real life, not so much.

I recently became a mother-in-law myself, and writing this book was basically a "Things I swear I'll never do" list.

I hope you enjoyed Chandler and Oren's story as much as I enjoyed writing it. I know it was a little different than the other Hickory Hollow novels since this is the first book where the couple is already married and has little kids (Maddie was a blast to write!).

As we get deeper into the Hickory Hollow series, I expect to see a bit more character crossover from previous books.

Huge thanks to Magan at Court of Spice Editing for helping me to make this a better book! If you spot any errors, they are 100% mine. (I'm a little stubborn with my commas.)

My undying thanks to Jen and Laura for being the best writer besties a girl could ask for. IAA 4-EVAH!!!

And of course, thanks to Scott for being my own personal patron of the arts, my biggest support, and my real-life hero and happily ever after.

Lastly, thank you to YOU for reading this book! If you enjoyed it and have a moment to spare, leaving a review online would be very helpful to me. (Even if you didn't buy it online, you can still leave a review.) If you'd like to hear more from me, sign up for my newsletter! You'll get exclusive sneak peeks, behind-the-scenes info, notice of upcoming releases, and all that jazz. (Sign up at carriejacobs.com)

You can also follow me on Facebook (facebook.com/writer-carriejacobs) for notice of upcoming events and more importantly, pictures of my furry editorial assistants.

Best,
Carrie

About the Author

Carrie's love of storytelling began in early childhood and never wavered as time marched onward. She reads in pretty much every genre imaginable, but found her writing happy place in small town contemporary romance and romantic comedy.

From that love came Hickory Hollow, a mashup of her hometown and places she's either visited or would like to. Her favorite part of Hickory Hollow? The residents don't have to drive an hour to get to Target, like she does in real life.

Carrie lives in beautiful central Pennsylvania with her family and very spoiled furry editorial assistants.

Connect with Carrie through her newsletter or social media!

Website: carriejacobs.com

facebook.com/writercarriejacobs

instagram.com/carriejacobsauthor

goodreads.com/carriejacobs

www.ingramcontent.com/pod-product-compliance
Lightning Source LLC
Chambersburg PA
CBHW061606190726
48288CB00007B/2205